The Lies of the Lion

Book One of the Lion's Trace

Suellen Ocean

The Lies of the Lion
by
Suellen Ocean

Published by:
Ocean-Hose
P.O. Box 115
Grass Valley, CA 95945
http://www.oceanhose.com

Also by Suellen Ocean:

Acorns and Eat'em
The Acorn Mouse
Poor Jonny's Cookbook
Secret Genealogy
Secret Genealogy II
Secret Genealogy III
Secret Genealogy IV
The Celtic Prince
Black Pansy
Evaline's Fiddle
The Guild
The Last Quadroon
Gold River
Gone North
The Common Sense Guide to Good Sex
Chimney Fire

The author has given this book an R rating due to its sexual content.

Table of Contents

ONE

June 1450 *Amsterdam*

Jacob's almond-shaped, hazel eyes darted self-consciously as he walked the canal trail that led to the bridge. He stopped and rubbed his neck. During the night, a cool breeze caught his flesh unprotected, now his muscles were stiff. He walked a little further then stopped at the bridge, slowly absorbing the warmth of the sunrise. The clanking of hammers and the shaking of heavy carpets told him his neighborhood was waking. Painters, metal workers and potters inside their studios prepared the tools of their trade. A chorus of brooms swept away what happened yesterday and birds chattered about what might happen today. Jacob would soon be busy with his own creativity, for he was a writer, a chronicler of events and each day his ambitious inquiries were transformed into a steady flow of news.

Jacob belonged to Amsterdam's community of Sephardic Jews who kept a low profile amidst the city's Christian majority. Most had not converted and would not hear of it, but there were a few families who had outwardly converted to Catholicism, while in the privacy of their homes continued eating kosher diets and secretly observing the beloved holidays. Those that chose to pose as Catholics, the church called Conversos, Marranos or New Christians.

Inside Jacob's neighborhood they were known to one another as the descendants of the Jews of Spain and Portugal, the *Sephardim*.

1

Seeking peace, they'd travelled north but most of Jacob's community did not feel secure in their current surroundings. Living and posing as Christians was humiliating and many pondered their fate. 'How long will we be able to stay?' they asked one another in lively debates. 'Where would we go?' was another question to which few had answers. They shared the belief that one day they would feel as free as other citizen of the Netherlands. Jacob kept these thoughts constantly in the back of his mind even though his nature wasn't suited to dwelling upon the dismal. He was by nature and nurture, an optimist.

Periodically, Jacob took work aboard ships loading and unloading cargo. Each excursion reaffirmed in him that there were no finer cafes nor culture than what he found in Amsterdam. He would forget, then travel to London, Paris or Rome, returning only to tell the others how fortunate they were to live amongst a community of diverse thinking and political organizing. For Jacob, Amsterdam had it all.

After allowing the sun to warm his body and the breeze to tussle his hair, he straightened his posture, took several deep breaths, ran his fingers through his hair and began his daily ritual of walking the streets, poking his head into different stalls to see what had been produced or imported and followed his nose toward any fresh baked goods, especially the undisputable smell of challah.

He walked from the hub of Amsterdam toward the farmland, to record the comings and goings of newsworthy people. Whether they be well-informed farmers, shoemakers, sailors, fishermen or chatty womenfolk, he plied them for information pertinent to the future of the Sephardim. He headed for home again and, like a puzzle, laid his notes out on the table, next to his bread, herring and cheese. He elevated his leg on the table and pondered over what the youngest prostitute in the Oude Zijda had told him. She said that two men, a sailor and a wealthy man, told her that someone in the Rhineland had devised a method to mass-produce manuscripts and books had begun to reach cafes in Paris. Jacob set that note above the others. He would seek to verify the damsel's account. It would not be easy for him to sneak back to the prostitutes. If anyone saw him, he hoped they would understand that it was only to procure information. But there were idle minds and busy mouths, and there had been that one incident, just the one.

The next day Jacob continued his information gathering.

"What's the news from Belgium?" a farmer shouted from his field as Jacob passed by.

"Two rogues stole two crates of Burgundy wine in Rouen and were caught in Belgium."

"Hggg... This is the story you bring me? My daughter goes off to Antwerp," the farmer rounds his hand over his belly to display he thought she was pregnant, "no word of her?"

Jacob shook his head. He knew the farmer's daughter. She was probably not pregnant nor had she run off with a man. Antwerp was an exciting place to be and it must have been especially refreshing to be removed from her father's presence and all his imaginings.

Wandering through the farms was pleasant but brought Jacob no new stories. The few remaining warm summer days were intoxicating but the vague story about books in mass production ate away at him. He walked back to the city to inquire if others had heard this intriguing news.

"Jacob," a gentleman greeted him before quickly ducking into a café, the aroma of fresh bread oozing into the street. Jacob followed him inside where several other men enjoyed fresh pastry.

"Morning Jacob," they greeted then waited for his rendition of the daily news. One man fondled his beard, another ran his thumbs alongside his rough whiskers. It made Jacob uncomfortable, these elder men, waiting for his news, believing that he held the barometer of their day. He purposely bumped against a chair creating a small racket then spoke, "Do you hope for good news to bring joy or something to contemplate all day long?" He joked while looking about the room. The men smiled uneasily. Most of these men had seen more troubled than peaceful days and Jacob's jab at them was hurtful. That was not his intention but he knew that because of their past, they were comfortable with a bit of bad news each day. For these men, life had held more pain than pleasure and as strange as it was for Jacob he often played their game and fed them their daily dose of fear.

"I have heard news from the Garonne basin," he told them respectfully.

"Ah, Garonne," one after the other nodded, looked at one another and repeated again, "Ah, Garonne," their eyes telling him, 'please continue'.

Jacob's hazel eyes focused on the men. "So close to the Pyrenees..."

"Yes, yes, yes..." they looked about in agreement. All were aware that there were Jews living and trading in the Pyrenees, the territory between Spain and France. Their Christian pretense was no secret, but because the stories had become elaborated upon, many were beginning to doubt their authenticity.

Jacob had nothing new to tell the men. He had told them last week what he'd heard while snooping around the dock but the men needed something and he would provide it.

"A birth of knowledge is growing in that region. There are powerful influences wishing to squelch that growth." he said remembering what he'd heard from the prostitute. "The tortured souls hiding behind Christendom are soon to have a voice."

One man begged him to continue. "Who will speak for them?"

"They shall speak for themselves," Jacob said coolly.

There were faces of disbelief and nods to the contrary. These men knew better than to believe that Jews pretending to be Christians, would be speaking out. Such heresy would only bring their death.

Most of the others chuckled at Jacob's audacity, except one who shouted from the corner, "The young man has lost his mind," he said then hid behind the large brim of his black hat.

Jacob looked down after catching the eye of one of the men. "There is word. I cannot reveal my source..." he said wondering if the man knew the information had been retrieved from a prostitute. Jacob shook the thought, looked away from the man and continued.

"Someone has devised a method to manufacture many manuscripts."

"How many?" the man next to him asked.

"Yes, tell us how many and how Jacob!" another cried out.

Jacob knew very little about the invention so once again relied on his creativity to get him out of a jam. He changed the subject. "Spain's anti-Jewish rebels are gaining ground."

A voice was quick to criticize. "You spoke of this a week hence, tell us something we do not know!"

"I'm telling you there's a new invention. It prints masses of pamphlets. The intellectuals will make great use of it. Spain will be liberated."

The wise old men were thoughtful. Jacob had once again succeeded in keeping their hope alive and provided them with something to debate and banter throughout the day and hopefully for several days. He respected the old men but they never failed to leave him shaking. As old as they were, each held power in the community in one way or another and had a sharp, keen mind and could win any argument he presented. As they began to discuss this new invention amongst themselves Jacob quietly slipped out the door.

Jacob spent the afternoon prying his friend Abraham for something pertinent he could chronicle.

"Lope de Montalvo is one of the most powerful officials in the Spanish Castilian government," Abraham said to Jacob who accepted the statement apathetically.

"We have known one another since we were boys, you have always looked toward that which is bright but you should remember, Montalvo is now a Christian."

"But he will make things better and in his heart he will always be a Jew," Abraham shot back.

Jacob would not budge, "Yes, he has great skill. Yes he lectures tirelessly. His work is beautiful. He is a true scholar but he has become a Christian."

Abraham frowned. His eyes were blood-shot and his thick skin was creviced beyond his years. He always grew impatient with Jacob. "Why do you argue with me? Others tell me, 'Jacob is so full of hope, he never fears', my mother tells me, 'think like Jacob, be uplifting', she does not know how you trouble me."

Jacob went to a jug in the corner, swung it up to his lips and gulped loudly then looked intently at his friend. "It is through dissent that we will win the right to practice our religion, without fear of punishment. One day this will be so, but you wish to see New Christians as Jews and they are not."

Abraham stepped so closely, Jacob could feel his breath, "But they were," he pointed his finger into Jacob's face. "They were born Jews, out of fear for their lives they converted, it is still in their hearts."

Jacob shrugged. He knew his friend spoke the truth but once again it had gotten late into the evening and he was tired of the discourse.

Abraham continued. "Come to me tomorrow evening and I shall tell you what I know. I am having a conversation with Rabbi Samuel and he has told me some things."

Jacob straightened his back. Did Abraham have a jewel of information? Why didn't he tell him now? He called Abraham's bluff. "Rabbi Samuel has not been out of Amsterdam except to Antwerp in many a year, he's secluded and short sighted."

Abraham did not waste the opportunity to torment Jacob. "Rabbi Samuel has..." he leaned forward stealthily, lowering his voice into the mocking tone he'd used with Jacob many times, "tomorrow evening I will tell you." And when Abraham laughed his wrinkles and worry seemed to disappear.

Jacob was quick to respond, "I will come tomorrow night because we meet most every night but I will not spend my day anticipating you have a great, important story, I believe you do not," he said going right up to Abraham's face before he went to the jug in the corner and took several large gulps before departing. Once outside he pulled up the fabric of his thick shirt to protect himself from the late afternoon wind.

Jacob had given many of his peers an opportunity to tell him about Rabbi Samuel and any delicious rumors they may have heard but by the next day, he still had not heard anything out of the ordinary, making him all the more excited to greet Abraham. Not wanting to appear anxious, he stalled and kicked around later than usual. He had a late supper and lingered longer with the fisherman's wives, as if they would have anything new to tell him since the morning.

In the evening, Jacob meandered into Abraham's small studio below the home of their friend, the merchant, Jean La Roz.

He stepped down the stairs and into Abraham's organized but moldy-smelling room.

They both stood squarely. Abraham ready to defend, Jacob ready to dispel.

Jacob nervously gave a tap tap, to his writing board. "You were to tell me, something you deemed important...Rabbi Samuel," he reminded Abraham.

Abraham walked to the massive wooden door that had warped with the rise of the winter's floodwaters. He had to bend down and lift it to get it to close. His muscles were taut and his curly white hair flew wildly as he came back up again. He wanted to make certain no one heard the information he was about to share with his friend.

Jacob was stunned at the secrecy but grew excited, no longer trying to conceal it, "You've got my curiosity up my friend, please..."

Abraham glared at him then walked to the windows and drew the curtains. Flying dust caused him to sneeze. He'd turned the pantry of the merchant Jean La Roz's home into a daytime workshop. At night he used the pantry to study religion before retiring upon a make-shift loft. Usually only Jacob came by. Many of the other men who shared similar political views and enjoyed conversing were older and a bit more conservative and met at the home of Peter Le Sueur.

"It is only me," Jacob grunted impatiently as his friend continued securing the room for secrecy.

"It would be all of them if they knew what I am about to tell you."

Jacob, who had decided to relax, let out a deep sigh and began fumbling with grape rootstocks ready for export.

"Don't touch those, you'll bruise them. The growers are strict about that." Abraham scolded.

Jacob let go, turned and stared. Abraham stared back.

Finally, Abraham looked at Jacob and spoke genuinely, "Spain's renegade New Christians have succeeded in bribing the Pope."

Jacob was thoughtful. "Have you told the others?"

Abraham shook his head, "I have only told you. The men that meet at Peter Le Sueur's, they probably already know. The Pope can be bought with art from right here in Amsterdam. The more art he receives for his collection, the more power he gives to Albert Barrents and Montalvo. Do you know all that these men can do for our plight?"

Jacob looked dryly at him. "They are New Christians, or as some in Spain refer to them, Marranos."

"They're Jews!" Abraham pounded his fist on the table, knocking grape rootstocks across the room. He was furious with Jacob for using the derogatory term, Marranos. "The New Christians are allowed to write publicly and have their arguments heard respectfully. They portray the Jews in the light they deserve. And..."

Jacob rudely interrupted him. "And?"

"My friend," Abraham grabbed the top of Jacob's hand, his voice was soft but his clutch was threatening. "They have succeeded in altering the historical record."

Jacob laughed. "This can't be true. The hold that the Pope has on Catholic Spain... it cannot be true. But if it is… it is an affront, albeit an interesting one. Tell me, what historical truth has been altered?"

Abraham hesitated, and with an ironic smile said, "The Bible."

Jacob's laughter filled the room and surely spilled outside upon the street.

"Shhh." Abraham scolded, "It is not meant to be for your humor. Rabbi Samuel speaks the truth."

Between chortles Jacob spoke, "Let's get these facts aligned. Are you telling me that Albert Barrents and Lope de Montalvo come to Amsterdam, purchase art and sell it to the Pope and he lets them alter the Bible?"

Abraham finally smiled. "Not those words exactly. Albert Barrents and Lope de Montalvo send others to Amsterdam and have art commissioned and give it to the Pope as gifts. In turn, they are given powerful positions in the Spanish government which include..."

Jacob stopped him, "Please ... allow me," he said, his eyes alert and his mouth turned sarcastically at the corners, "powerful positions in the government which include ... lying?"

"Jacob, I knew you would twist it, I suppose one could see it that way, but they are divine lies."

"Divine lies?" Jacob laughed heartily and feeling ornery he fondled one of Abraham's grape rootstocks. "I need to return home. This will require deep thought. I am grateful that you shared this tale with me. You needn't worry that I spread it as I do the other information, I would not want trouble to come to Barrents and Montalvo. There are stories in the Bible that have led to war. Perhaps we can convince the Pope to excommunicate the anti-Jewish rebels."

"I thought you'd see it my way," Abraham smiled, patted his friend on the back and the two of them, side by side, heaved the massive warped door open.

Abraham sat down upon his favorite carved chair. The fingers of his left hand followed the grooves that formed the wings of the bird that created armrests. His right hand cupped a clay vessel that held a stimulating herbal beverage that had been gifted to him by the rabbi. Letting out a deep sigh, he dropped his head, closed his eyes and sipped. Jacob's visits were never without confrontation. Abraham knew Jacob would busy himself with the Rabbi Samuel story. No matter how hard Abraham tried to remain calm, Jacob's visits left him feeling frayed. But now the herbal tonic both soothed Abraham's nerves and aroused his senses. After finishing his cup he rose and returned to his tasks. His rootstocks were due to ship in two days. One by one he heard the final sounds of doors shutting. The city was soon quiet except for the rhythm of water swooshing about the canals and rats scratching beneath the foundations of the homes along the river's waterfront.

Powerful positions in the Spanish government, Jacob could not remove those words from his mind. Jacob propped his boot upon his cracked and crumb-filled table and began attempting to solve this new puzzle. Dozing off in the chair, reawakening to ponder a bit more, then finally removing only his boots, he crawled into bed.

Jacob hadn't bothered to remove his clothes the night before so the next morning he was dressed and set to begin his day. Shuffling to the basin, he splashed the cool water upon his summer-dried skin, still lost in thought about the two New Christians bribing the Pope. Could it be true? How could he prove it and why would he want to? He knew he had to give this new investigation time to percolate. He'd drop a few hints at market stalls, toy with the produce vendors and even sneak over to the prostitutes to see if there were any pieces of this puzzle yet to confirm. It was late morning and his eyes suffered from dryness. He hated starting the day like this and would avoid running into Abraham, he wouldn't want to give him the impression that he had lost any sleep over such random prattle. He returned to his bed and sat squarely, boots flat upon the wooden floor, elbows upon knees. Why would he bother asking produce vendors? It was the art vendors he needed to ask but they wouldn't tell him anything. All the Jews spoke among themselves, secrets were rampant, that was how they survived and now, yes, as a matter of future survival, two well-heeled Jews, New Christians really, Jews no more, were busy changing history's story. Though deceitful, the scheme was altruistic and designed to protect the Jewish community from further harassment. Jacob's peers could all read Hebrew. If they read the altered version they would know. But Jews would not be reading the New Testament. Could those in the know keep quiet? Besides, what monopoly did the Papacy have on God? But how, who and what would prevail?

Jacob whistled and kicked debris that came in his way as he walked along the canal. The coolness provided by the brick homes and the breeze blowing in from the water made his walk pleasant. People were doing chores, repairing crooked doors damaged by floods, washing windows and a beautiful young girl was upon her stoop brushing her long, wavy, light-brunette hair. Her posture was upright as her slender fingers combed through her hair. He tried to analyze her unfamiliar face but was spurred on by pedestrians from behind. Although his heart quickened, he had to keep up his pace and headed for the dock.

"Nicolaes! My friend! How is the sea today?" Jacob shouted to the skipper as he jumped down into the ship, startling the gentle man who smiled, apparently pleased to see him.

"Ah Jacob, are you looking for work?"

Jacob jumped down further into the ship. His feet landed firmly. "When are you shipping out?"

"Not for three weeks," Nicolaes said putting his head down. "I need to rest and care for the wife and children."

Jacob understood how the life of a Seaman caused conflicts. Nicolaes suffered tremendous guilt at being away for such long periods.

"How are your stories?" Nicolaes asked, his face browned from the constant sun. His dark eyes sparkled. "Anything of interest?"

Besides their cryptic practice of hiding and gathering for Shabbat and other holy days, Jacob's stories were one of the few ways this small, secretive community of Sephardim could stay connected.

"Yes, good news," Jacob told him as he used his boot to kick an empty crate around turning it so that he would have a better view of the dock and the comings and goings of pedestrians. He finally settled down and sat upon another crate and began telling the news. "An enterprising man has created a way to mass-produce pamphlets. My understanding is that he writes one and from that one is able to duplicate many more." He waved his arms about passionately. "The streets of Paris are littered with pamphlets."

The skipper looked at him warily. He didn't always believe the entirety of Jacob's stories, which were credible but prone to exaggeration.

Jacob saw the skipper's doubt and reinforced his news. "I have heard it from two sources."

"Well Jacob, I shall confirm your tale in July. I sail to Roen. Close enough to Paris to have received these pamphlets you speak of."

"Roen? Where else do you sail?"

He dropped his head but did not speak. Jacob attributed the silence to another long trek away from his family. Or was it that Nicolaes didn't wish to speak of his business ventures? As Nicolaes looked up with a slight apologetic smile Jacob backed away and stopped questioning. The skipper let strangers assume he was a Protestant, a common practice amongst Sephardim merchants employed in Amsterdam's docks.

"Have you seen any paintings lately?" Jacob asked.

Nicolaes laughed but kept his mind on his task of securing the cargo of his ship, "No, no art. The sea would have surely destroyed it."

"I don't doubt the power of the sea, nor your skill. You humor me Captain but I expect you will soon be enjoying the delights of your wife and children. Perhaps someday I too will be proud to have a family."

Nicolaes nodded while he worked. His coarse, nimble fingers kept to the task. "Yes, you will be proud."

Jacob asked more questions of the Captain and took notes regarding the ship's departure times and inquired about destinations, a routine he practiced regularly. Jacob quickly eyeballed the dock for any signs of art shipments. Though one masterpiece could fetch a hearty favor, he soon realized how trivial that approach was. If art was shipping out, it would be crated. At that thought, Jacob gave the Captain a hearty handshake and then headed past a row of homes along an adjacent canal to one deeper into the old city where a community of artists had recently settled. About five minutes into his jaunt he spotted a bench and sat down to think and began mumbling aloud to himself.

"If the Pope is acquiring artwork it is of course religious in nature. That would eliminate Jewish artists. No, they should not be eliminated, of course not." He closed his eyes and took the cool summer sea breeze into his lungs. Deciding to stay put, he stretched his legs and slumped down into the bench while the puzzle pieces floated through his mind. Needing more puzzle pieces stimulated him. He rose from the bench. Despite his impatience he continued toward the homes of the artists. When he reached their street, he decided to focus on the tall, slender brick homes attracting visitors. He saw that patrons were knocking on doors. Some were allowed in while others tried without luck to stir the artists.

"How do you expect the artists to create if the whole city is upon their stoop?" Jacob called to one of them.

He shouted back, "How do you expect them to pay their rent if they do not sell?"

Gathered at the door of what must have been the home of another artist, Jacob saw a cluster of young people loitering, not caring whether the artist made an appearance or not, they appeared happy to have a meeting place. He believed the crowd to be a testament to the fame of the artist and entered upon the crowded porch; pleasantly surprised to recognize the young woman he had seen earlier, brushing her long locks. Her beauty wasn't as stunning as he had first thought. He stared at her, analyzing what her future might bring. Her hair was brunette. Her skin was a dark olive. Her dark eyes smiled at him then looked down. He edged his way through the group, drew closer to her and made his presence known. She looked up. Suddenly his impression of her station in life was altered. She was older than the others. What were her intentions? Before Jacob had time to question her, the door opened. A man's hand reached and pulled her into the residence leaving Jacob perplexed.

"I didn't expect to encounter female painters. I would think them too busy sewing, cooking and entertaining."

Three out of the four boys shrugged.

"You believe she enters because she paints?" one of the boys volunteered. "I believe she poses for the artists and when she's done she's paid for her patience." He laughed loudly and looked toward the others for approval.

"Sir, may I speak my thoughts?" a girl asked.

Jacob turned, "Your thoughts are vital. Women procure art as well as men, is this not true?"

"Yes. But it is the man of the hearth who purchases the work, and not without the approval of his wife. I have spoken with this woman before. She is not a model. There is something..." she paused, and with a far-away smile leaned against the porch railing, "alluring about her."

"Alluring?"

She turned and faced Jacob. "She is different."

"In what way?"

"I doubt she busies herself performing the duties of sewing, cooking and entertaining. She may be a patron, I've seen her clasp her money purse when she exits."

Jacob saw the light peeking through one of the stained glass windows and bent down to have a look. He saw no furniture. Instead, there were easels and spirits for mixing paint, but no paintings on the easels.

"This is the preparation room. Why do you loiter?" he asked the youths. "Do grand artists reside here?"

"They give us food," one of the boys told Jacob. "Patrons are attracted to this spot. They are given food and drink to liven their spirits so they will feel giddy and want to buy."

The girl nodded, "We receive several fine meals a week."

Jacob stooped down and peeked another window.

"Wealthy patrons come from Iberia, France, and the Rhine and..." one boy began.

"Nobles maybe," another boy interrupted.

"No, they are not Nobles," the girl shook her head. "These are wealthy patrons but not Nobles."

Jacob grew tired of the banter but asked one last question. "Do you ever see Holy men?"

None of the youth responded. Jacob waited but when he received no response, he walked away and headed toward Abraham's.

The door was open so Jacob barged in. "I've come to several conclusions. My emotions guide me to abandon the story of the paintings and the Papacy. I care little about the Pope or the fact that New Christians are bribing him," Jacob told his friend who was busy slicing grape rootstalks.

Abraham looked up suspiciously. "You? My most curious of friends? If that is your wish it shall be my wish as well."

Jacob was surprised that Abraham did not argue. Thirsty, he eyed his friend's water jug in the corner but dared not go to it. "Well..."

he said, then paused, leaving an opening for Abraham to speak more on the subject. Jacob thought of fondling one of the grape rootstalks but decided against it, "Shalom," he finally said.

"Shalom," Abraham said with a resentful nod.

Jacob walked along the cool canals towards home, happy to be free of the disagreement. The lightness brought him joy. Lost in his thoughts, he was startled by a horse and carriage and the familiar whistling of an old Hebrew tune. It was Rabbi Samuel cheerfully maneuvering his carriage up the cobblestone street. Jacob saw several large, flat, rectangular shaped objects draped in black and carefully arranged to look like caskets.

"Good day Jacob," Rabbi Samuel said with a wry smile. Jacob could only stare, his mouth agape.

Day after day, Jacob returned to the street that housed the painters of Amsterdam. He told himself it was to search for clues regarding the Papal bribery scandal but in his heart he knew better. He would never turn against his fellow Jews and reveal the workings of a system that was serving his people well. And it was no secret amongst northern Europeans that Rome had improprieties, especially with Cosimo de Medici as head of the bank. And then there was the subject of the Pope's nephews who were really the Pope's illegitimate sons. At least Rome was encouraging the arts and the arts were where Jacob's heart led him. But each day he was disappointed at not seeing her. He did not know her name, how old she was, or what she found interesting in the artist section of Amsterdam. He knew he would encounter her. When he caught sight of her several blocks down from the artists' neighborhood, he developed a nervous stomach and hid from view. He hid quietly for half-an-hour until he heard her footsteps and the rustle of her dress. His courage and self-confidence returned and Jacob jumped out in front of her, startling her.

"Good day Madame," he said, tipping his tattered hat.

"You startled me Sir," she said, frightened there may be others waiting to assault her.

"You have nothing to fear," Jacob told her. "I have seen you in the artist's neighborhood."

She was relieved but took one last look around. Assured this was not an assault in progress, she smiled and was quite friendly. "Amsterdam is full of wonderful artists. It has only begun. Patrons are coming from London, Paris, Barcelona..."

"And not Rome?" he asked, wondering if she knew of the Papal's hunger for art from his local rabbi.

"Rome?"

"Forgive my abruptness. I am Jacob," he said with a bow.

"Ahhh..." she smiled, "another Jacobi."

He frowned. His parents had called him that. He could still hear it echoing throughout Friesland. 'Jacobi do this, Jacobi do that'...

"Did I offend you Jacob?"

"If thinking of Mamma and Papa are offensive then yes," he said with a laugh.

"You're a nice lad." Her eyes were dark. She wore her hair tousled, twisted and pinned.

"I *am* a nice lad. And your name?"

"Marie Belle."

"Ahhh..." he smiled, "another Marie."

Swinging her foot out from underneath her fashionable skirt, she feigned trying to trip him. It was apparent she was older than he yet she was childish and he liked that.

"Are you from France?" he asked.

"No, are you?"

"No. Are you from..." he said but she stopped him.

"The Rhineland? No," she said, enjoying the banter.

"Are you from..." he pretended to be concentrating fiercely, "one of the Italian States or Greece?"

"No," she said, still appreciating the game. "I am from right here in Amsterdam."

"No," Jacob told her.

"No?" She said with a fetching smile.

"No," he stated again, behaving like a know-it-all. "I have lived in the Netherlands all my life. I am certain you are not from Amsterdam. London maybe?"

"No, London would not..." embarrassed she stopped herself. Her face grew crimson.

Was she a Jew? London had a ban on Jews. Few Jews chose to risk oppression and live in England. He was relieved to be in Amsterdam.

She stood poised while he admired and analyzed her.

"Your skin... a Mediterranean quality to it, sun-kissed, if you will," he said, pleased with himself for choosing what he felt were the perfect words.

"I will accept that as a compliment. Keep guessing."

"Spain?" he asked.

She laughed and swung her market bag towards him.

"Oh, the lady is Portuguese, I see that now. It should have been my first pick."

She averted his eyes. "I shouldn't have played this game. I wish I could tell you that I had a homeland but it would be false. My father is in the money-lending business and we move about." She sighed and looked around. The tall red brick homes in the Jewish neighborhood, made her long for the permanent home she has never had. "I've lived in Rhodes, Palermo, Barcelona, Tarascon, Valencia, Turin, Murcia ... I've even been to Jerusalem. We are never at any one place for long."

"Your father is a money-lender?"

"Yes, and a very intelligent one. He is prudent and does not expose his clients to risky endeavors," she said proudly, with a hint of the class she knew she held.

"Does your father lend to the Papacy?"

Her laugh was hearty. "No. My father would *not* lend to the Papacy," she said confidently but then thought again, "I would not think so..."

Jacob jumped in. "The day shall not go on forever, would you care to walk towards the fish market?"

"I have my father's business to attend to, then I must care for my son," she said, disappointed that she had to decline.

"Your son?"

"Yes," her eyes glowing with talk of her young son David. The boy impressed all who met her family, the Soeiras. He was extremely bright and his grandfather, Monsieur Soeira had seen to it that his tutors were well versed in literature, mathematics and science. Marie Belle oversaw his artistic and cultural instructions. "David is my beloved son." Her mouth formed cute little wrinkles as she smiled.

Jacob knew something must have happened to the lad's father. He waited for her to broach it.

"His father..." she put her head down.

Now it all made sense. She was older and now that Jacob thought about it, did hold a bit more weight about her body, as many women do after childbirth. The thought of her having a child was quite freeing to him. He was in no position to burden himself with a family. He would withhold further charms and flirtations. There was only one more question.

"Is your father here in Amsterdam?"

"No, he's in the north, in Friesland. He has business there. He'll be back soon."

Jacob was struck by her beauty and felt the strongest sexual urge toward her. He did not know what prompted his sudden feelings but wished he could grab her and push his chest against her full breasts.

"Jacob?" she asked, her voice concerned by his change of character.

"Yes, yes, of course, I am feeling hungry though," he said smiling at the thought.

"Yes," she said, "I am hungry too."

Jacob lied. He had not needed to visit the fish market and he was not hungry. Returning early, he tossed and turned in his bed in his small quarters. Why had he become smitten with her after she spoke of her father's trip to Friesland? What manner of man was he that her father's power should entice him about his groin? Or was it really such? Perhaps it was the way the light hit her dark eyes at just the right moment, or the way the muscles of her cheeks tightened as she smiled. Was it the way her vest fit tightly about her full body, or that he knew underneath that abundance of linen on a hot day were two warm breasts that would delight him on any occasion?

Jacob prayed. *Lord, please guide me. I am not a great Jew but I am a Jew none the less and I believe in your power. I will trust and depend on it when I meet Marie Belle again.*

He thought of grabbing himself and relieving the need that welled in his groins but stopped when he heard a rap at his door.

"Yes, Jacob is here but he is napping. If it is not important, please go away."

"Open the door, it's me Abraham."

"I am weary. I no longer have an interest in pursuing the story. Let me be."

"Jacob, open the door. There's more to the story."

"Go away Abraham. I have no further interest."

Abraham pounded louder and Jacob knew the whole neighborhood could hear. Jacob rose, re-united his leggings and ran his fingers through his oily brunette hair, looking back longingly at his bed where he was sure he would have enjoyed himself were it not for the interruption of his friend. His bare feet touched the cool floor as he looked about for something to cover his erection. He grabbed his writing tablet, stepped to the door and pulled it open to find Abraham pushing his way in forcefully.

"What is it? Why do you push your way in here while I nap?"

"It has been done," he said, shaking his head.

"What has been done?" Jacob who had never seen such trepidation from his friend.

"The man with the contraption to print multiple copies of pamphlets. He has begun printing a Bible."

"Old or New Testament?"

Abraham responded. "Both. And what I have feared has come about."

"What's that?"

Rabbi Samuel has involved us in something we should not be involved in."

"Us?" Jacob shouted. "I told you I want no part in a conspiracy to change the history of the Jews."

Abraham was distraught.

Jacob was more secular than Abraham who gathered with other men in orthodox homes for study and prayer. These men feared God but a few had become involved in a dishonest translation of the Christian version of the Torah and now Abraham feared the wrath of God.

Jacob tried to calm him. "I've decided that if they change the wording here and there it will not be such a frightful move."

Abraham stared in disbelief. He had hoped for his guidance.

Jacob tried to comfort him. "Moses will not come down from the mount and strike you. There have been worse offenses."

"We made sure Rabbi Samuel commissioned the art exactly as the Pope ordered. For months we knew that as the artist painted away we would be changing the history of the Jews," he confessed to Jacob.

Jacob was thoughtful before he spoke. "You're a part of this scheme?"

Abraham nodded, his curly white hair thick about his head, his eyes as large as clamshells.

"Now while they print this altered Bible, you fear the morality of your decision?"

Abraham nodded.

Jacob was pragmatic. "I have little faith that the changes or omissions will be relevant. Perhaps it is God's plan. Throughout the ages, the stories and ancestral journeys have been adjusted. The books of Genesis and Exodus were not written at the time but centuries later. Do not doubt that Albert Barrents and Lope de Montalvo are sincere Christians who desire to record history accurately."

"They are Jews!" Abraham shouted and kicked at the chair he sat upon.

Jacob shouted back, "They are Conversos ... Marranos ... and the Catholic Pope will be sure that they record the historical record accurately. Now may I return to the slumber at which I was about to enter?"

Abraham was not appeased. Jacob surmised that Abraham knew more than he was telling but Jacob's interest was in the beautiful young woman, Marie Belle and the curious travel of her father to Friesland.

"I question your Hebrew roots," Abraham said cruelly.

Jacob froze.

Abraham could see he'd made his friend uncomfortable. For a fellow Hebrew to question the ancestry of another man was a serious accusation but Abraham continued, "I have never seen your mother nor your father and from what the others say, Friesland, and especially Leeuwarden has intermarried Jewish families."

Jacob's anger frightened Abraham, so much so that he rose for the door and flashed an apologetic look but not in time.

Jacob trembled, sensitive to the fact that his mother's Jewish ancestry was not clear. He shook his finger at Abraham. "Not many know the significance the lion has to my family. The flag and all of Leeuwarden's sculptures were done under my father's guidance. My family brought the lion to Leeuwarden! They journeyed to Friesland to be free of persecution," Jacob screamed.

Abraham was ashamed that he'd tormented Jacob with hurtful accusations. He knew that the Jewish community might not trust Jacob if they believed he was not a *true* Jew. He reached and put his arm on Jacob's shoulder. In anger, Jacob pulled back and Abraham saw the tears in his eyes.

"My brother, I *know* you are a Jew. Your mother's family line is of no significance."

"There were rumors about her family but we found documents. My mother is a Jew," Jacob said with a long face.

"I heard it many years ago. I have never heard it again and I shall not repeat it," Abraham said kindly.

Jacob nodded and pursed his lips.

<u>TWO</u>

Every day Jacob saw Marie Belle somewhere in the city. Following her around was exhausting, especially darting behind buildings, trees and pedestrians so she would not see him. On more than one occasion, he was sure she might have. Running low on money, Jacob wandered the docks asking for work, hoping to find it in Amsterdam instead of shipping off for a couple of months. Every time a position was offered him, he was too busy chasing after the prettiest mother in all of Amsterdam.

Jacob had not seen Marie Belle with her child so assumed the grandmother or a nurse was caring for him. Late one afternoon, with the summer in full, he saw her at one of the canals, entering a small boat. He grew anxious as he watched her gather her skirts, balance herself and step into a boat. He recognized her big smile and lovely eyes but winced when she bent over and her buttocks shot prominently into the air. She would have not thought that flattering but as Jacob stood peering at her from afar he found it stimulating. She carried her son onto the boat and saw to his safety. As they drifted along the canal Jacob lost sight of them and did not see her for several more days.

"Marie Belle," he smiled as he ran up to her one morning, forgetting the affect she had on him. He remembered as he drew closer.

"Good morning Jacob," she said, returning the smile and delighted to see him.

Jacob had his hat in his hand and bread and fish rolled in paper tucked under his arm. He truly was hungry and was not about to let his emotions get away with him this time. "I saw you with your son this week, he looks a fine boy."

"Yes, he is. I didn't see you. Why didn't you approach us?"

"I was far away. You would not have heard me. I would have had to shout."

"It pleases me that you don't shout at women but the next time, if I am anywhere near, you must at least raise your voice."

"I'll do that Miss Marie," he said then nodded politely. "Has your father returned from his business in Friesland?"

"Yes, returned and left again. Now he is in Florence meeting with the banker Cosimo de Medici." She looked around to see that no one was listening, "Refuting my statement that my father would not ... or ... does not do business with the Papal. I'm not sure of the nature of my father's business but Cosimo de Medici is tied with the aspirations of monks ascending to the throne. Have we come so far as to have Jews as liaisons between monks and influential bankers?"

Jacob squinted and took a step back. "I think it strange you pose the question. You know your father's business better than I. Do I hear sincerity in your voice, or is it doubt?"

"I'm afraid it's both."

"Marie... if I may be frank... your presence makes me forget about political maneuvering and religious manipulating." He flashed a crooked smile. His wavy brown hair hung in his face. "Your presence makes me forget about this bread and fish I have under my arm. It's growing warmer from the heat of my body which you do nothing to cool."

Marie was accustomed to socializing with those who spoke their mind. Her life included travel throughout the Mediterranean and she had seen much of Europe. "Would you enjoy meeting my family?" she asked, her dark eyes looking straight into his. "My father will be home for Shabbat dinner. An extra plate on the table will be welcomed. Especially when he sees your smile and hears you speak with such grace and intelligence."

"I would be honored to meet your family and I will be there at precisely the correct time. And your son?"

"David," she said, pulling at her scarf. It did a poor job of controlling her thick locks of hair. "He turned five when we arrived at the beginning of summer. And what a delightful summer. I am enjoying Amsterdam immensely," she said wistfully. "I would love to stay," she planted her eyes directly into his.

He didn't know what to say but the reality of it hit him square in the belly. What was the son of a cabinetmaker, a lad from Leeuwarden, doing pursuing such an exquisite woman? He looked down at his clothing. It was not the fine clothing of the wealthy Jewish Sephardim, it was the clothing of a peasant. Jacob ran back to the docks and had to give his fish to an old man but quickly ate the bread while waiting the rest of the warm day making sure he was available for work.

"You're working hard lad," the Skipper said to Jacob who hoisted barrel after barrel off of the ship. "You came around here looking for work then never returned. Now you beg for work."

Jacob took a rag and wiped the sweat from his face and neck, hesitant to divulge his innermost thoughts to Skipper Nicolaes. "A very fine woman from a wealthy Sephardic family. I don't know what prompted me to take up with her. She's beautiful." Jacob shook his head. "My body is heated to a boil when I go near her and I feel hers is the same. She has invited me to meet her family."

The Skipper laughed. It had been a dull few days and he welcomed the male banter. "I see your dilemma. Many a man would be delighted to marry into a wealthy family but it is not without its inconveniences."

Jacob waited for an explanation but the Skipper's mind seemed lost in a memory. Jacob shrugged and continued lifting the heavy barrels, working until the sun had almost set.

"Son," the Skipper said, "we're finished for the day. Come sit with me and watch the sun set. Today we are not at war and no one is inquiring about our religion. Our families are safe. Let us toast to that which is good. I always save a bottle of the best wines. Romainville, Suresnes and Montreuil are all very good wines. Take your pick. And when you finish the job tomorrow you will leave with two bottles for your Shabbat. I wish you luck. A man should never miss an opportunity for love; there is nothing finer ... not even the wines of La Montagne Saint-Genevieve. Someone should have warned me long ago." The skipper winked the wrinkled skin around his eye and made it clear to Jacob that he had once lost a chance at a special love. Jacob knew that his one chance was before him. He held up his cup to toast the skipper. As the evening sun reflected off the water, the wine went down smoothly, warming him to his groin. It had been a good day. Life was not so bad in Amsterdam for the peasant son of a cabinetmaker from Leeuwarden, Friesland.

"I can't fit into these," Jacob said, squirming and twisting nervously in the clothes the tailor had given him to try on.

"But it is what I have son. You come to me today, the day before Shabbat and expect a miracle. I do not perform miracles, only Adonai performs miracles," the tailor told him.

Jacob hoped flattering the tailor would speed him along. "The Lord will perform wonders through you and I will tell all of Amsterdam that the tailor performs great miracles. You will become very prosperous."

"Hggg," the tailor uttered. Though frustrated, he was able to piece together a set of clothes from garments that had been left for repair and no one had returned to pick up. Jacob gave him a nice sum for his success then left and headed toward his friend Abraham's where he found him as usual laboring over his grape rootstock.

The door was ajar and Jacob quickly walked through. "And all of Paris is covered with vineyards," he said to Abraham who looked up and then back down at his work. Jacob could see that his friend was no longer angry but that their last dispute had left Abraham saddened. Jacob tried to cheer him up. "Along the road to Falise the troubadours sing of their love for wine, stopping at each castle hoping for a beautiful maiden. But I, Jacob, a peasant from Leeuwarden, have been invited to Shabbat dinner with one of the finest Financiers in all of Amsterdam."

Abraham smiled. He was happy to see Jacob in good spirits but he spoke with an element of doubt in his voice when he inquired of Jacob's dinner invitation. "What family?"

Jacob was caught by surprise. "Oddly I neglected to ask the family name, my lady friend is Marie ... Marie Belle."

Abraham looked down at his work. Once again he had hundreds of rootstocks to prepare for shipment and though he could converse, he had to keep working. "Is this Financier Sephardim or Ashkenazim?" he asked Jacob.

"What does it matter?"

"I need to be with the Sephardim because that is how I have lived and studied. There are so few Ashkenazim here in Amsterdam. I had a dream not long ago. The Ashkenazim were coming to Amsterdam in masses. I spoke about the dream with the others, especially with the rabbi and they were not surprised. They expect the Ashkenazim will one day be plentiful here in Amsterdam."

"Ashkenazim, Sephardim ... we will merge and become one," Jacob said.

Abraham gave Jacob an elite air of dismissal but thought again, "We always do. The brotherhood has lasted for thousands of years, we take care of one another and we always will."

"Shall I bring one bottle or two of my finest wines for the lady?" Jacob asked.

Abraham shook his head, disgusted that his friend desired to go no further with the politics of religion. "Some of Amsterdam's canals do not run as deep as others."

Not wanting to respond to Abraham's taunting Jacob looked the other way, and through the opening of the big door he captured his first glimpse of Marie Belle with her father. He was shocked at what he saw. "Abraham, come see Marie Belle's father," Jacob said, with a lump in his throat.

Abraham scurried to the door to have a peek. He smiled then turned to Jacob, "This is her father?"

Abraham and Jacob stood aghast peering at the tall and lanky financier, Monsieur Soeira with his beautiful daughter. The father wore a finely woven wool suit and his silver-streaked black hair and beard were impeccably trimmed. He looked as though he were waiting for common folk to come out of the shadows and ask for pittance.

"Oh Abraham," Jacob whined and pinned himself up against the wall behind the door. "What does she see in me? Her father is handsome beyond all others. He is wealthy and without doubt of the highest intelligence. He conducts his business with Europe's most brilliant men. I can't measure up to that."

"Pull yourself up off the floor Jacob!" his friend said to him before turning back to the door to have another peek. "The daughter is not a girl. She is a woman!"

"I agree, yet when she speaks she has a girlishness not seen in the girls of Amsterdam. I thought it was because she was fond of me," Jacob said while taking another peek. "Which way did they walk?"

Abraham strained to look further. "They are heading straight to Rabbi Samuel's!"

Jacob made his way to Marie Belle's and arrived on time but felt uncomfortable in his new suit of tailored clothes. The tailor had done his best to fit him for the occasion and considering Jacob's lack of funds it was an honorable attempt. Still, the crotch was a little short and the jacket fit tight across the shoulders and the way he kept twisting prompted Marie Belle to enquire.

"Are you uncomfortable?"

His shiny, almond shaped, hazel eyes looked perplexed at her question. "No, I feel well. I'm pleased to meet your father and," he put his head down as he fumbled a linen napkin on his lap with one hand and a sharp meat knife with the other, "so sorry about your mother, I had expected..."

"It was long ago. My sorrow is that I don't remember her. My father keeps her memory alive."

"Are you speaking of me?" her father asked playfully, ducking while coming through the kitchen doorway of the narrow five-story house. Monsieur Soeira's hair was freshly brushed and oiled, darkening the silver and increasing the blackness of his natural color. His teeth weren't perfectly straight but the uniformity of them and years of a good diet kept them attractive. His eyes were crisp and bright for a man his age. His skin, especially his hands, were soft, not rough like those Jacob saw at the waterfront or like Abraham's from his agricultural endeavors.

"Father, I was telling Jacob how you have kept mother's memory alive."

"If she hadn't had such a good heart she would be with us today. I suppose we must care for those less fortunate. Do you agree Jacob?"

"I do indeed," Jacob agreed. He cared for the plight of others, he had seen desperate living conditions when he went to foreign ports. "It is often grotesque."

"What's that?" her father replied. "Oh yes, the plight of the needy. I do care for them... but Jacob, we must remember... many of the less fortunate lack the initiative to better themselves, don't you agree?"

"Monsieur Soeira," Jacob said, leaning forward, forgetting that he was Marie's father and a man of power and influence. "I do not agree. The majority of the less fortunate lack opportunity."

Monsieur Soeira raised an eyebrow. "Jacob, there are very few who enjoy social opportunities. The masses are ignorant. Many of them are happy to have a warm meal once a day and stay dry. If they have families, the men are fortunate to have enough work to feed them and a woman who cares for the home. A man is doing exceedingly well if he can school his children for the first few years."

Jacob stated more of his case. "Amsterdam has many opportunities for improvement. If we can offer the ability for all children to learn to read it will be a glorious achievement. I heard just this week that a man has invented a machine that can print books. There is no longer the need to transcribe by hand, provided of course..."

Monsieur Soeira spoke up, "Provided the community has the resources to purchase this new printer."

Jacob became excited, "Can you imagine what a printer like that could do for the hamlets? Everyone could learn to read. We could teach art, science and religion. We could share the stories of Moses and the songs of David. We could teach numbers and astronomy."

Monsieur Soeira again raised an eyebrow. "Jacob, are you familiar with science and astronomy?"

Embarrassed at his outburst Jacob calmly tried to rephrase his thoughts. "No, but I'm acquainted with those who are. I am friendly with Nicolaes, a sea captain who draws maps and knows how to follow the stars. I learn from him."

"Ah, Nicolaes," Monsieur Soeira jumped in aggressively, "I know Nicolaes, your impression of him is different than mine. I see him as a very stubborn man."

"Nicolaes? You do business with Nicolaes?" Jacob was astounded.

"I said he is a very stubborn man." Monsieur Soeira said, and then his beautiful hands picked up a crude large copper bell and rang it. Jacob cringed at the loud noise and Marie Belle giggled. Marie's little boy came running in along with their servant, a fair-skinned Eastern European girl that couldn't have been more than fourteen. In her arms she carried a large hot platter that held a steaming game bird surrounded by boiled root vegetables and greens. The spices she used wafted a wonderful aroma into the room.

"Climb up here young man," Monsieur Soeira said to his grandson and placed him upon his knee.

Marie Belle shook her head in dismay. "What kind of manners are you teaching my son?"

"David has plenty of time to learn manners. His manners are finer than most," her father said.

Jacob stared at the little boy whose golden hair was shoulder length, soft and curly in little ringlets. His cheeks were pink on top of a lovely light-brown skin, his eyes sparkled and he had just a hint of a dimple on one side. His teeth were slightly crooked, taking after his grandfather, and he laughed heartily as if no one had ever hurt him nor ever would. Jacob's staring caused young David to grow shy.

Jacob turned to Marie Belle, "In your travels did you see this printing machine?"

Monsieur Soeira laughed, "You are very interested in this machine. I have seen three. A man in the Rhine, Johann Gutenberg has printed the Bible."

"You've seen these printers? Have you seen the booklets they print? Is it clear? What kind of parchment do they use? Does it rip?"

"Jacob you are the most inquisitive young man I have ever met. You fire questions much too quickly. Would you like to see it?"

"I would love to see it. Where is it?" Jacob said, forgetting his table manners.

"I can arrange to have one brought over from the Rhine," Monsieur Soeira bragged.

"We could have one here in Amsterdam?" Jacob smiled and winked at Marie Belle.

"I could easily arrange that. Provided..." Monsieur looked up from his food and Jacob suddenly lost all interest in his, "provided you help me persuade Nicolaes to do a little business with me."

"Father!" Marie protested, "I have not invited Jacob to dine with us so that you can recruit him into your business."

Monsieur Soeira raised an eyebrow. He backed away from his request. "I beg your pardon Jacob. I am very engrossed in my business at present and Nicolaes is a skipper with integrity. My understanding is that he will be shipping through the Strait of Gibraltar and extensively into several ports along the Mediterranean. He shall be gone for some time. No other skipper will be traveling that far. I have cargo I need sent to Rome. The man seems to want nothing to do with me, I thought perhaps."

Jacob looked at Marie Belle's flushed, embarrassed face but she did not look away. She made direct eye contact with Jacob who turned to her father.

"I am on very friendly terms with Nicolaes. I will see what I can do."

After dinner Jacob gave a polite thank you for the Shabbat dinner, said shalom to her father and allowed Marie to escort him to the door.

She tried to reassure Jacob. "You don't need to procure the Skipper's..."

He put his hand upon her forearm. "Shhh... it's fine. I know Nicolaes well. He's an honorable man and a fine skipper."

"But..." she tried to interrupt but his eyes told her different. Suddenly she realized that he knew about the bribe and the trade for power and her manner changed.

Jacob spoke reassuringly. "There are those things which we know of but of which we do not speak."

"Jacob, where is the honor? Is it for the benefit of people's lives or for the procurement of wealth?" she asked. He could see she was distraught.

"Both." He said courageously. "Without reward many good deeds would go undone. I shall see you soon with the news of Nicolaes. Shabbat Shalom," he said and bowed his head.

"Shabbat Shalom," she said and slowly closed the door.

Shortly after Jacob finished his crispy morning meal of bread and herring, he put away pieces of one of his stories and walked briskly to the dock. He had not expected to see Nicolaes, he knew the skipper was resting with his family and would not take lightly to being bothered. Jacob pondered the morality of disturbing him. He was, after all, seeking the Captain for his own self-interest. If he could draw Nicolaes into the clandestine scene he'd found himself in, he would probably win the respect of Monsieur Soeira. He hoped to draw closer to Marie. He feared she was becoming a friend instead of the romantic partner he'd hoped for.

One of the most valuable attributes that helped Jacob with his chronicling, was the ability to analyze all aspects of a situation. The bad habit of jumping to conclusions had put him in precarious positions where he lost face with members of the community. Fortunately, due to the quality and accuracy of his news, his reputation was quick to rebound.

If there were war skirmishes within five-hundred miles, Jacob would know. He'd been the first to inform the community that Pope Nicholas V had ascended to the throne. He warned his friends when influenza was sweeping towards the Netherlands or when acquaintances of his peers had succumbed to malaria in the Holy Land. He knew when Grietje's cow gave birth and he knew when fishermen would arrive with fresh catch. But now, as he walked vigorously away from the dock and toward his friend Abraham's to ask for advice, he pondered the fate of Marie's dead husband. How could the young man have died?

"Abraham!" Jacob shouted to his curly, blonde-haired friend. Abraham's long legs moved quickly down the street and he did not hear him.

Jacob knew where Abraham was headed and was not interested in following him to the homes of the devout to pray with the orthodox men of the community. Jacob felt he could pray at home and a little piece of his thoughts told him he was not sure he wanted the Almighty in on this one. Not just yet. He knew Abraham would ridicule him for changing his mind about the scholars, Barrents and de Montalvo, and their gifts of paintings to the Pope, in exchange for rewording the Bible. Making a full turn in the middle of the street, Jacob did what he knew was right. He headed for the prostitutes of Damstraat to see if any of the women knew. The information that came through Damstraat was reliable and from a variety of originations. All the news was heard first in Damstraat.

"Ah Jacobi," several of the young prostitutes said as they greeted him, making him feel boyish. Two years ago he'd recognized one of the pretty young women from his childhood in Friesland. She'd wanted to experience cosmopolitan life in Amsterdam and had aged a lot since arriving. It was difficult for him to see her. She'd once been fresh and in her bloom. She'd called him Jacobi in front of the other women and the name stuck.

"Morning," he said with a smile. "Is all well and have you any news?"

"Jacobi," one of them addressed him while putting her hand upon his forearm. "If all were well we would not be in this business, we stay as well as we can. We take time off but most of us have grown accustomed to the large sums we receive. It isn't easy to acquire a husband after this line of work but we are well enough. The day just got better seeing your smiling face."

"We've heard some news of you Jacobi," another said. "One of the damsels returned from market and reported she saw you with a certain fine lady. Is this true?"

"Am I not always with fine ladies?"

The laughter was unanimous and Jacob blushed, he hadn't realized his romancing reputation was so thin. He quickly changed the subject. "Well ... albeit you are all well. I see plenty of smiles, is there any disturbing news I should know of?"

They shook their heads no. He could tell by their straight eye contact there was no news to be found at their house of prostitution so he bid them a fine day and wandered into the narrow corridor that ran parallel to their establishment. The corridor had been designed to let the women come and go freely and as a private escape route for dignitaries who were *just visiting*.

The damsels and their poking fun at his lack of romance laid heavily upon his mind. He swallowed his pride. After all, if the damsels had laughed so heartily at his lack of romance didn't that give more reason to procure love?

It was a long walk to the farmland where Nicolaes had a homestead. Jacob hurried as he passed grazing cows and tall grasses and the occasional friendly traveler on foot. He saw several new faces and witnessed new farmhouses under construction and was shocked at the large barn being erected by a group of both young and old able-bodied men. When he finally arrived at Nicolaes's farm, only his wife was about. Jacob greeted her and she welcomed him in for hot milk and cheese.

"Your milk and cheese is the finest," he flattered her. She smiled and accepted it graciously.

"Nicolaes has taken the children to the dock. He needed to check on things before sailing out after Shabbat."

"He's sailing so soon? He told me he intended to stay awhile, to be with family for a long rest."

"Yes, he had intended to but we have thought that it best that he sail before the big storms come. If all goes as planned he'll be home for Chanukah."

"I'm sorry to hear he must leave again, I truly am," Jacob told her sincerely, forgetting his own agenda. "I'll see if I can catch him at the port."

She smiled politely. "If you're unable to meet with him, is there something I can relay?"

"You could tell him that Jacob was here modestly asking to consider a request."

She nodded. Jacob could see that she was disappointed at her husband's having to leave again.

He reached for her hand to bid her good bye, "Perhaps your loss should be my temporary gain but an issue where we all gain." She gave him a strange look. He'd seen it many times before. It was all part of his job as Chronicler.

Jacob found Nicolaes doing a serious walkover on his vessel while his five small children played about the deck. Nicolaes, glancing over regularly to see that the children would not endanger themselves, appeared to Jacob to be out-of-sorts.

"Ahem," Jacob cleared his throat and caught the skipper's attention. He nodded but only gave a half smile.

"I'm sorry to hear you'll be off again. You've just returned," Jacob said.

Nicolaes frowned and looked out at the sea. "Families need food. If I leave soon I'll beat the storms."

"Your wife tells me you'll be home for Chanukah. Sounds like winter weather."

"I presume. If the weather is bad it will be Passover before I see my family again."

"I'm sorry," Jacob told him genuinely.

"Why are you here? Do you want to come along?"

"No, I have a favor to ask."

Nicolaes ran his hands up and down the thick ropes that held his sails secure. "Look at the fray here Jacob," he shook his head. "Can you imagine being out in the rough seas with such a frayed rope?" He scorned and then hollered at his children to be more careful while they played.

"What favor do you need? If I come across stolen bounty would I save you some?"

"No, if I may be frank, it has to do with love."

"Love… we spoke of love the last time. Did she enjoy the wine?"

"Yes, and so did her father. And he knows fine wines."

"Who is her father?" Nicolaes asked nonchalantly as he walked to another huge pile of ropes and sat down next to them to begin the arduous task of checking them carefully.

"Monsieur Soeira."

Nicolaes dropped the rope. He raised his eyebrows and his ears followed. "Monsieur Soeira is her father?" Do you realize who he is? My God, he's a prominent banker and world traveler. He dines with Cosimo de Medici. I've no doubt he associates with Royals. He's probably the wealthiest man to walk the streets of Amsterdam."

"Don't frighten me Nicolaes! His daughter is a gentle lady. And she is a mother."

Nicolaes glowered at him.

Jacob glowered back but wondered... *does he know something about Marie Belle?* He knew that look upon a man's face. *What does he know?* Jacob prompted him. "Do you think I should inquire about the identity of the child's father? Would that be improper?"

The skipper ignored the question and returned to Jacob's original request. "What is this favor you need?"

"Uh... I need you to... uh ... Monsieur Soeira has requested I ask you..."

"I have already been asked and I said no."

"I haven't asked you yet."

Nicolaes rose from a sitting position and jumped onto a crate. His height was intimidating, especially since the crate gave him another foot-and-a-half to his already six-foot frame. "I know all about it. *We* all know about it. There are many things in this community that you know nothing of."

Jacob responded quickly. "I question that. I'm very well-informed."

"No, you aren't..." Nicolaes blasted him, his voice direct and angry. "Because you tell. Your job is to go around telling everyone everything. You cannot keep a secret. You are a Chronicler. If one wishes to keep a secret he does not tell the Chronicler." He laughed, heartily. "Can you imagine if we told you everything?" Then he looked straight into the young man's eyes and realized he had hurt his feelings.

"I beg your forgiveness lad, I'm tired and saddened that I must return to the sea." He waved his large calloused hands toward his five children. "Try to feel as I do. It's painful knowing that the seas may take me and that I may never return to my family."

Jacob nodded but Nicolaes still felt bad that he'd blown up at his young friend.

"Go ahead lad, ask me your favor, perhaps I am wrong."

"Monsieur Soeira has pegged you as a stubborn man and..."

Nicolaes scoffed and Jacob glared at him. The skipper waved his hand several times dictating Jacob to continue.

"And he wants, uh… needs you to speak with him. He has business he wishes to discuss."

Nicolaes returned to being ornery again. He agreed to meet with Monsieur Soeira but not without first telling Jacob, "You tell Soeira that I'll meet with him but he'd better be prepared to offer me a large sum for this *favor*. I shall be expecting great compensation for the risk that I, a Sephardim skipper, will be making with his *Papal exchange*."

"I'm not privy to what Monsieur Soeira will ask. I have heard some talk though, of course," Jacob lied about knowing of the scheme to curry favors with the Pope in exchange for altering the Bible.

"Yes, of course," Nicolaes said with a smile and then jumped down from the crate, startling Jacob. But when he broke into the crate and pulled out another bottle of wine, Jacob smiled.

"Working men have their rewards lad," Nicolaes said proudly.

Jacob had succeeded in setting up a meeting between Monsieur Soeira and Nicolaes but he was troubled by the look the Skipper had given him when he spoke of Marie Belle's child. What did he know? Without haste and without thought to the tattered clothes he had on, he headed to Marie Belle's.

"Good day Sir," the servant girl said. Jacob remembered her from the dinner he'd shared with the Monsieur and Marie. Today she looked more rested. She was obviously well cared for, treated as part of the family.

"I'm seeking either Marie Belle or Monsieur Soeira, are they about?"

"Monsieur Soeira is meeting inside with Rabbi Samuel. Would you like to wait?"

"Yes, of course," Jacob said nervously, shocked that Rabbi Samuel was there. This business transaction was becoming conspicuous.

"Please make yourself comfortable outside the door. When they're finished, Monsieur Soeira will exit and see you there. Then you may speak with him."

"Thank you," Jacob said and sat himself down into a tall, stiff chair then let out a deep sigh. He could hear talk but their voices were muted and Jacob was so nervous his ears were ringing and his head spinning so he could not hear much. But as their conversation became heated, Rabbi Samuel and Monsieur Soeira's voices became quite clear.

"You owe it to the boy," Jacob could hear Monsieur Soeira say to Rabbi Samuel.

"Yes, I am so sorry it happened," the Rabi replied. "I should have never let myself be so captivated by her beauty."

Jacob froze. *Was Rabi Samuel the father of Marie Belle's son? Old man Rabbi Samuel?* Jacob lifted himself quickly from the chair and ran out quietly not wanting them to know he heard. He ran to the docks and out to the end where there was no one to hear him cry. He pulled at his hair and rubbed at his tearing eyes. He felt dirty. He'd thought of himself rollicking about with Marie Belle. He'd made love to her in his mind. He'd imagined he kissed her nipples when they were soft and again when they were erect. He'd held his hard manliness and pushed up against his bed pretending again and again to thrust into her. He'd imagined that he had let go of his semen inside of her, hoping to make a child of his own. Oh now he was ill. *Rabbi Samuel? How could he?* He must seek out Abraham and tell him of the rabbi's obscene nature and he must immediately cease thinking of Marie Belle.

"Lord forgive me for excluding you from my thoughts. I shall not do that again for it has brought me less wisdom and I feel a fool," he said then set off to warn Abraham.

Jacob was relieved to find his friend busy working with his rootstocks. Abraham looked up as Jacob entered the large door he usually left open to let the sun and fresh air in. Jacob could immediately tell Abraham was in a good mood.

"I'm sorry to destroy this gorgeous day by telling you that our holy man is undisciplined," Jacob remarked rudely.

Abraham wrinkled his nose and stared at Jacob. He had no notion of what his friend was talking about.

"I'm sorry that holy men are dirty," Jacob said again, this time louder.

Abraham was beginning to wonder if Jacob hadn't been nibbling the little golden mushrooms that spring up in the cow pastures after the rain.

"Holy men ... dirty? Jacob, if others heard you speak of the Rabi this way, you would not be welcome in the Sephardic community. You'd be returned to Leeuwarden to spend your days."

"Rabbi Samuel is dirty. He has erections just like all of us, only he takes young women into his arms, beautiful young women and he spreads his seed. I know this."

Abraham thought Jacob toyed with him and was dismayed at his friend's poor taste. "How do you know this?" He took a step toward Jacob with the thought of throwing him out of the room but gained composure. "Rabbi Samuel was married. His wife died and he has spoken of nothing else since. All men struggle with the flesh but I know he would not be… dirty as you say."

Jacob pointed his angry finger at Abraham. "I'll keep this between us and you'll do the same. But when I have proof, I'll go to the others and it will be another one of my stories for all to hear!" He stamped his foot, turned and marched out the door. He returned home and threw himself down on his bed and sobbed.

Jacob lay sobbing for quite some time. He could not remove the image of Marie Belle fornicating with Rabbi Samuel. Did it feel as delightful as he'd imagined? The thought of Rabbi Samuel delighting in Marie Belle's wonderful, full breasts added a vicious jealousy to his angry emotional state. He thought of Rabbi Samuel's cat-like smile and knew that he must have worn that grin after delighting himself in her youthful, moist opening. Oh, it was sickening, why did he have to know? Did they still fornicate? Did Rabbi Samuel sneak off and meet with her so he could hold her again in his arms, feel her flesh as he, Jacob had longed to do? He lay sobbing until the sun lowered for the day. He lay sobbing as the sounds of the city grew quiet. But by the time the city began to sleep, he was thrusting his pelvis angrily, pretending he was making love to Marie Belle. Someday, he would enjoy her pleasures as no one else had. If Rabbi Samuel could have her flesh, he would have her too.

Jacob did not seek out Marie. It had been three days since hearing the bad news and three days since he spoke with Nicolaes. He hadn't inquired to anyone about anything worth chronicling, he just sulked around, eating very little. He avoided Abraham and was not sure how to recapture his daily routine. Sooner or later he would meet Marie Belle on the street. She loved fresh air and the outdoors. Perhaps he should inquire about going to sea. It would be good to get away. With that thought, Jacob headed to the port where he thought Nicolaes might be. The afternoon was growing late. The sun hit the water, and brought warmth as he walked along the sea wall. He wasn't thrilled when he looked up and saw Nicolaes working on the sails. He'd hoped Nicolaes wouldn't be there and he could think twice about leaving Amsterdam. From up in the sails, Nicolaes had a great view. He'd seen him coming for quite some time.

"Shalom, Jacob!" he called out. "I've not heard from Monsieur Soeira. Has he found another skipper?"

"You can forget about that. I have another favor to ask," he said sullenly.

Nicolaes hollered back, "I will probably say yes if it is more desirable than the last. Let me climb down and show you the new map I've drawn."

Jacob hefted himself onto the ship as Nicolaes climbed down from the sails and then retrieve some warm milk he'd kept tightly wrapped in a blanket. Jacob admired the eloquence at which Nicolaes settled comfortably on the deck and unrolled his new map. Nicolaes's navigational wisdom was artistically displayed on thick, crisp parchment drawn in dark ink. He knew the seas well. As an accomplished artist he unfolded it proudly.

"Jacob," he put his index finger on Amsterdam, "We are here, at the North Sea. And here is Lisbon. As long as they don't ask if I'm a Jew, life is good in Lisbon. I will go through Gibraltar and sail to Valencia. From Valencia I will sail to Palermo then head north to Rome then return again when the winds are favorable. Do you like my map Jacob?"

"Yes. Your knowledge of the stars is accurate. Everyone is secure sailing with you. No one is afraid. Nicolaes never gets lost."

"My father taught me to navigate the stars. He was taught by an Arab who was a dear friend of my fathers. They shared the same passion for knowledge when others were focused on the simplicities of the day... eat, sleep, and find a woman..." He looked at Jacob wondering if he had gone too far but Jacob nodded. He understood.

"My father's Arab friend spent his lifetime in the desert. He knew the constellations. My father adapted them to his sea-faring. He made mistakes and we have both learned from them."

Jacob didn't seem to be paying attention.

"Jacob, are you ill?"

"I've seen better days. I feel as though I've grown twenty years older and forty years wiser in the last three days."

"Why? What's happened since I last saw you?"

Jacob stared at Nicolaes. He wanted badly to confide in him about Rabbi Samuel. He keeps secrets well. Perhaps he can keep his mouth quiet about Rabbi Samuel.

Jacob began, "Nicolaes I am very disheartened. I have learned that Rabbi Samuel is an evil imposter of a man. I have discovered that he is the father of Marie Belle's child, David."

Nicolaes broke into a spontaneous, booming laughter that could be heard up and down the port. His laugh was so loud and hearty, poor Jacob thought he would never stop. When he finally did, he looked at Jacob's sad expression and started up again until tears welled from his face. He put his hand on Jacob's shoulder.

"Oh lad, I don't know where your information comes from but you'd better check your sources," he laughed heartily again.

Jacob continued to pout. "Why do you laugh? It's true."

"No, it isn't. I've heard of Monsieur Soeira's lovely daughter. Her child is not fathered by Rabbi Samuel," he laughed again just as heartily.

58

"It would be humorous if it were not true," Jacob complained. "What do you know?"

Nicolaes grew serious and ended his laughter. "You're the Chronicler. Find out on your own. But I can assure you, it is *not* Rabbi Samuel," he chuckled.

Jacob picked himself up from the crate where he was sitting and bolted for home.

After a good night's sleep, Jacob was ready to begin a new day. He combed his hair carefully and refrained from his morning ritual of herring so his breath would not be fishy. Today he would speak with Marie's father.

"Good day Jacob," Monsieur Soeira's servant said with a smile.

"Good day," he said politely.

"Are you here to see the Monsieur or Marie Belle?"

"Is Marie here?"

"No Sir, she is not."

"Then I'm here to see Monsieur Soeira, please."

She led him through the open door that led to Monsieur Soeira's study and seated him in a chair at the table. Jacob thanked her. There were maps and parchments strewn about the table. Someone was doing research. Jacob analyzed the chairs and came to the conclusion that several people had sat there recently.

"Jacob!" Monsieur Soeira spoke when he entered the room.

For the sake of love Jacob held steady.

"Good morning Monsieur Soeira, it is nice to see you again," he lied. "I have spoken with Nicolaes and he has agreed to meet with you. Although I am not quite sure of the matter," he said, hoping for some insight.

Monsieur Soeira refreshed his memory. "As I mentioned before at dinner..."

"Yes and thank you for the wonderful dinner. I enjoyed it and I do remember... you have *cargo* bound for Rome."

"Yes. And I need a skipper who will be discreet. The goods are to be delivered personally."

"Personally?" Jacob grew angry. "He will bid you good day if you ask too much."

Monsieur Soeira pulled at his mustache thoughtfully. "So be it... I'll hire an attendant," he said referring to Jacob.

"Oh no Monsieur, I don't want to go to sea."

He eyed him thoughtfully. "If you have a change of heart..."

"Of course Monsieur, of course."

Their conversation was broken by the entry of Marie and her child, David. Jacob blushed at the sight of her when he saw how delighted she was to see him.

She'd just returned from a hearty walk. Her chest rose and fell with each breath. "Jacob!" she said between pants.

"Jacob!" little David repeated.

"You're a popular man," Monsieur Soeira said genuinely. At that moment the two men's eyes locked and Jacob knew he was sitting with a man of depth and complexity.

"I hope so," Jacob said, and then looked down at Marie and her son. "I hope so."

"David, please go help in the kitchen, I would like to speak with Jacob alone."

"I will, but can we go back outside again for another walk before nightfall?" the boy asked.

"He loves to walk," she said apologetically. "Yes, David, we'll go for another walk, a longer one and perhaps... Jacob would like to come too."

Before heading into the kitchen, David clapped his hands and raised a tight fist into the air, amusing them all.

"I have not seen you up and around," she told Jacob.

Feeling chastised, he put his head down. "I've been ...following a story."

"Is it interesting?"

"No. Do you have anything to drink?"

She frowned at his abruptness. "Do you mean Father's strong drink?"

"No... no... I'm sorry. I'm thirsty but it can wait."

"I get you a fermented beverage that will not inebriate you. It will delight your palette."

She returned shortly and Jacob gulped it down. He couldn't help the edginess he felt. He needed to discuss the matter of her child and he had no idea how to broach it... until she created an opening.

"David's father loved this drink."

Jacob stiffened, took a deep breath and awkwardly asked, "And David's father was?"

She stared straight at him and answered. "David's father was a Christian."

"A New Christian?" he asked, referring to Jews who converted to Catholicism to avoid persecution.

With a sweet smile, she shook her head no. Jacob detected that her smile was a little mischievous.

"A Christian ... *Christian*," she answered.

"Not Jewish?" Jacob asked, "One of those Christians?"

"Yes," she laughed. "One of those. But I am a Jewess so my son is a Jew. David's father has passed so I needn't worry about religion for my son. David shall be raised with the rest of the Sephardim. I may never tell him his father was a Christian."

Jacob nodded and let out a big sigh, relieved that he had been wrong about Rabbi Samuel. He didn't think to ask how David's father, the poor man, had met his demise. His only desire now was to sit back and relax at the table. His legs were wobbly but she'd not invited him to sit down after she walked into the room, so both stood staring at each other, neither knowing what to say.

She finally broke the silence. "How's the deal coming along?"

His face told her he didn't understand.

"The arrangement you've made with my father to have a printing machine come to Amsterdam."

"Yes," he said, remembering Gutenberg's new printing apparatus. "I'd forgotten about that. It was implied that if I help your father secure shipment of his cargo to Rome that Amsterdam shall have a printing machine." He smiled at her affectionately. "Did someone say something about a walk?"

After walking with Marie and little David, Jacob was in high spirits. He headed toward Abraham's. A different route took him past the favorite cafe of his Sephardim brothers. He poked his head into the cavernous room and waved broadly. He could tell by their grins that Nicolaes had not had the will to keep quiet about something as scintillating as Jacob's blunder regarding Rabbi Samuel.

"Wonderful story Jacob the Chronicler," one of the men shouted as the others joined in laughter.

Jacob was embarrassed but did not let the old men get under his skin. He was relieved when he finally arrived at Abraham's flat. "Abraham! Dear friend!" Jacob greeted him.

"What are you so happy about my misdirected friend?"

"I was mistaken about Rabbi Samuel, please forgive my transgression."

Abraham's expression was unpleasant. "I knew you were wrong. Rabbi Samuel is a good man. He would be the last..."

"Yes, yes, I know."

"And the young woman? Marie Belle? She would not bed an old rabbi. My friend where do you invent these thoughts?"

"I was outside the study of Monsieur Soeira and I overheard them talking. Monsieur Soeira told Rabbi Samuel that he 'owed it to the boy' at which Rabbi Samuel replied, 'Yes, I am so sorry it happened. I should have never let myself be so captivated by her beauty'." Jacob hung his head, "Wouldn't you have believed that Rabbi Samuel was the father?"

Abraham laughed.

"I'm tired of the laughter. It feel like all of Amsterdam is laughing at me."

"It will be fine Jacob," Abraham reassured him. "I know who Rabbi Samuel was referring to when he spoke of being 'captivated by her beauty'. He was talking about the daughter of a prince. One with whom he had done some wrangling. The Prince sent his daughter to charm Rabbi Samuel."

"What?"

"A boy was crippled and maimed from a carriage accident the prince caused. He was to be compensated by the prince but he and his daughter left the night before the morning they were to pay up."

"Ah... so Monsieur Soeira believes that Rabbi Samuel owes something to the boy who was a victim in the carriage accident?"

"Yes. Exactly. Rabbi Samuel was so captivated by the beauty of the prince's deceitful daughter he allowed the prince to leave without payment."

"I believe this issue is now closed," Jacob told him. "Shalom my friend."

"Shalom," Abraham said and with his gentle proficient hands he slowly turned to the hundreds of grape rootstocks that would one day become the vineyards of Europe, the Mediterranean and the rest of the known and unknown world.

Jacob and Marie Belle are privately wed

"Your father cares deeply for you Marie but I don't believe he wanted to draw attention to our marriage because David's father was a Christian."

"We had no papers confirming the legality of our marriage but I tell you Jacob, we were legally married. David is not illegitimate."

"Of course not," he assured her as he held her tightly. Illegitimacy had not even occurred to him.

"I had been left a widow through most unfortunate circumstances. It was of no fault of mine that my husband took that deadly fall from a horse. He should have known better than to ride in that storm."

"Sometimes our fate is changed by storms that come upon us unexpectedly."

She agreed and wondered what fate their lives held in the palm of nature's hand.

Marie Belle had grown moody over the winter and he'd assumed it was due to the colder, shorter days. But there was something on her mind that she would not speak of. Finally, one evening when her father was away from home, she admitted to Jacob that she was feeling cut-off from her normal activities.

"I used to be so free. Little David and I would roam the streets of Amsterdam and walk along the canals. We'd watch the musicians as they sang for their evening meal. I also helped my father. I made arrangements for business meetings, and scoured the neighborhood searching for new artists. Now..." she looked at him with tears in her dark eyes and long eyelashes. He respected her sincerity and knew by her face that she would tell him what was in her heart.

"You have taken my place in Father's life. You're doing what I used to do."

He sat motionless at the table where they'd just finished dining. His straight brown hair hung in his face. They were alone. The daze in his comely, almond-shaped, hazel eyes saddened her as she looked into them. He thought for a long while before he spoke. When he did his words were frank.

"This is not what I wish to do for my livelihood. If it's not what you wish, we should combine our talents. We'll tell your father that we have issues and we need to rearrange the situation."

"I doubt father would approve. He is so domineering. He has David under his complete command. You would think he was David's father."

"Yes you would. Perhaps we should break away. We could visit Paris."

"It's worth thinking about. We could be away from Father and still attend to business. He travels to Paris frequently. Perhaps he'd be pleased."

"He has us perched in his claws."

"Yes he does." She wore a sorrowful face, no different than Jacobs.

"We must accept his graciousness. He's been kind to the community and has promised to provide a printing house for Amsterdam. I could busy myself with that. I want to teach David the art of retelling stories." The thought of passing along his occupation to was a pleasant one.

"You want to teach David to be a Chronicler?"

"Yes. I could teach him a skill that would be both interesting and beneficial to any community he became a part of. He could teach his children as well."

She rose from her chair in a dreamy trance. "I don't think father would mind. He may be quite proud." She let out a sigh of relief. "I'll talk to Father about Paris and your return to chronicling. With you busy, he'll have more errands for me."

THREE

Amsterdam where Jacob and Marie Belle have grown elderly. They reside quietly and prosperously thanks to the generous estate of Marie's father, Monsieur Soeira. Marie's son David, is forty-three-years old and lives in the same neighborhood he has since childhood.

"Rabbi Amos, it is with pleasure I come here tonight," David said, greeting thirty somber faces of men attending the Friday night Shabbat gathering at the home of Jacques du Veaux.

"Jacob has successfully taught you the trade," Rabbi Amos said admirably, referring to David's skill as Chronicler.

David smiled and nodded in agreement. His step-father Jacob, whom they fondly referred to as *the Lion*, had taught him well. Even today, Jacob coached David adamantly about the correct way to approach the group with the news that had spread like a fire through the Jewish neighborhood. Jewish refugees from the south were escaping to the north to join their communities. Jacob drilled David about clarifying the issues and insisted he maintain calm. A worrisome future demanded they remain composed.

David finally spoke. "I have the full story and when all are present, I'm ready to report."

"Everyone is here," Jacques du Veaux said impatiently, motioning for David to sit on the empty chair at the top of the room where the others had gathered around.

David sat down with the men. Half of them were well-dressed, wealthy Sephardic merchants who had made fortunes through family connections to Spanish and Portuguese trading. Amsterdam had proven a safe place of refuge for their Jewish ancestors, provided they kept silent about their origins and their religion. And provided they gave their children names that on outward appearances appeared Christian but had a Sephardic meaning or double meaning. Occasionally, a name was creatively adapted to blend in with the Christian community. As businessmen, they were welcome in the Netherlands. Their affluence helped the North Sea hamlets prosper.

The other half of the group was not shabbily dressed but one could say their clothing was drab and one often did. These were the workers of the community and David respected them as well as the others, sometimes even more so.

"Monsieur du Veaux, I want to thank you for opening your home this evening for Shabbat as well as every Shabbat. It's much appreciated," David began.

Jacques du Veaux motioned with his hand to cut short the introduction and begin the serious discussion.

"Yes, well..." David continued. "I know you've heard about the period of grace the Church in Spain has given heretics to confess their sins and convert."

"We are not in Spain," a voice spoke from the back.

Another man from the back, who David knew as the neighborhood glass blower asked, "I've not heard this word before, *heretics*, what does it mean?"

"It refers to someone one who believes other than the doctrine of the Church of Spain," David answered.

"That would make us heretics. We are Jews... not Christians," Jacques du Veaux spoke dismally.

"I'm afraid Monsieur du Veaux is correct. This is a period, a very short period, perhaps only a month, in which the Inquisitional Authorities want all of Spain's Jews or non-Christians to convert."

"Tell them what the authorities want the new converts to do," Jacques du Veaux spoke again angrily, making David uneasy and wondering why Monsieur du Veaux who seemed to know the situation so well, did not tell it himself.

But David spoke up. "After approximately thirty days they expect the New Christians to report heretics," he said, his voice trailing off. The situation appeared worse each time he spoke it, whether it was to Jacob, his mother, or any others he'd spoken to during his rounds as Chronicler.

The bread baker stood up. "May I speak?"

"Speak, speak," several shouted.

The baker continued. "The church is demanding the Jews convert and report all un-converted Jews to the Inquisition? They expect us to betray one another?"

"Yes," David said. "I wish I could tell you that the stories I hear are fabrications but they are not. I've heard it everywhere. On the docks, along the canals, in the market. I've even heard it spoken from the mouths of the inebriated in the dark shadows of the alleyways." David kept his head down then brought it back up in strength. "We need to prepare for hundreds, perhaps thousands of families. We need to prepare for this and be welcoming."

The ritual slaughterer, the *Shochet* stood to speak. "What will happen to the heretics if they ignore this period of grace?"

Rabbi Amos, who had remained silent, finally spoke. "We won't speak of the consequences that beset heretics who ignore this. Not this evening. Not on the Shabbat. As most of you know, there has been pressure on the Iberian Sephardim to convert to Christianity, and many have. The situation would be worse if prominent New Christians hadn't worked their charms within the Inquisition. But there is a growing hatred of New Christians by the common people of Spain. They still see them as Jews."

One young man jumped from his seat, knocking over an empty chair to his left. He kicked it loudly. "I find it abominable that they became Christians!"

Rabbi Amos defended the New Christians. "Let us not judge our brothers. They love their homeland. If you'd been asked to choose between your orchards and livestock, loving children and grandchildren ... to once again wander in the wilderness..."

"Is it true they changed their names?" another shouted.

71

"Yes, very often after conversion they take the name of their Godfather," Rabbi Amos replied. "Many still hold onto their sacred names."

"I have heard they are referred to as swine, is this true?" a younger man asked rudely.

"Yes, it is true," the Rabbi told him as he pulled a handkerchief from his pocket, removed his hat and wiped the sweat from his forehead. "Fear has led many New Christians to put swine into their stew to prove they are no longer Jews. They are called *Marranos*. It means swine. They are afraid for their lives and the lives of their families. Let us not speak of the darkness that may befall upon our Iberian brothers. Let us focus on the light of he who brought us from the desert so many years ago."

"Yes," David pleaded with the group. "There are issues we need to discuss. The families that will come, many have been practicing Christianity, only to protect themselves. I am told they will eagerly shed their Christian pretenses. They await the opportunity to enter the homes we use as synagogues. We must be patient and kind. Open your hearts. Find work for them. My grandfather told me that the Marrano Sephardim have strong connections in the shipping industry. Over time we shall all prosper."

"Rise," Rabbi Amos told the group. In devotion they all rose. They joined hands. In unison they reached their clasped hands to the ceiling. The men's dry, cracked knuckles revealed they all labored tirelessly in one occupation or another, whether they had their hands in the soil or upon wood or wheat.

"Brotherhood... love," the rabbi said and they all shouted back again, some stronger than others, "*Brotherhood love.*"

"Are we ready Brother?" the rabbi asked David as the men slowly filed out of Jacques du Veaux's home.

"Yes, we are ready. And with the arrival of the newcomers will bring a new prosperity. Will it not Rabbi?"

"Yes it will. Our connections in Portugal are solid," he said, and David could see the hope in the rabbi's eyes and his change of spirit. "And the good news that Da Gama has found a direct route to India's Malabar Coast will bring prosperity to the diamond trade. There will be new diamond cutting houses and jobs for hundreds of diamond polishers. If anyone should know this, it should be you."

David put his hand on the rabbi's shoulder. "There are many in this community who know the answer to that question better than I. I must be off."

"Oh David," the rabbi said smiling, "one more item."

"Yes?" David asked. Most of his golden hair had faded to gray and the lovely light-brown skin of his youth had aged.

"The community at large has decided that it's time you took a wife."

"A wife?" David said, as if he had not heard correctly.

"Wives are always chosen for the young men David. You were never given the opportunity," the rabbi said, surprised that David didn't appreciate his meddling.

"Rabbi Amos, I was not given the opportunity, my family has always..." he stopped short for he did not want to remind the rabbi that his family was not strict about Hebrew scriptures and the laws regarding marriage, so David just smiled and left quickly.

David's mother Marie, and his stepfather Jacob were old but their minds were sharp. Marie's father, Monsieur Soeira took a permanent residence in Paris where Jacob and Marie visited often. As young David grew older and after his grandfather, Monsieur Soeira died, he too enjoyed Paris and the surrounding villages, where he mingled with both Christians and Jews. Sometimes David associated with Cathars and enjoyed a drink in a pub with militants who would have loved to ax him on the spot. David was far from Orthodox and enjoyed frequent sexual proclivities with beautiful Parisian women. He hadn't given much thought to marriage and no one had chosen a wife for him, as was usually the case with most of the young men of his era.

"Mother," he addressed her one evening.

His mother's external beauty had faded. Her skin draped as much as the shawl about her arms. "Yes David."

"Rabbi Amos spoke with me today about a wife."

She raised her eyebrows.

"Yes Mother, a wife! I'm afraid the Sephardim have gotten together and have chosen a wife for me."

"Oh my," she said smiling. "Finally after all these years. Perhaps I shall have grandchildren?"

"Mother I know you've always wished for little children and to continue the family but I am content. I am quite busy..."

Jacob came shuffling into the room. "Did I hear David?" He used a cane to walk but his mind had not dimmed. David helped Jacob into a chair. The old man fell into it but smiled as he did.

Marie's voice was agitated. "The men at Jacques du Veaux's home this evening hinted that they had a wife for our son."

Jacob squinted his nose and peered at David and then looked at Marie. "I thought David had a wife in Paris. I thought he had two," he said then laughed whole-heartedly.

"It's not humorous," David said crossly. "I believe they may be speaking the truth and I don't know what my response should be."

"Dear boy," Marie said to her son.

"He's no longer a boy," Jacob told her.

"He'll always be my boy."

"Please... Father... Mother... what should I do?"

Jacob told him frankly. "You must respect their choice. This is how it's done."

"Who is she, this woman who will bear my grandchildren?" Marie asked frankly.

"Mother please! Don't make light of it. I'm deeply concerned. I'm considering leaving Amsterdam for good and taking up residence in a hamlet where grandfather left me a cottage."

Marie turned her stiff neck toward Jacob. "He's serious. We can't let him leave."

"I would visit often," David told his mother softly.

"Or…" Jacob said tersely. "You could marry her."

David grit his teeth. "I will think this through," David told them both, then rose and left the room.

As soon as he was out of hearing range Marie spoke fondly. "I remember walking all over Amsterdam with him."

"Yes. I remember it well. He was a handsome boy and you were the envy of all the Amsterdam artists. But now he's an older man. It has surprised me that the community never spoke to him about a wife."

"I heard rumblings. The other mothers always hinted but I just smiled and nodded. I thought one day he would bring home one of those pretty Jewish girls from the wealthier Sephardim neighborhoods on Paris's Left Bank."

"You always loved Paris."

"David and I accompanied my father often when his business led him to the Left Bank, along the River."

"The river that cuts the city in two. Paris was not always safe."

"Yes, but with father's influence we were protected. Such a fine life we led."

He reached for her hand. "Marie, thank you for sharing your father's wealth with me."

She brushed aside his praise.

"You could have been selfish but you chose to spend your life with a poor fellow who squandered about the docks looking for any morsel of a story to barter for an evening meal."

Her eyes held the beauty of her youth and the depth of her wisdom. In them Jacob saw their intertwined souls.

"La Rive Gauche," she said, still lost in fabulous memories of her youth. "La College de Sorbonne brought handsome men to Paris, from all over Europe."

He smiled at her taunting.

"David was born in the Jewish Quarter of Paris, it was just a swamp."

Jacob eyed her curiously. This was one story he had not heard.

"David's father was a Christian, yet the family carried the name of the swamp, *Marais*. Perhaps they were Christians who used to be Jews," she mused. "Marais is French for swamp and my father would not have his grandson called, David of the Swamp. After David's father died we went by Soeira. The name has served us well."

Jacob laughed. "And it has served me well too."

She smiled. She had always been pleased with her choice of Jacob for a husband.

"France's Jewish history has always fascinated me," he said.

She had wondered about her first husband's ancestry. He looked a Jew but his family were Christian and none would speak of their past. The history of Jews in France dated back to the first century. "The Romans went to France after they conquered Jerusalem and brought boatloads of Jewish prisoners."

"Many of the prisoners gained their freedom. Their children grew to be prosperous in medicine and viticulture." She wasn't telling Jacob anything he didn't know.

"The Jews supplied the grapes for Mass."

She laughed.

"What's so humorous?"

"Oh I don't know," she said shaking her head in disbelief. "Just the thought of Jews providing grapes for Mass. It is an odd world we live in."

Their son David wasn't laughing. He didn't find anything humorous about the rabbi finding him a wife. He was extremely nervous when he returned to Jacques du Veaux's to meet with Rabbi Amos and the others who said nothing about his tardiness.

"David!" Rabbi Amos greeted him, and with a chorus of "Shalom," from the others, he was escorted to a chair. He sat nervously as each of the men nodded and smiled. Rabbi Amos was the first to break the silence.

"We have our rituals to attend to but there is a matter concerning David, of which I'm sure he will be pleased. David cringed and shrunk lower in his chair. His eyes wandered around Monsieur du Veaux's home. Du Veaux's wealth had allowed him to acquire several large Biblical paintings, Christian in nature. David wondered why the other men had not chastised him for displaying Christian art that proselytized. But, had not his own grandfather marketed Christian art? And hadn't he prospered greatly from it? David's attention was pulled away when he heard Rabbi Amos speak his name again.

"David?"

"Rabbi, yes, I was just admiring, the art."

Every man in the room laughed. Rabbi Amos had to bang on his cup to get their attention, which had turned into a lively conversation regarding du Veaux's art. David made a mental note to look into it, as it seemed there was a bit of a story that he, as Chronicler, had neglected to follow.

"And ... thinking of what we spoke of last week," David said nervously, "the families coming north because of Spain's Edict of Grace."

Rabbi Amos's mind was on another track. He turned and smiled at the other men who nodded. "We have found you a delightful bride." The men clapped.

David's body heated and his face reddened. He looked to the Christian paintings for help. Could there be something Christians found soothing in these paintings? Hadn't thousands died for their beliefs? The paintings gave him no answers. He looked at the men in the room, their faces swollen with joy. The blood-shot eyes of the oldest lunged at David and he saw the younger men's smiles as atrocious. He needed to defend himself. He tried to speak quickly.

"No, no, we are not here to speak of women. We are here to..."

"Yes we are," Rabbi Amos said, ignoring David's protests. "We have found you a bride!"

"Who is she?" David finally asked.

"She?" Rabbi Amos said comically and the others laughed again. "You refer to your future wife as she?"

David was beside himself with the bantering at his expense and ready to excuse himself from the room.

"Magdalena!" Rabbi Amos said with a toothy grin.

"The Shochet's daughter?" David asked, not sure he could believe the drama unfolding. "The young woman whose father performs the ritual slaughters?"

"Yes!" the rabbi said with a big smile.

David wanted to run from the room, out the door into the streets of Amsterdam, and into the arms of his mother and the comfort of his father Jacob. "She is too young and I travel continually. I would make a terrible husband."

Rabbi Amos grabbed his hand with a grip so tightly David winced. "We love you David. You love us David. This is the Jews. We love!"

"Yes, yes," was the cry from the other men. "We love you David." One by one they rose from their chairs to congratulate him. As each came to touch his shoulder and look into his eyes to congratulate him, all David could see was a blur and out of the corner of his eye he spotted the only Hebrew painting in the room, Moses and his parting of the Red Sea.

David had lost the battle.

His mother told him several days later, "You can't be serious about going through with this wedding."

All Jacob could do was shake his head at his poor son. "I don't know how to resolve this," he told him, "You should have spoken up. The poor girl. What's her name?"

"Magdalena," David said hanging his head.

"How old is she?" Marie asked, fixing her eyes on him.

"She's just a girl," David said weakly.

"And a very big girl," Jacob said, his eyes widening. He had seen the Shochet's daughter.

"You're not helping!" David glared.

"Jacob!" Marie scolded. "It's what's in a woman's heart. That's the center of her soul."

Jacob raised his eyebrows at his wife and she uncomfortably gathered the cloth of her skirt in her wrinkled hands. "It's just that David has grown accustomed to some very fine ladies. There was that one in London and several in Paris. When he travels to Portugal they are absolutely smitten with him."

The reminders did nothing to soothe David who hung his head.

"When is the wedding?" Jacob asked but looking at Marie who had not taken her eyes off of her son.

"Soon. Is there anything you can do Jacob? Or you mother, to help make this union, just a quiet ceremony?"

"Perhaps. I'll have a conversation with the wives."

Marie Belle was successful spreading the word that the union of David Soeira and Magdalena Shochet was to be a small affair, immediate family only. And it was, except for Magdalena's two sisters, three brothers, the bride and groom's parents and the gaggle of on-lookers who gathered outside the fence. Outside the gate, uninvited people pushed and shoved for a better position to watch the ceremony, especially the tradition of breaking a glass. David tried desperately to pretend he was happy. The wine was vintage Burgundy. Marie had promised her father, before he died, that she would save it for the day David was married. She smiled at David as he and Magdalena climbed into the ritual slaughterer's family wagon pulled by oxen.

With his hands at his side and an expressionless face, Jacob stood watching. "I never thought David's marriage coach would have blood stains on the side."

"Yes, he is a good sport."

David's parents stood with their feet planted in the soil and the sun going down slowly. They watched the wagon roll off towards the countryside where David would temporarily reside with Magdalena and her family, in a small outbuilding on her father's farm. The sun reflected off the water and hit two tin buckets that were hanging from the back of the wagon. The jingle jangle of the buckets coupled with the oxen harnesses made a rather odd music for the two newlyweds.

"Perhaps David of the Swamp would have been a fitting name for him after all," Jacob said jokingly. Marie did not appreciate his humor. He put his arm around her tightly and walked her back to their fine brick home along the Amstel River.

Upon his arrival at the Shochet's farm, David was pleasantly surprised at the tidiness. He was asked him to wait outside while the women finished decorating the outbuilding where he'd be living with his new bride. The waiting gave David time to look around. Because he'd married the ritual slaughterer's daughter, he'd expected the place to be a bloody mess, but all the bones were burnt regularly and it had been cleaned for his arrival. They kept animal stock for themselves and David couldn't help but marvel at the health of their cattle and how content they were. Their black and white spotted fur was thick and clean and the air was crisp on this early fall day. There was plenty of grass in the pasture and the fences were taut and in good repair. The home was not towering like those in Amsterdam but had a sprawl to it. David could see that it had been added on to over the years and in a tasteful way. The outbuilding that was to house him and Magdalena was very small. It was very tidy and there were colorful flowers scattered all about the property. His thoughts returned to his dilemma and he hung his head. Magdalena was a nice girl but his feelings were only of a friendship nature. How could he perform his duties as a husband? Soon Magdalena's mother and two sisters came out of the outbuilding… all smiles.

Magdalena's mother took David by the hand. "It used to be an animal pen but now it's a small home. I'm sure you'll be comfortable."

"Thank you," he said averting her eyes.

"She's waiting… inside," her youngest sister said while the other one giggled.

"Thank you," he said wondering what he should do now. He looked at the outbuilding. The doorway was so short he worried he would hit his head. The building was so small he wondered if the bed would be long enough. The three women nodded that it was time for him to go inside. He tried to smile but wanted to cry. He nodded politely. The women walked away but not without turning around several times to peek.

David ducked his head and walked into the outbuilding where he was shocked to find his new bride had removed some of her clothes. He didn't know what the rules for Jewish wedding nights were, and it was apparent Magdalena didn't either. It made him question her father's ability to perform ritual slaughters. But when Magdalena smiled at him, and the clothing that held her breasts intact fell to the floor, he didn't care about kosher meat or Jewish dietary laws. What a surprise it was for him to see the beauty this young woman held under her clothing. His whole body was immediately warm. Yes, she was big, as Jacob had joked, but if the old man could only see her now with her warm full breasts spilling out and the delightful curve of her waist he would understand David's not knowing how to contain himself nor that he should. In all her innocence Magdalena was seductive just standing there. The smile she held grew larger as she saw his eyes widen. She giggled when she noticed his penis had grown hard. David assumed she was a virgin, and her sweetness about her now did not belie that. How was he to treat this damsel that he wanted to move so fast with? Gathering his wits he motioned for her to sit down on the straw bed. She did. She was shy about what was about to commence and trying to be brave, closed her eyes and leaned forward to kiss him. Seizing the opportunity he kissed her back and slid his hand behind the back of her neck to gently hold her aloft. She went limp, and the weight of her body fell upon David's arm. They fell back upon the bed, which made them laugh. Her dark eyes stared into his as she lay upon her back. Her brunette hair feathered out and David did not refrain from touching it. He wondered what paths her family line had taken that had given her this beauty. He could feel her rapidly beating heart. She turned and one of her breasts eagerly fell into one of his hands. *How could God have known what pleasures man desires?* He rubbed it gently and the desire began to rise so quickly, he paused. And at that moment she helped him help himself to her other breast and when he had caressed them both, she rose. She stood in front of him half dressed. He wanted to know what the other half looked like, and she could sense that. She pulled at the ties that held her skirt. The big beautiful woman who was all his, stood before him. Her beauty the grandest surprise of his life. He stood up and hastily removed his clothes. Her smile told him she was pleased. He grabbed her wealth of brown flesh. She placed her hands just above his buttocks. With vitality, he entered her. He slid easily into her and moved quickly and rhythmically. There was no blood and she knew what she was doing better than she'd let on. *She's not a virgin!* David grabbed her face and looked into her eyes. She cast them down. What farm boys had rolled her in the hay? What young man had delighted in this wonderful body? Their sexual dance became more dramatic as he knew… and *she knew he knew*. It was only the two of them. No rituals. No pretending. Just raw, earthy instincts. They went for quite some time. She was a perfect match and he enjoyed every sultry minute of it. There had been London, Paris and Portugal but there had never been Magdalena.

FOUR

Though Magdalena was young, she was a fine wife and David was pleased at the rabbi for choosing her. They would soon be parents.

"How does my wife feel today?" he asked as she struggled to keep up with him.

"I feel hungry always but the fresh air is nice. Where are you taking me that we should walk so far?"

David was a Chronicler and just as his father Jacob had done, he walked through Amsterdam's Jewish neighborhood, *Jodenbreestraat* seeking the day's news. "It is a surprise."

Even though her father's farm kept her busy, going to Amsterdam with a Chronicler required lots of walking. She wasn't accustomed to it. They came to a quiet area near one of the footbridges along the canal. Birds scratched at leaves that had fallen from trees during the first of the season's fall rains. The air was crisp.

"It's getting colder, winter's coming," she said apprehensively, wondering where he was taking her. As the daughter of the Shochet, she'd led a simple and protected life. David sought to educate and culture her. He'd been teaching her to read and today she truly wondered what he was up to. He sensed her impatience but did not provide clues until he led her up a small flight of stairs into a tiny but respectable home. He reached for her hand and together they stood at the door of the home. She assumed he was to meet someone but when he pulled a key from his coat pocket and opened the door, she was confused.

"Magdalena, enter our new home."

"Our new home? I thought my family's farm..."

"It's been difficult traveling back and forth. My work is in Amsterdam. We'll raise our children here."

"Here?" The stone building was dank. She shivered.

He led her to the hearth. "Here's where we'll have our fires."

"It more respectable than the converted animal shed we're in now. But I'll miss my family," she said, looking around dejectedly. "I understand about your work. Not much news to gather on the farm."

"Don't lose touch with animals, Magdalena. One day, we'll have our own farm."

"Perhaps," she said absent-mindedly. Her eyes wandered around the room, imagining how she would arrange their things. "I'm afraid you'll have to do more than share the latest news. Your grandfather's inheritance must be almost gone."

"No. Grandfather's businesses have grown," he said enthusiastically.

"He must have been very wealthy."

"Magdalena, my mother and father have not been well," he said, changing the subject. "They've requested to go to Paris to spend their last days."

"I'm sorry. I know how close you are."

"There's more to the story."

What more could he trouble her with? She had enough to worry about with the baby coming. Now she had to tell her family she would be leaving them?

"Mother and Jacob want to use Grandfather's wealth to buy several pieces of land. They're certain that their close friends will be forced to leave Spain. They'll need sanctuary."

"Your grandfather had that much wealth?"

He nodded.

"Where do they want to purchase land?"

"They want to buy a large piece of land, south of Amsterdam. Jews in Spain are terrified of the *Edict of Grace* that the church imposed. Many are moving to Portugal. Other Jews have been moving there and they feel safe."

"What effect will this have on us?" she asked.

David reached for her hand. "I will be away from you for long periods."

His words startled her. He could see she felt dejected.

He spoke up quickly. "I'll hire a nurse for you and the baby. You'll have fresh milk and cheese delivered every day. You'll want for nothing. I love you with all my heart… but we have ties to people who are having a difficult time and..."

She looked at him skeptically and he knew that look, not just from her but he had seen it all his life.

"We'll do all we can to make both properties profitable. Cattle ranching offers opportunities. And those less fortunate…"

She shook her head. "I think I understand. When you speak of those less fortunate… are you talking about slaves?"

"Yes. From Africa and from the east."

Magdalena's father had been opposed to anything that resembled slave trafficking. He believed in using his own two hands and enlisting his wife and children to help. That was all.

"I've seen the slaves from the Mediterranean and I have seen the men and women from Africa… and the blondes from Poland."

"Yes! And they all need a job and a roof over their head."

She continued expressing her discomfort. "I don't know that I could rest at night knowing we profited from slavery."

He argued with her. "As long as we don't enslave other Jews, it is not immoral."

"Whether I approve or not you will probably purchase humans to resell. I don't wish to hear of it. My father always said we are here to make others' lives better, not worse."

"Yes… of course. I will see to it, that if any of my negotiations involve human trafficking, the lives of the captives will be improved."

She winced and put her hand on her body where her unborn child lay. She looked away and let her eyes roam around the empty flat. The distraction did nothing to repress her distaste for the subject.

"I'll continue as Chronicler. I'll hear grand stories from Spain and Portugal, shall I not?"

"Yes you shall David. We'll hear grand stories," she said, trying to be lighthearted. It had not been the best of days for the daughter of the Shochet but she had married into prominence and wealth. If that brought with it, the task of working on the morals of mankind, then she would accept her role. "I shall have stories to tell one day too David."

She had just belittled him, but he was not sure, so he said nothing. Together they walked back into the heart of Amsterdam where a cart waited to return them to the farm, where her family warmly awaited their return.

When David was in Holland he spent as much time with his mother and father as he could. One evening David asked his father, "Do you believe it is against God's will to profit from the buying and selling of another human?"

"I do, but I'm probably the only man in Amsterdam who feels this way."

David's mother spoke up. "Of course you're not the only man in Amsterdam against slavery. I've heard many complain... it isn't decent."

David sat down. "Must you go to Paris? I agree that we should buy land south of Amsterdam. But Paris is..."

"Unsafe?" his mother interrupted.

"Yes, that too," David said waving that aside, "but that was not my thinking. I don't want you to go to Paris. Magdalena is with child and it will be difficult for us to divide ourselves between Paris and the Netherlands. If I could spend my time building a farm south of Amsterdam I would make my wife happy."

"Magdalena is a fine wife ... considering," Jacob said winking at his son.

"Yes father. She has changed me in many ways but lately she has given me a cool shoulder because of my business dealings that involve the selling of other humans."

Marie Belle stood up, lost her balance but regained it just in time to prevent a fall. Her voice was shaking. "Then refrain David. Do not do it. There will be those who do and they'll provide the domestic help we need." She paused making sure her voice was out of range of the housemaid. "House servants, well," she whispered. "That's a different issue. We make their lives better."

Jacob lifted his elderly body up and paced the floor slowly. He thought deeply. "David, you have grown accustomed to a life of abundance but it does not need to include trafficking human cargo. You're too fine a man. Do what you can to ensure you have wealth but most of all go about your job as Chronicler. Continue telling Amsterdam what goes on in the world. Tell your news to all who will listen. Through you son, our storytelling will live on. Teach one of your children to tell the stories of the times and have them teach one of their children. For what better way to learn but from the mistakes and successes of our elders?"

David knew his father was right. Jacob had been a wise and loving stepfather and David had always tried to be a good son. "I shall try to keep the promise of the Chronicler Father."

David knew his parent's idea to move to Paris was a silly dream of two old people. Still, they could easily find someone to make the trip to Paris and care well for them once there. To David's relief they did not ever mention it again. One day when David was visiting, Jacob put his hand out for David to come to him in his chair.

"Lift me up son, I want to see the sunset of old Amsterdam."

With Jacob's hand in his, David took his trembling father out to watch the sun set upon the canals of the city he loved.

"I may not live through another cold winter but remember what I told you about teaching one of your children to tell our stories."

"Yes Father."

"And David..." Jacob said, his wrinkled almond eyes twinkling, not with joy but a hint of sadness.

"Yes?"

"Kiss your mother very delicately this evening before you go. She has not been sleeping well and she has been missing breaths."

"No!" David turned and looked back at the home.

"But she must live to see our children, she has always wanted children!"

Jacob shook his head. "I'm afraid your mother shall not live to see your children. Stay as long as you wish tonight, and any night, for it may be her last. She has been a fine woman. I hope Amsterdam's artists will remember the beautiful woman she was and how she helped her father procure paintings for..." Jacob paused, and David smiled for they both remembered the role his mother had played in procuring art for the Papal, ensuring the New Christians a place in Spain's government where they had at least some power and influence over the fate of the Jews.

"She has made her place in history son."

David glanced back again to the tall building that housed his mother and had kept her safe through the years. He then looked at his feeble father Jacob, who smiled peacefully while watching another sun descend from the sky that loomed over the city he had always loved.

Marie Belle did not live to see the birth of her first grandchild, a healthy boy David and Magdalena named Akev. Nor did Jacob. One morning, Jacob awoke to find Marie had died in her sleep. The night before she had been happily recounting her fondest memories. He wrapped a finger around a lock of her silver hair. He kissed her cheek and prepared to tell the rabbi that burial preparations needed to be made. When the rabbi and four other men came to retrieve her body, they found Jacob, lying next to her with a pleasant smile on his face. Never to awaken again. The old Chronicler was dead.

"You're like your father," David said to Stephen. Abraham was a good friend to my father Jacob."

"Yes," Stephen smiled. "Right down to the grape root stalks."

They both laughed as Stephen lifted the heavy sacks of salt into the wagon and swooshed away flies from the two oxen about to pull the load.

"Older people have walked up to me and stared, as if they were seeing a ghost." Stephen was a tall, skinny man with curly, white hair just like his father, Abraham, Jacob's friend.

David was thoughtful as he also waved away flies. "But you don't share your father's religious beliefs."

Stephen was amused. He hefted another sack of salt into the wagon then turned to David. "My father was stern. The memories I have with my father are pleasant but they were not harmonious. Jacob had the same problem with him. He was very set in his beliefs. That was his nature."

David nodded and pulled a fig from his pocket, offering one to Stephen. "Jacob loved Abraham but they used to argue. I know your father took his rootstocks seriously. Why do you labor so hard over the salt when you have the rootstocks?"

"People need salt. All of Europe and much of the Mediterranean is planted with vineyards."

"I suppose there is more profit in the wine itself."

Stephen shot David a wary glance. "I have prospered from my father's grape rootstalks. As a Jew, I was forced to leave Spain and have left behind important contacts. Today in Portugal no one bothers me..." Stephen grabbed another salt sack. It seemed heavier this time. "I was able to sell my land in Spain and relocate to Portugal. For my safety, I am a Crypto-Jew posing as a Protestant. I unload salt from ships and redistribute it because it keeps my body strong and it is discreet. I make a handsome profit. Everyone needs salt."

"The last years have been uneasy for the Sephardim," David told him.

"I don't understand why you don't hide, like the rest of us. Your business ventures, your money lending and land purchases. And you don't draw the attention of the Inquisition?"

"My grandfather was wealthy and knew how to appease people in high places."

Stephen looked down.

"I know other Jews questioned my grandfather's motives, but I assure you, he was a good man and he loved his brothers. His actions saved thousands of lives. Here… in Portugal," David waved his arms at the rocky countryside. "Had it not been for my grandfather, Monsieur Soeira, the Sephardim would not be living and prospering in these lands. I still worry. We have work to do."

"Are you still searching for farmland in the Netherlands?"

David smiled at the thought of new land where he and his wife could build a homestead. He took pride in Magdalena's ability with animals and delighted in seeing her at her family's farm milking cows. Her gentle hand with the horses while birthing was invaluable. "I hope to raise our children in the countryside. It has been hard pulling Magdalena away from her family but I finally did. She visits frequently and has a hand in the raising of the farm stock. She found land south of Amsterdam, suitable for a farm," David said and then corrected. "Several farms. There's room for you and your family Stephen."

Stephen shook his head no. "I've just begun to work my new land. We will prosper in Portugal."

David was disappointed and he spoke solemnly. "We have avoided speaking of the thousands of our brothers and their families who have perished in Spain. We want to build a community consisting of several farms where we can all live without fear."

Stephen looked directly into David's eyes. "Will you live as Jews or will you pretend to be Protestants?"

David was firm. "We must continue posing as Protestants when we go to the cities. But when we are alone on our farms we will celebrate Shabbat and hold Synagogue… as we should."

David could not understand how the public executions of thousands of Jews in Spain did not weigh heavily on Stephen's decision to stay in the south. Especially when so many other Jewish Sephardim had gone north. David respected the son of his father's friend, Abraham. He put his hand upon Stephen's shoulder. "I hope this land provides well for you and your family."

They grabbed the last remaining sacks of salt from the wagon. Stephen went to the donkey that stood patiently. He stroked his gray fur and rubbed his ears. "There has been an offer," Stephen told David.

"An offer?" David was perplexed and nervously brushed his hand across the floor of the cart, brushing out spilled salt.

"A Noble has offered to buy the land next to ours. He wants us to work his land. There is an issue though."

David was both captivated and distracted. His hand had picked up a splinter from the wooden cart. "What's the issue?" he asked while trying to remove the splinter.

"The Noble knows we're Jews. He saw a menorah… we neglected to put it away. I think we can trust him. He desperately wants us to work his land. He'll reap a handsome profit."

"You trust this fellow?" David said eyeing him dubiously.

Stephen was angered by the doubt he heard in David's voice. "You profit from your money-lending to the Nobles. Why shouldn't my family prosper? Must we starve?"

"It's a difficult situation," David said crudely. "Thousands of Sephardic Jews have been killed because they remained true."

Stephen gestured to the hills surrounding them. "Or they've exiled themselves to the high country where they struggle with the rocky soil. Just like their fathers."

David looked at the hillsides. There were miles and miles of rough donkey trails made by other Sephardim who had fled. "For generations the Jews prospered in Spain. But many have been executed and their rancheros have become the property of the church."

"The ranches the Sephardim left behind were beautiful."

"There are many who stayed," David said dryly.

Stephen scoffed and roughly pulled on the donkey harness, startling the animal. "Yes they stayed so they could keep their grand estates. They became New Christians to the world but remained Jewish inside their homes. It is a sad day when someone finds we are Judaizing."

All the talk left David feeling anxious and distressed. "If you change your mind about joining us in the north... I assure you, the church will not get their hands on our land. Never," David told him.

"Time will be our witness," Stephen said with a deep sigh.

The two men embraced and said their good-byes. David had his own business to attend to.

Upon David's return to Amsterdam he found Magdalena was not at home. It appeared she had not been there for quite some time. He understood and had half expected her to return to her family's farm but was disappointed nonetheless. After resting for the evening he rose the next morning and headed to the Shochet's farm north of Amsterdam. When his stocky cart horse finally pulled up to the farm he could see Magdalena's silhouette. The afternoon sun cast her shadow. As usual, she was tending to the livestock and appeared healthy as ever. Her smile was warm when she saw her husband. Gathering her skirt she ran to greet him. The years had made his body stiffness but he hurried toward her. He looked at her rosy cheeks, soft full body and clear eyes, and wondered how a man his age could be so blessed with such a fine woman. She wrapped her arms around him as a child would, and he put his hand upon the small of her back. He loved the fullness of her backside and her rich curves. She could not hold back her grin, nor the joy she felt in his return. David laughed when he saw that a small clump of cow manure and straw that had gotten stuck in her hair. He gently removed it as she leaned back in his embrace.

"Where is our son Akev?" he asked.

"Sleeping. Oh David, that boy sleeps and eats too much. You should see how large your boy has grown." She rubbed her stomach and smiled.

"Another child?" he beamed.

"Yes. Why do you think I work so hard? We have mouths to feed."

He smiled and played along with her little game of pretending she needed to work hard to provide for her children. They both knew he had enough resources to provide for as many children as they wanted but working with animals was in her blood and she enjoyed every minute of it.

"I need to rest for a few weeks," he told her as his eyes wandered around the farm wondering what had changed since his last visit. "The journey was difficult, especially on my emotions. But as soon as I'm rested, we'll break ground on our new land."

She shouted gleefully while dancing barefooted in the loose soil. "Please don't go away again, say you will never go away again David, please!"

"I wish each and every night I could hold you and love you as we did in that shed on our wedding night, but I have obligations. I promised my father that I would write more and that I would teach one of our children to continue the profession of telling the news. Do you think our son, Akev would be a good writer?"

"I think not David. Perhaps this next child," she smiled, "or the next one," she smiled again and led her husband toward the cozy home that held her family. They would welcome him, feed him heartily, laugh and tell jokes and stories. The sun would go down and place a chill upon the home from the outside but a strong fire would burn inside each of the family members that were so pleased to see David return.

FIVE

It was a long drive from Amsterdam and Magdalena's family's farm but she hoped that eventually all the Shochets would come join them. David had his doubts.

"Your father will never leave," he said to her one day while at the Shochet farm. "He has his work and he makes a nice livelihood. He enjoys his farm and the community needs kosher meat. We'll be an afternoon's ride to Amsterdam but we'll be closer to Antwerp, Paris and Roen. If I need to go to London it won't be as far."

She rolled her eyes. "You're too old to roam. When did I ever express an interest in going to Paris? I love living here, in the Netherlands by the sea, where the grasses grow and the cattle are flourishing. It's colder than Paris but they have more problems."

David looked around at the Shochet farm. Her parents had grown older and a few of the children had become adults, living nearby with their own farms. Even Magdalena spent time away at her flat in Amsterdam and had not had as much time to care for the Shochet farm and it had begun to show the beginning of a fall into disrepair. David felt responsible for that. He only wished the old man would let him hire some help to tidy things up. There were old carts outside that had broken and had not been repaired. The fences had broken often enough and Magdalena had piled up rocks and buckets to keep the livestock from getting out. The place her parents called home looked primitive compared to new dwellings in Amsterdam.

David turned his thoughts to the future. "When the summer comes we will build our new farm. I have good news. Stephen from Portugal has changed his mind. He's decided to join us."

"Stephen?"

"Yes, he has a wife who's creative and three children... boys. They'll be a big help building the barns we desperately need."

Magdalena had grown accustomed to her privacy. She knew David's grand plan was to build a large, secure community. She found it difficult to accept the lifestyle change.

"You'll enjoy having other women around," he reassured her. "Stephen's young boys will soon be men and they'll bring wives. One day our son, Akev, will be a man and he'll bring a wife. And I hope he becomes the next Chronicler. There are too many stories to tell."

"Yes. Perhaps he will be a fine writer."

When Stephen and his family arrived at Amsterdam's port, David was alarmed at their appearance. They looked as if they'd left with only the clothing on their backs.

"What's happened?"

"The Noble..." Stephen began but David interrupted.

"The one you trusted?"

"Yes. The one I so foolishly trusted. All five of us rose early every morning to work his land. We spent weeks removing rocks then several more weeks terracing in the hot sun. We carted animal manures and dug them into the soil. We neglected our own land, so we could work his. We lovingly planted fruit and nut trees. One morning he and five other men demanded we leave. They threatened us with pick axes. We had just finished planting his orchards."

David didn't know how to respond. It grieved him to see his old friend arrive under such dire circumstances yet he'd warned Stephen but his friend had not taken his advice. "You're here now. You and your family will be safe with us."

Stephen had developed a small twitchy habit. He kept shaking his head as if he was still shaking off Portuguese flies. "The man had no intention of sharing the profit. He told us he was as a Spanish Noble. We have since discovered he is from Poland."

David looked at Stephen's tired and disillusioned wife. She had gone through the move from their beloved Spain and fled to Portugal where they thought they would be safe only to be tricked by this unethical man. The three boys looked confused but they were strong and curious. They would do well in the Netherlands. David knew the boys had learned the painful lesson to keep quiet about their Sephardic origins.

"The boys have grown. They are soon to be men, yeah?" David asked.

"They will soon be men," Stephen's voice was tired but proud.

"We will put everyone to work," David told him as he helped them load what few belongings they had onto his cart for the long trek to his land south of Amsterdam.

"Wait, wait!" Stephen said. "I have seven crates of wine and many sacks of rootstocks. Is there somewhere safe we can keep them here in Amsterdam until we have an empty wagon?"

David was pleased. He put his hand on his friend's shoulder and stepped past him and walked further onto the ship seeking the captain. David's business connections were vast. He was trusted and well connected. The crates of wine and sacks of rootstocks would arrive in no time at their newly acquired land south of Amsterdam.

1491

It had been six years since David and Stephen spoke among the beauty of Portugal's hillsides. In those six years David's farm in the Netherlands had begun to take shape. He had invested much more than he had planned. The community was now his sole inspiration. He had never imagined that he would enjoy farming as he had. Magdalena's skills had proved invaluable. Stephen, his wife and their three sons had built several barns and a home. David saw to it that they used good stones and quality lumber.

David was growing older but continued making his Chronicler rounds in Amsterdam. One day, after arriving home late, he rose early the next day, barely spoke to anyone and then headed south. He was gone for many days.

Stephen confronted him. "David, we've been worried about you. You're too old to be traveling,"

"The cart and horse serve me well."

Stephen could see David was not well. "You look concerned."

"Not one person I spoke with had anything good to say. The Papacy continues its cruelty. Even the Catholics are worried. Cardinal Rodrigo Borgia is a monster who continues to gain power. Many fear his rise to the Papal throne as just more problems for the church all over Europe."

Stephen grew angry remembering his hardships in Spain and Portugal. "Isn't it bad enough that Jews can't settle land claimed by either Spain or Portugal? Isn't it bad enough that thousands have been executed? And for what? Being a Jew? Will we be safe here, south of Amsterdam, pretending to be Protestant? Will all the world be making the sign of the cross? What will become of Magdalena's father, the Shochet? Shall he abandon his belief in ritual slaughter? Shall we all eat swine like the Christians so they will leave alone?"

Stephen's wife went to his side. Their boys heard the commotion and came to hear the conversation.

David was not deterred. "We have animals for food. We have shelter from storms. We have wives to keep us warm at night and children to care for us when we grow older."

Stephen nodded.

"It's time we welcomed more families to join us here."

Stephen disagreed. "No. It's time you returned to money-lending to save our families and our heritage. We must use the resources we have at our disposal. Our Spanish connections are what we have. We need that influence."

With Stephen's encouragement, David returned to money-lending. It was a time of change throughout Europe's political landscape. The Catholic monarchs wanted a united Catholic kingdom. In March of the following year, Ferdinand and Isabella issued their Edict of Expulsion. More than 100,000 Jews left Spain. Those who said yes to Christianity and no to Judaism were the only ones allowed to stay. Many chose both. Outwardly they were Christians, going to church, even throwing swine into their stew to show that they had shed their Judaism. But at night, in the solitude of their homes and especially on Friday nights they practiced their own beliefs and rituals. But they practiced in deep fear, for if they were to be discovered practicing any kind of rituals other than Christian, they might be killed.

1492

"Akev," David's elderly voice said softly to his ten-year-old son. "Do you know what your name means?"

"Yes Father, it's Hebrew, I'm named after my grandfather, Jacob."

"That's correct. And I made a promise to your grandfather."

"You did?"

"Yes, I promised him that one of my sons would continue to report on the day's news."

"You mean the stories that you tell Papa? The real stories? The stories about all the fighting and hiding and even those stories I hear you tell late at night when I'm asleep?"

"Yes. And do you think someday you can persuade your son to be a Chronicler?"

Akev shook his head yes and looked up at his father. They both had the beautiful eyes of their ancestors.

It was dark when Magdalena came in from the dairy where she'd been caring for young calves. Her hands were dirty and so was her apron. She was humming a tune when David stopped her. He put his hand to hers, his finger to his mouth expressing her need to shhh... and pulled her aside, out of reach of Akev's listening.

"Jews are fleeing Spain by the tens of thousands. They're going to Portugal where the government is taxing the wealthy 100 cruzados to stay permanently."

"One hundred cruzados?" Magdalena was shocked. "How can they pay it when Spain has already taken everything?" She looked to David for answers. This time he did not have one.

"Many are unable to pay the high tax. They've been told to pay eight cruzados each. But this will only enable them to stay for eight months."

"Eight months?" She let out a deep sigh. Their farm south of Amsterdam had already been accepting desperate friends and family, helping them in any way they could. Homes and animal sheds had been built to accommodate the added population. Other refugees ventured farther north and into Amsterdam proper.

"Eight months is all they're allowed to stay if they don't pay the higher tax. After eight months they're asked to leave but it's not always easy. Sometimes ships are scarce." David hated telling her but knew he must.

"What happens to those who can't leave or don't have one hundred cruzados?"

"They're labeled as heretics and told to convert to Christianity or they'll be..."

"Don't speak of it."

Magdalena was younger than him and he wondered why they had not conceived more children besides the two boys. Perhaps it was the will of God. Why bring children into a world where they are controlled by cardinals and kings? He thought of his boys and knew the lads would survive the coming years. He smiled thinking of how pleased Akev had been with the storytelling promise he'd made. He wondered how many generations would be Chroniclers and what stories they'd tell. He threw his tired head back and leaned against the wall as Magdalena walked into the kitchen. He had stories to prepare and was to return to Amsterdam in the morning and meet with the Sephardic community. The Sephardim wanted to know the latest news regarding the Inquisition. They wanted news of their family and friends in Spain and Portugal. The mood in the Jewish quarter of Amsterdam had grown dark.

Men from Amsterdam's Sephardic community came scurrying out of shops and cafes. "What news do you have of our family who have fled Spain?" one of the men asked when he saw David walking down the street.

"It is not good news."

They could see he had dark circles under his eyes and they worried about his health but nothing was more important than finding out the future of their loved ones in Spain and Portugal.

"Portugal's King Joao is preparing to go to war against the Moors," David told them. "To finance his war, King Joao will be collecting taxes from the Jews."

They looked at him not understanding the height of the tax fees nor the dismal penalty for not paying.

"One hundred cruzados."

"One hundred?" Shouts of unfairness could be heard around the room and David had to quiet them down before he could speak again.

"King Joao is recruiting Jews skilled in weapons-making. Many of our brothers have exceptional forges. King Joao does not want Jews making weapons for Moors."

Heads nodded. Most understood the value of a good weapon's mechanic and could understand the king's desire to utilize their skills.

"All Jewish weapons mechanics will be granted permanent residence. The King has promised to provide ships so that others may leave. If they are unable to leave..." David's voice trailed. The men stared blankly at him until one spoke.

"If they are unable to leave?"

"If the king does not keep his word and provide sailings away from Portugal, they will become slaves of the king."

Anger rose amongst the men. Talk of revenge and vendettas fired from their mouths, the older the man, the angrier. The younger ones were stunned.

David continued to stand before the small crowd of his angered brothers. "I shall not lie to you, nor try to make you perceive the days will be brighter. My instincts tell me these problems will not improve. Continue to keep your religion to yourselves and tell your families to do the same. Do not let your children speak of their Jewish families nor the troubles they faced in Spain or Portugal. There will not be peace for many generations. I will continue to gather what news I have as the information slowly arrives. We will continue to hold Synagogue at our farm south of Amsterdam and enjoy Shabbat services. You are all welcome."

"And you David, are always welcome in Amsterdam's homes open for Synagogue. Come and bring your beautiful Magdalena and the boys. How old is Akev now?" an old friend asked.

David smiled for the first time. "Magdalena is busy with the birthing of the calves, which she delights in and Akev has promised he will be the next Chronicler of the family."

There were plenty of affirmative shouts and smiles. Chronicler was a job that no one else wanted, yet it was an invaluable asset to the secretive community. It was a relief to all that young Akev would be learning the skill.

"Shalom," David said to them as he hurried out the door, anxious to return to his home in the south and his loving wife.

"Shalom!" the men said as they began gathering into small groups to discuss what could be done to help their families stuck in Spain and Portugal.

SIX

David yanked on his coat and pulled the fabric to protect his neck as the cool evening bit at his elderly skin. He should have left Amsterdam earlier while the sun was still high. He would not make it all the way home, the drive was much too far. He needed somewhere to spend the night. Fellow Sephardim had formerly lived along the route between Amsterdam and his farm but had either moved onto the farm with him or bought property of their own and lived on adjoining acreage near them. The only accessible shelter David knew he would find would be with former business acquaintances he'd known through his grandfather, Monsieur Soeira. They were Christians, and among the few in Holland who knew that he was a Jew. They were the children of the men who helped his grandfather set up liaisons between Papal monks and influential bankers. When David was young, he accompanied his grandfather and played with these children in their lavish homes while his grandfather conducted business with their fathers. He saw them from time to time, once in Antwerp and once in passing on the streets of Paris. He'd spoken lately to one of the gentleman, when they chanced to meet one afternoon in Antwerp. The man had given David the opportunity to continue business but David had shied away from it. His grandfather had left such a large group of assets, David had not needed the connections. Besides, his step-father Jacob had warned that they conducted business contrary to what he'd been taught from his parents. But now, here he was, out in the cold.

And recently he'd been contemplating re-establishing his grandfather's connections to Royals. How could he swim without getting wet? How could he go home to his warm Magdalena if he made deals and prospered from the ill gains of others? But without funds how could he build a strong community for his own family? And what was to become of the Jewish families coming north to escape the fires of the Inquisition?

The cold air blew up against his face as he turned the cart and horse toward Leiden. The recent rains softened the ground but it was not too muddy to travel. The frigid temperatures hardened the ground. David felt excruciating pain in his back. He wondered how much longer he could continue, such an old man, gallivanting about the countryside. His horse grew nervous as they approached a cluster of wealthy homes. David comforted his horse. A flicker of candles and lanterns lit up the front of the home of a former acquaintance. Inside the home, the host was entertaining. There were several horses and carts in front and he could hear music, like the minstrels he'd heard in Paris.

He shivered in his cold, damp clothing, uncomfortable with the imprudent intrusion, but some impulse pulled him toward the other carts. He stiffly swung himself out of his cart and eagerly went to the front of the home. The door was opened before David had time to rap on the door. A male servant, whose job it was to open the door and greet guests, could see that he was chilled. Compassionately he motioned for David to follow him. He gave David a warm coat, scarf and felt hat. David thanked him and entered the home full of guests, both men and women. The men were gathered in groups, as were most of the women. All were dressed in early autumn clothing, bundled much warmer than they'd been weeks ago when the summer was still young.

"David! It's been years! What brings you here?" the host greeted him.

David struggled to banter and cajole as his grandfather had. "I was traveling through. I was headed south toward home." He looked toward the women for a warm smile. After receiving none his eyes continued around the room where they met with the male servant's eyes. David found comfort and support in his gaze.

"We have not seen David since the era the church declared Pico a heretic for publishing his philosophical treatises," one of the male guests quipped. All the men laughed except the host of the festive gathering. He quickly defended David.

"You're forgetting who protected Pico. The de Medici family, who David's grandfather, did business with." He had put the other men in their places for disrespecting David, who was embarrassed but relieved. The host then escorted David, alone, to another part of the home so they could talk. He put his hand on David's shoulder.

"How have you been? I've heard you have a young wife. Is this true?"

"Yes," David almost told the story of the rabbi who arranged the marriage until he remembered he was speaking to a Christian.

David changed the subject to business. "I have connections with Portuguese merchants. In the event you need anything shipped or goods you need... let me be of service."

"We need loans David. Everyone needs loans. We'll be happy to do business with you. Diamonds and gold are always welcome."

"I have connections... in diamonds," he stammered.

The man smiled. The years had made an old man of him too. The man's teeth had yellowed and one of his molars was missing in the back but it was just barely visible and when he saw that David was looking, his smile grew shorter. They both had their pride.

"We have room for you my friend. Be our guest for the evening. If you walk outside and look to your right, there's a small cottage. There's a lamp burning inside. It's the servant's room. Please, reside there for the evening and we shall talk in the morning."

David was confused. "And the servant?"

"The servant? Oh, the servant. Well he shall sleep in a chair!" he laughed and David felt unfortunately odd as he walked past the kind servant and out into the man's dwelling to sleep.

David had not been in the hut long before he heard a knock at the door. Still dressed, he opened it and to his surprise it was a young woman.

"Master of the home has sent me," she said, her dark eyes glowing in the candlelight. She couldn't have been more than seventeen and David wondered how many of the host's guests she must entertain.

He knew his grandfather, Monsieur Soeira, had taken advantage of the gifts his hosts provided. Some of the Sephardim from Spain and Portugal, had grown accustomed to sleeping with their servant girls. But the rabbi had made it clear that it was unacceptable.

David's thoughts returned to the beautiful girl in front of him. Her well-rounded body aroused him. He could not tell her origins, only that her mother and father must have also been beautiful. He did not send her away without first staring at her beauty and pondering what a small taste would be like. He smiled politely but shook his head no. She put her head down but David could see the poor girl was relieved she did not have to submit. He wondered if she was close to the servant who had so kindly greeted him at the door, given him warm clothes and now whose bed he had taken.

David regained his place of respect within the Christian business community. Eventually David's time for this life ran out and it was up to his descendants to carry on his work. His son, Akev kept his promise to be the Chronicler for the Jewish Sephardim community south of Amsterdam where they struggle against the pull of Christianity.

SEVEN

Akev is now sixty-four years old and speaks to his grandson, Jacques

"Mother tells me you want to speak to me," young Jacques said respectfully to his grandfather.

Stiff and feeling his years, Akev smiled fondly at his grandson. He put his hand on the boys shoulder before he spoke. "Jacques, I want to tell you about a promise that runs through our family. It was passed from my father to me and now I want to pass it to you," he told his grandson.

"Is it a secret grandpa?"

Akev laughed. "I have many secrets, but no, this is not a secret. It's about telling secrets so that there may be justice."

Little Jacques looked puzzled.

"The world is ruthless and waiting to be tamed. I want you to promise me that you will do as I have and my father before me."

"What is it grandfather?"

"I want you to pay attention to your father Solomon. He is the Chronicler of the family. Notice how he speaks to everyone. Notice how he returns to his family in France and comes back with stories that he shares with the community."

Jacques wrinkled his nose and asked his grandfather, "You want me to tell stories too?"

"Yes Jacques. But I want you to tell true stories. Listen to your father. He will teach you to be the Chronicler. It is very important.

We want our children to know these stories and we can't always write them down. It is most often through the spoken word that the family history is kept alive. There is a fire that we must keep burning."

Jacques was still puzzled. "That will be fine Grandfather. I will remember to tell the stories. Can I tell them about you?"

"Yes, please keep my memory alive. My father David, died when I was just a boy and my mother, Magdalena, taught me storytelling. She became the leader of our family. Everyone in our hamlet came to her for advice. The stories will be essential for this family's survival. I do not expect life to get any easier."

The boy put his head down. He wanted to sit on the floor and play with his wooden blocks and blow his new whistle. He did not want to be troubled by the worries of today and especially about what was to come. Akev patted him on the shoulder. He was content that he'd fulfilled his promise and he was sure that Jacques would carry the torch. Akev rested well that night and within several months the old man passed away.

Leaving a void that could not easily be filled, Akev's passing was difficult for the community. He was one of the last original Sephardic men whose families had come to the Netherlands from Spain, Portugal or France fleeing the Inquisition. The hamlet they built south of Amsterdam had grown into a prosperous bustle community. Every year, new babies were born and animal stock was regenerated. There was always a new cottage erected with the help of friends, family and neighbors. But today, a black draped wagon carried Akev's body. It lumbered through mud and rocks until it reached the only quiet, unseen place the Jews had to bury their dead. They hung their heads as they forsake their Jewish customs and accepted Christian funeral traditions. After all, the hamlet of Akev, as they had all voted to begin calling it, posed as a Christian community. The pretense had existed since their arrival in the 1400's. The Inquisition had grown stronger and was no longer just a threat, but a reality soon to be at their hearth. So it was with long faces that the elders buried Akev, the last of the true benefactors of the Sephardim. Little children walked the trail behind the wagon tossing colorful flowers. They were well fed; their chubby cheeks were rosy and their eyes bright. Their sense of the future was not marred by the solemn day. One child saw the events of the day in a different light. Akev's grandson Jacques. He'd made a promise to his grandfather that he would be the new Chronicler. He listened carefully to the ceremony, understanding that one day he would tell the story.

Within days of Akev's funeral a community meeting was organized and seven-year-old Jacques was in the crowd.

The rabbi led the meeting.

"What shall we do?" a man in the crowd asked.

"Share what you know," the rabbi told the residents, then looked down at Jacques.

The rabbi had been unable to influence Jacques to study the religious books. Instead, the boy liked listening into everyone's conversation. He learned about Judaism, business, agriculture and what the adults did for pleasure. The boy was a sponge for all that went on in the hamlet. Every chance he had, he hopped in the back of a wagon or onto a horse and headed to Amsterdam. He became a valuable resource, especially through his relationship with the skippers and the dock workers. It was there where he received both compensation and information.

"I say we gather the whole hamlet together for a meeting," Jacques gestured toward the barn. The men looked down at the short, stocky boy. His aggressiveness irritated them but because he stood in line to be the most powerful man of the community, he was treated with respect. His mother was Akev's daughter. She still held the purse strings of Monsieur Soeira's remaining wealth. Her father was the wise old man, David, who reestablished his money-lending connections with European nobility. It was that wealth that built and held this community together. The merchants of the hamlet were conscientious of the effect they had on humanity. They got along well with the Christians and many a night was spent discussing new religious theories. Many in the hamlet began embracing them as their outward Christian front.

As the rabbi stood in front of the large crowd he told them, "The lad is right, go home and have your suppers. Return to the big barn where we will make plans for the future."

A young man hollered from the back. "I'll tell you what we should do. I don't need to compare notes with anyone. I say we join the revolt!"

The crowd was ominously silent. Most knew that the Spanish crown had infiltrated Holland. They worried that war was imminent.

The rabbi shouted back angrily. "Go have your evening meal! Return to the big barn later. We will discuss our options."

The group wasn't quick to disperse. Instead they gathered in small circles to whisper and talk loudly amongst themselves but as it neared time to eat they gradually filtered out with a promise to return.

"Spain is here to remove the Jews!" a man in the back of the barn shouted. Jacques looked at him and then to the group. It was a chilly evening. Women and children were snuggled in knitted woolens and the men donned their beloved prayer shawls.

"They are coming to make us all Catholics!" the man shouted again. Most of the crowd nodded in agreement.

Jacques appreciated his new position as Chronicler. He'd told no one of his promise to his grandfather, but his mother, Sarah, had told a few of her closest acquaintances. Word had gotten round but Jacques was oblivious to anyone's knowing. All were in agreement that the boy showed tremendous promise, looking as though he may be the best Chronicler yet and any time they had a good tip they made sure Sarah heard of it. Jacques had the knack for piecing together gossip and hearsay and making sense of it. He stood on top of a stiff mound of hay and struggled to see the people's faces and pair them with their voices.

A man from England who'd come to the hamlet to visit family, walked to the head of the crowd and stood next to the rabbi. "I know it will not calm everyone's fears but there is talk that England will assist," he said.

A woman whose face was hidden shouted, "The Protestants are all the hope we have."

Another woman's voice shouted angrily, "If Spain takes control we will be forced to become Catholic."

The rabbi tried to calm the fervent crowd. "We must have faith."

An old woman pleaded with the rabbi. "In Spain my family pretended to be Catholic. In Portugal my family pretended to be Catholic. Now in the Netherlands we pretend to be Protestant. When can we return to the faith of our ancestors?"

The man from England, still standing at the front of the crowd next to the rabbi replied to her, "Perhaps not in your lifetime I am afraid."

Jacques dark eyes looked sympathetically at the despairing faces. Even little children were grim faced and huddled in groups asking the older children for explanations.

"Spanish ships have surrounded British slaving ships," the Englishman continued.

The crowd began to argue about the evils of slave trading. Jacques knew the controversy well. It was a contentious issue and some of his family wealth had been made through slavery, horrifying his grandmother, Magdalena.

A man walked up to the front beside the rabbi. His beard was white and coarse and Jacques could see he was drunk but he was well spoken. "There is truth to the rumor that the British have retaliated. They are raiding Spanish ships in the Atlantic and the Indies to the west of Africa."

A scruffy man in the back seated on a stool, spoke sarcastically, "It's pirate monks! Their revenge against the church."

Jacques smiled. He was familiar with the stories of the Templar monks. His grandfather drank too much wine one night and told him of the connections between his family's money lending and the monks. The monks and his Sephardic ancestors practiced money lending together.

An old woman loudly chided the man. "We are not here to hear your tired old stories about the Templar Monks."

The rabbi agreed with the woman. "We're here to discuss the Inquisition at our door, not the crusades of yesterday."

Once again there were mumbles in the crowd and discussions broke out, this one harder to squelch than the others.

The rabbi was firm and in command. "Silence!"

"I respect your wisdom Rabbi," a man came forward.

Jacques could see he was another well-dressed visitor and the boy was beginning to realize what an important community the hamlet of Akev had become to attract such an interesting stranger. As the man continued, Jacques noticed how effectively he spoke and how refined his clothing was. Jacques imitated the man's hand movements and the slight tilt of his head. A woman glared at him thinking he was mocking the speaker.

The man continued, "The Inquisition forbids Judaism. Their wish is that we become Christians. Otherwise... death."

"Yes, yes," the rabbi said impatiently. "We are well aware of the facts of the Inquisition, look around you, do you not see the faces of those who have lost family? We will not speak of this now. We are here to compare rumors. I plead with you all. If you have heard nothing new, be silent. If you have something of value to add, please step up. This is your chance. We need all the information we can gather. Has anyone been to the north, to Leeuwarden or come lately from the south?"

A voice asked. "I heard that Protestants from the south and Huguenots from France are fleeing to England. Is this true?"

Another loud voice asked, "Will they accept Jews?"

"Please," the rabbi pleaded. "Let's not think of fleeing. We even have our own burial ground here!"

"It is but a Christian burial ground," a woman scoffed.

"But it is *our* burial ground and one day we will have a burial ground where we can bury our dead the way our ancestors did. Most of us would have perished long ago had we not taken on a Christian pretense," the rabbi shouted, growing redder in the face.

A pretty young woman slowly walked to the front. All eyes were upon her. She wore a colorful hooded cape intricately embroidered. Jacques could see that a fine artist had woven it and someone had paid handsomely for it. He could not see her face.

"I have heard from Flanders," she said.

The Englishman asked her, "Are you from Flanders?"

The girl shook her head no. "My aunt is."

The rabbi was growing impatient and so was the crowd, "What have you learned from your aunt?"

The young woman answered eagerly. "Many are embracing Christian Calvinism. They are converting. Both the well-to-do and the peasant populations."

The frustrated rabbi began looking around for some place to sit. "Is there any good news?" he asked.

"I heard something," Jacques spoke from his perch on top of the hay. Every head turned towards him especially the children's. "The old men in Amsterdam told me that Protestants and Jews are gaining favor. It's the Catholics who are being persecuted."

The crowd was amazed at such wisdom coming from the boy.

The rabbi pleaded. "Please... let's not be rash. We must stand our ground."

"Do you mean fight?" a young man asked.

The rabbi shook his tired head and waved everyone on. They all walked slowly from the barn and met in groups outside the big doors. Most of their faces were grave and showed not much hope except the face of the hamlet's namesake's grandson. Jacques found it challenging and exciting. He planned on hitching a ride to Amsterdam to meet with the rabbi and the men and women of Jodenbreestraat, the Jewish neighborhood where he could learn more about the unfolding developments.

"What have you found out son?" the rabbi asked Jacques upon his return from Amsterdam.

"The proclamation against un-baptized Jews in Utrecht and Gelderland still holds," he said.

The rabbi stared. "You're wise. It is beyond belief."

"Thank you very much Rabbi, Grandfather would be pleased."

"Yes he would. And what else did you learn in Amsterdam?" the rabbi asked anxiously.

"I learned that there is a whole street where women wait for men to come," Jacques said innocently.

The rabbi stiffened but the boy didn't notice his discomfort and continued. "These men come at all hours of the night and they come and tell the women all kinds of stories."

The rabbi's eyes widened but before he could respond Jacques continued.

"They have stories from the Nobles, stories from the seamen, stories from the merchants, stories from the..."

"It's fine son. I understand your interest in finding good sources for your stories but these women are not to be trusted."

"Oh but they are. The men of Jodenbreestraat say the stories that come from these women are the most to be trusted."

The rabbi was livid. "The men of Jodenbreestraat spoke this way? Which men?"

"There were many. And the more I knew about these women the more likely it was that the men would tell me more."

"What did they tell you?" the rabbi asked angrily.

"They told me that my great-great-grandfather, the very first Chronicler, Jacob, used to visit the women all the time!" Jacques said earnestly.

"I had not heard that," the rabbi said, his tone softening hoping that soon the subject would change.

"Yes. I am so proud and excited. I went there and spoke to the women and..."

"You went to Damstraat?" the rabbi raged.

Jacques smiled. The rabbi could see just about every tooth in the boy's mouth.

Jacques looked at the rabbi curiously. "I see you know about the women of Damstraat. Why has no one told me?"

The rabbi sighed and knew it would be of no use to counsel the boy who was too fascinated with his stories and too involved with the dangerous politics of the era.

The rabbi had only succeeded in teaching Jacques the basics of Judaism. The boy was just not particularly interested in religion. Yes, Jacques loved Purim and the telling of the Megillah. He respected Yom Kippur, the most sacred Jewish holiday. And he participated in prayers and fasting. But business, politics and the recurring wars were what fascinated him.

"It's important that you study the religions of other cultures. Not only should you study Christianity, but you should know how Muslims worship. And never forget the ancient Greeks nor the Romans," the rabbi told him.

"I will study as you suggest," Jacques promised.

"Study their language." The rabbi grew very serious. "You must learn to read and write Hebrew," he said proudly. "I can tell you something no one else ever told you."

He had Jacques complete attention.

"If you master the ability to read and interpret the ancient Hebrew Scriptures, you'll have great power."

"The Christians are always asking me questions. My ability to answer will give me great status."

Fear rose in the old rabbi. "Jacques? Are you telling me that there are Christians in Amsterdam who know you are a Jew?"

Jacques put his head down. He knew he was supposed to keep quiet about his origins but it had been difficult, he was young and loved to talk. "Yes, there are some nice ladies."

"Not the same ladies, the ones on Damstraat?"

"No, not them, I don't go there so much. It smells bad and after what you advised..."

"Yes, yes, go on son, which ladies?"

"Well Rabbi, you know there is a strong Sephardim quarter in Amsterdam, everyone pretends they're not Jewish but it's quite apparent they are."

"No, I didn't know it was apparent, perhaps to you but..."

"Well, as I was saying Rabbi, the Sephardim quarter runs into the other neighborhoods and I have met some nice people, especially the ladies, they are quite wealthy. Did you know that these families paid handsomely to the municipality for the privilege of building wider homes?"

"No son, I did not."

"If they see me they visit with me. They're very good Christians. They ask me questions about Hebrew scripture and how similar it is to their religion. They love to hear about the Jews. It's strange Rabbi, they're just as hungry for stories about the Jews."

"Are they?" the rabbi said dryly.

"Yes. And they would love to attend Synagogue. They tried to get me to tell them which homes are being used for Synagogue but I..."

The rabbi was furious. "Jacques, do not ever tell! Never! They may pry you for information so that they can shut the synagogues down and lock everyone up. Or worse! Keep your mouth shut! Please! The Inquisition arrested people for something as small as changing linens on the Sabbath."

Jacques soon realized he'd been careless. The talk with the rabbi was a turning point. From this moment on, the lad was more cautious.

1564   *Introduction of tobacco into Europe, Jacques is fifteen*

In a most irritating voice, Jacque's young friend Rebecca asked, "What are you doing Jacques?"

"I'm smoking," Jacques replied between coughs.

Rebecca continued to berate him. "The smoke is everywhere and my father will be here soon. What's he to think?" she asked as he towered over her. He had out-grown his youthful chubbiness and had begun to grow tall and lanky, much like his great-great-grandfather, Monsieur Soeira but without the poise.

Jacques personality resembled none in the hamlet of Akev, nor any other young man in any province for hundreds of miles. Jacques was the product of the times and the prodigy of many. His influences included the rabbi, the old Jewish men of Amsterdam, his father and grandfather, his mother and grandmother and his closely-knit community. And in their own way, the Christian women of Amsterdam had influenced Jacques. His thinking had also been shaped by the skippers at the docks and to some extent the women of Damstraat had helped to develop the well-rounded, street-smart lad. And now he was fast becoming a handsome young man and more than one young lady coveted his presence. The one he was currently spending the warm day with was Rebecca. Her father was Isaac, a well-respected Akevian farmer, originally from Gelderland. Isaac grew grain on about ten acres of the community's land and he was always sought after when Passover neared, for he never failed to accumulate the bitter herb, horehound, for the traditional ceremony.

Rebecca was smitten with Jacques but was afraid to show it. He treated her as he did all the girls, but she caught him staring on several occasions. Today, they'd come to Amsterdam in the back of a wagon. The warm sun and the rocking motion had put them to sleep. They'd left Akev in the early hours when it was very dark. Now, as they waited for her father to return from a business meeting, they were alone in a home that served as a synagogue. Jacques grew impatient waiting for Isaac, because in Amsterdam he usually scurried around and gathered information from his usual sources. But he felt a responsibility to watch over Rebecca.

"I'm glad you stopped the puffing," she said as he shook the tobacco from the pipe.

"I don't know whether I enjoy this New World product," he said.

Rebecca rolled her eyes. She usually found herself wishing he would speak plainly and quit trying to talk like an adult but what she didn't realize was that Jacques had spent his childhood around adults.

"I'm glad that tobacco has come to Europe," he said.

"Why? It stinks."

Jacques told her matter-of-factly, "I suppose it does but it is in great demand and the demand grows larger every day. You wait and see, men will become very wealthy with this new agricultural product. They'll fight wars over it."

"They'll be sick over it too. It truly stinks Jacques and I don't wish you to puff it around me again."

He shrugged. He'd only tasted it twice and there was very little tobacco in the pipe. If Rebecca didn't wish him to puff it, he would not do so in front of her. He looked forward to the day when he could taste a full pipe load of the dried herb. Before the two could begin any other conversation, Isaac burst into the room.

"Gather your things. Quickly!"

Isaac grabbed his daughter's hand and they ran into the street, away from Amsterdam's Jewish Quarter, Jodenbuurt. They ran along a canal toward the markets and to the Amster River where a large, flat barge was docked. Maneuvering alongside it, Isaac managed to hoist Rebecca unto the barge. Perplexed, Jacques followed the girl's father onto the barge and sat down on a pile of hemp ropes as Isaac instructed. They were to wait until his return.

Jacques understood the importance of obedience but found it hard to stay put, knowing there was a story unfolding. If he hadn't felt the need to protect Rebecca, he would have disobeyed Isaac and followed his nose to the center of whatever political storm was brewing. The afternoon moved at a painful pace but as it slowly turned to evening they saw Isaac's shadow approaching.

Isaac hugged Rebecca tightly, "We can stay here tonight."

"I thought we were staying..." Rebecca was cut off before she finished.

Isaac shook his head. "Some have been arrested, accused of Judaizing."

"I thought the authorities believed we were Christian Calvinists." Rebecca could see by the looks on her father and Jacques's faces that she had a bit to learn.

Before they could explain, the owner of the barge walked up. "It may be cold tonight, but you'll be safe. You can return to Akev in the morning."

Jacques spoke up. "I want know what happened."

They looked at him in disbelief but Jacques was not deterred. "I must follow the story. The knowledge will keep our community safe. The rabbi told me there is great power in knowing."

Rebecca's father spoke to the lad in an adult manner. "You are a man now Jacques. What you say is true. But Rebecca..." he looked at her knowing she would not like what he was about to say. "You must not come to Amsterdam again. It isn't safe."

She nodded and looked wide-eyed at Jacques who was not thinking of her but wondering how he could get away to find out what had happened. If members of his Sephardic community had been arrested, there could be more arrests. Before Isaac could stop him, he scurried off the barge.

"Sorry Isaac," Jacques said, stopping and looking at them both. "You said I am a man."

Isaac nodded, knowing it would be of no use to try to stop him. He waved the boy on, rather relieved to have his burden lightened.

Jacques ran alongside the river, then cut across and ran along one canal after another until he found himself in the heart of the city. He knew where he must go. Somewhere he had not been in a very long time. His heart raced as he ran through the dark towards Oude Zijd and to Daamstraat. The street was dark. With the sun down, the evening was quickly chilling. Knowing he would be noticed, a young man amidst the older, he cast his face away from all the lanterns and hurried to the business in the very middle of Daamstraat. One of the young women recognized him as she was drawing a heavy curtain across the small windows the girls had displayed themselves for sale earlier in the day. When she saw Jacques she knew immediately why he had come. She did not smile.

"Go to the back," she told him in whispers from the doorway.

Jacques pointed to the right, questioning just how he would reach the back entrance and she nodded. The boy ran all the way back up the street and found a narrow alleyway and methodically worked his way down to what he assumed was the back of the establishment. He stood leaning against the brick wall, his hat pulled down over most of his youthful face. He could see that the evening had already begun. There were sounds of the approaching drunkenness that was sure to follow as the evening wore on. There was the fake, yet sometimes sincere laughter of girls bantering with men. The frequent sound of horse hooves scraping the cobblestones and the lone sound of a man whistling added to the eerie mood on Damstraat as Jacques waited for his friend to meet him in the back.

"Hello," he said.

She didn't greet him back, instead taking the time to look right and then left. She pulled the lad into the building then spoke to him. "I knew the arrests were coming but I had no one to tell."

Jacques queried her. "Who told you?"

The woman offered information as best she could. "Several officials told me, they come often. Sometimes they come for favors, sometimes they come to check up on us."

"Why did they tell you?"

"They get drunk and speak of things. You should tell your Jewish friends to dress like everyone else. The Sephardim of Amsterdam are too obvious."

"Obvious?" he asked.

"Yes," she said angrily. "I'm not responsible for them. I tell you as a favor to your community."

Jacques shrugged and started to walk away. She grabbed at his shirt.

"Their names, they need to change them. Reverse the letters around, do anything but don't let them walk around with Portuguese accents and Latin names. This is Holland."

Jacques nodded; he felt he understood that part.

"And I have seen far too many men wearing their prayer shawls. If there is anything that distinguishes them from the Christian men it is those prayer shawls, especially on a warm day!"

Jacques nodded again. It was difficult for him to understand that men and women from his community had been arrested for little differences such as the wearing of a scarf or the sound of their name, but he knew that Judaizing was a dangerous offence. He would tell the community to dress and act more like Christians and look into altering the spelling of their names. He walked away perplexed. It was also difficult for him to comprehend that *his community had just been chastised by a prostitute*. As Jacques was walking back out into his world, he heard the girl's voice echoing through the streets, her voice bouncing off the stone walls that encased the alley where she had decided to relinquish her youth.

"And one more thing..." she said, half her body swung out into the street as she clung to the header above the door way, her wild curly hair and piercing eyes, bloodshot already so early in the day, "John Calvin is dead."

"They're all crooks," Isaac Hune said to the group of friends and family that came to his home to discuss the issues that were pressing upon all their minds.

"Father, don't be so bold," his daughter Rebecca scolded. She was married now to Jacques and they had three children of their own. He went to Rebecca's side and put his hand upon the small of her back, his unspoken signal for her to calm down. But Rebecca had a mind of her own. Her father had seen to that and Jacques found it attractive. They'd learned the art of love-making in the animal sheds, almost getting caught once but able to talk their way out of it. Eventually all could see the two were inseparable and even now after all these years their love was strong and their intellects were closely matched. Jacques was still the community's Chronicler and Rebecca forever setting up people and places for him to investigate. There were times when he had to remind her that he was only one man and would she please slow down in the running of his life. He never dared stop her intruding, as her keen intuition led him again and again to the most recent political and social dramas that were unfolding all around them in Holland and the rest of Europe. Today, they'd gathered to discuss the colonizing of the New World. Many of Akev's merchant residents had begun talking about making the voyage.

"Why are they crooks?" one of the farmers asked Isaac who was also a farmer.

"They are after quick riches," Isaac brandied his hand about, his white beard and ashen skin worn from years out in the sun near the sea. He'd spent years tilling the soil in Gelderland before arriving in Akev. Isaac's herbs were still sought after for the Jewish Passover Feast.

Several of the men chuckled and Isaac glared at them.

"It's what we want. You think you'll get rich with your horehound?"

Isaac shook his head dismissively.

Jacques shot Rebecca a worried look. When they agreed to have a meeting in their home, they had forgotten Isaac's latest hostilities. Rebecca stepped in to clarify what it was she knew her father wanted to say.

"The Europeans go to the New World in search of minerals and..." she spoke but was quickly interrupted.

One of the men spoke aggressively. "As should we! I find no evil in gold or silver. Even the mountains off the Caribbean can be mined for guano. There's gold in that too. There are profitable new trade routes. There's an abundance of animals that can be skinned for their furs. The furs bring high prices in Europe. There's human trafficking too if you've the stomach for it. There's a huge profit to be made, a man could..."

"Jacques could you bring the biscuits into the room?" Rebecca broke the man's speech. Immediately Jacques knew it was Rebecca's way of getting the subject changed. The women of Akev were not as hot on the trafficking of human souls as many of the men were, though there were plenty of women who didn't mind, as was the case in Europe and the East. Slave trading was fine as long as the slaves weren't the same religion as those holding their freedom papers. Jews would not enslave other Jews nor would Muslims enslave other Muslims.

The man could see Rebecca had changed the topic and his big angry face made her think what a horrific experience it would be to have him own anyone's freedom papers.

All attention was on Rebecca when she asked, "Jacques? Have you any news?"

Jacques was caught off guard by her question. He stood holding the basket of warm biscuits with an odd look on his face. All the men except Isaac smiled at her tone of voice at him. Rebecca was a beautiful woman and any man in the room would have been proud to have her as a wife, but they did not envy Jacques with her demanding nature.

"Biscuits anyone?" Jacques asked.

"Honestly Jacques, I wasn't that intruding," Rebecca said to him while they lay upon sheepskins on the floor in front of the fire.

"Yes you were and you embarrassed me in front of the group. Just try to remember that I am your husband and you need to treat me with more respect."

Rebecca took her slender hand and pulled a lock of hair from in front of his dark eyes. She could see he was pouting and it wasn't going to be easy to soften him up. But she knew she had to try. She moved closer. He slightly pulled away. She moved closer, reaching over him, presumably to pull a blanket, but what she really wanted was for him to feel her firm, full breasts tightly wrapped in her dress, rub against his arm as she reached for the blanket. She could hear his breath quicken. Jacques proudly and stubbornly tried to quell his excitement but Rebecca wasn't just demanding in the political sense. She leaned over again, this time both breasts resting upon his chest. She looked into his eyes. She knew he had opportunities to bed other women when he traveled, and as she looked into his eyes she tried to decipher if he had partaken of their feminine gifts.

"Why do you stare at me?" he asked, angry and sulky.

"Do I?"

"Yes you do. Are you trying to read my mind?"

"Me?" she asked, feigning ignorance.

"Yes, do you ... I mean ... no ...you don't read my mind!" he said but looked at her with that look that asked *do you*?

She threw her head back and laughed. She knew that they would soon be making love beside the fire. Her father had taken the children for the evening so the children could enjoy another family's cooking and toys. Isaac had sensed Jacques and Rebecca needed time alone. He wasn't senile, just the occasional fading in and out. He was basically still a very sharp man.

"Jacques, I don't read your mind but need reassurance."

"Mademoiselle needs confidence?" he teased.

"Yes," she said, falling into submission. "I need you to tell me how much you love me and miss me when you're away," she looked at him with her transparent green eyes.

He grabbed her and pulled her close and held her tightly. "I see women frequently, beautiful women especially when I go to Paris. But none as lovely as you," he said as she rolled her eyes. "Now wait Rebecca, I speak from my heart. You are one lovely woman. Even after all the labor you've been through to raise three children, you delight me and I can see it in the eyes of the other men."

"See what?" she asked surprised.

"The envy. You're a beautiful woman. Any man would be proud to call you his wife."

She snuggled up to him. The bodice of her dress was tight fitting. She had removed the woolen jacket she wore at the meeting. Jacques eyes grew large when he took a better look.

"Good you wore the woolen. Envy would have been the least of my problems."

She laughed. She thrived on his attention and praise. This was the game they played again and again, never tiring of it. Her breasts were tightly locked into the bodice making them appear harder and even fuller than they already were. She rubbed her fingernail on one nipple, making a scratching noise against the cloth. Underneath it had grown large and erect. He took his warm hand and pushed it into the tight fitting bodice, rubbing it against the nipple. The contrast of her soft creamy skin against that of her nipple was delightful for Jacques. He gently reached for her hand and led it down his trousers where she found his hardened erection waiting. She loved every section of his strong body. She loved hearing his quickened breath as they rolled together and his knee rose up between her thighs and he gently rocked it. His fingers felt for the secretion he knew she had. Sliding one of his fingers gently inside of her he felt around and opened her up. Now he could feel her breathing rapidly. Her eyes gave him a look that spoke of deep devotion and a sense of privacy that the two had. He knew he could delve into her body in ways that would seem abominable to the community outside their door but he knew that she knew the ways of the European world as they had heard many stories and there were many wonderful stories Jacques had relayed to her about Europeans and their sexual liaisons. The rhythm of their hearts kept pace with the in and out motions of their lubricated bodies. Had they not been alone, their indiscretions would have been offensive but to Rebecca and Jacques it was delightful.

"I have become a bit fearful," Jacques said to Rebecca the next morning.

"Fearful?" she asked, surprised that he hadn't mentioned it the night before.

"Yes, the Inquisition is striking fear within the writing community. Portugal... with its ritual burning of writers because of their religion."

"You confuse me Jacques. Does the Inquisition burn writers?"

He knew she was upset at the topic and knew he must address it. "No ... well, yes ... no..." he stammered.

"Jacques!"

"No. The Inquisition does not burn writers for writing. The Inquisition burns them for Judaizing but it is striking fear among writers. It brings negative assumptions regarding books and learning."

Rebecca said nothing but he could see she was angry. She worried constantly when he was away. She would only worry more now. Jacques was a well-known Chronicler and many had expressed concern that one day he would be tried in the courts, especially because many outside their community knew Jacques was a Jew. There were outsiders who wondered about the tightly knit community of Akev, wondering if they all weren't posing as Christians.

Jacques began again. "I've never seen so many Sephardim as I have these last few weeks. They're coming north in masses," he said.

She nodded. "I've seen them too. I'm sorry that our community is full."

"Yes." He looked absent-mindedly out the window. "There are other communities and they can find work in Amsterdam."

"There's always the New World," she said, also looking out the window.

He spoke honestly. "There's always the New World but Jews are forbidden to settle in any territories that have been claimed by the flags of Spain or Portugal."

They both stared opaquely out the window. In a voice Rebecca had never heard so thin, he said, "But when have we been Jews?"

1581

"Thank you for coming," Jacques told the crowd who'd gathered to hear what the Chronicler had to say. There was confusion in the hamlet of Akev and Jacques felt he could offer some good advice.

"There are too many religions here," he said, unable to hide a smile as he looked into the crowd of friends, family and farmers, "and too few merchants. Why no merchants at this meeting? I understand that their business takes them far from home. But when you see them, tell them that we need them to attend our community meetings. Their knowledge is valuable to those that spend their time tilling the soil or caring for stock. The weavers and the potters and those that care for our children often make important decisions without the shared wisdom of the merchants. Please... speak to them when you see them."

Wheat dust covered the hands and face of the miller who was still in his thick apron, "Jacques what are you saying? There is but one true faith in Akev. That is known by all."

Jacques nodded; he loved the people of Akev, especially those who gathered around him today. "We're trying to create a Christian image but when we have Calvinists housing with Catholics and relatives coming from the Rhine who are Lutherans, it will arouse suspicion. We are Jews but to survive we pose as Protestants. Most of the territories have converted to Calvinism," Jacques told the crowd, knowing he would incite anger. These were not wealthy Sephardic merchants. The members that surrounded him today were the glue that held the community together. They sheared the sheep, wove the clothing and milked the cows. They kept food on the tables and stood watch night after night protecting the community against invaders. They knew how to work hard yet when their tasks were finished they knew how to enjoy what their day's work had brought them. In the evenings, you could hear music coming from many of the cottages, children singing in Spanish or French, reciting literature, often in Hebrew or Greek. On frosty mornings, when the sun rose, their faces were the first you saw, their fingers numb from the cold. Without them there would have been no Akev. As Jacques looked out into the older faces he remembered that as children they had helped build homes and now as old men they still worked a day's labor, almost as well as the younger men. The women often worked beside the men, or performed tasks that were difficult yet suited for their physiques.

Jacques told them firmly. "We must make the decision to be Calvinists. Not Huguenots, not Lutherans and above all else we are not Catholics. Yes, yes, we are Jews but it is too soon to expose our identity. As I said before, for the sake of our safety we are Calvinists."

A woman with a face wrinkled from years in the sun asked him, "Who are you to say what religion we should say we are?"

"He's the Chronicler!" a boy shouted, receiving chuckles from the crowd.

"He's Akev's grandson. Akev is the Hebrew name for Jacob. Jacques is to be respected as Akev's Chronicler and the grandson of the namesake of this land," said the potter who brought the crowd to reason, most nodding affirmatively.

A deep voice from the back disagreed with Jacque's plan to be Calvinists. "The Union of Utrecht will make for religious peace. Holland is ready to welcome the Jews."

But Jacques continued with his argument. "We live in a time when there are not one but many religions. They're often used for political purposes, especially financial. If it would prove strategic, European Nobles would switch religions in a day."

The crowd laughed and Jacques furthered his argument. "In some instances, Holland is becoming more tolerant. The tide has changed. There are now more persecutions of Catholics. But these are confusing times... not many of Holland's Jews lay bare their identities. It is not wise. It is not time."

"When *will* it be time?" a young man with a frustrated face spoke out.

Jacques tried to calm him. "We all understand your anger. For too long, we've hidden our faith. But I speak to you today with fear for our hamlet. There are hundreds of us coming and going. Spread the word, we should embrace Calvinism as our outward religion," Jacques told them then turned and walked away, waving off any further comments but turning once finally to say, "You will do what you wish but for the sake and safety of your children, follow the Calvinist path."

EIGHT

1590   *Jacques longs for a change*

"Rebecca," Jacques said one morning, "let's go south."

She looked at him as if he had lost all senses. She loved Akev and despite the dangers that surrounded them, they had remained safe. With the defeat of the Spanish, the northern merchants had taken control of Antwerp allowing her brothers to enlarge their business connections to include the Asian pepper trade. Though she seldom saw her brothers, she was close with their wives, and loved their children as she loved her own.

"My brother's children are my children. I cannot leave them," she told Jacques.

He reached for her waist and looked into her eyes. Her hair was graying and her skin beginning to lightly drape but to Jacques she was still his childhood friend with whom he had learned about love. When he drew near her, his heart still pounded as it did for none other. Her hair smelled of the most delightful perfumes and her body was always brushing against his when they were in close quarters.

Jacques defended his stance. "We don't have to bring all our belongings, just a few things. I have business I can attend to regularly in Paris."

"Is it safe?"

"Nowhere is ever safe. We will always be skirting a war, famine or a plague. How much longer will our old bodies carry us around this countryside? If we live in a flat in Paris we can live simply and enjoy a city that every day is full of excitement," he pleaded.

"If there is a secret Jewish Quarter, I would think about an extended visit, just a visit. And I must insist we be outside the city, it must be somewhere that we can live unmolested."

Jacques put his head down. He didn't know anywhere that they could live without fear of persecution. All he knew was that he had tremendous connections in Paris and he felt something in his heart... a pull. Something strong and full of color and incentive, pulling him toward the very heart of Europe.

"It surprises me that you agree so quickly," he said, with a questioning tone and a scant eye toward her. He wondered now what could be brewing in that mind of hers.

She smiled and also looked down. "Ten years ago you hinted at going to the New World. It was a wilderness and still is. It was a dream. Your dream. I've fulfilled many a dream of my own. If you wish to enjoy Paris ... I have heard..."

"Ah, Mademoiselle has heard of Paris, of course, of course, of course," Jacques smiled broadly as that colorful, magnetic pull began to work its charm on his wife.

Though it had been weeks since arriving in Paris, Rebecca and Jacques were still travel-weary. Besides thousands of people crowding the streets and markets, there were thousands of horses, breeds from all corners of the earth, some well-cared for, many overworked. There was so much to see and many of the spectacles overwhelmed their senses, especially Rebecca's.

"Jacques," she said, out of breath from walking, "never have I seen so many people."

"Yes," he said with a light voice but his beleaguered face revealed his concern for bringing his wife and oldest son Daniel into this chaos.

She knew that expression and drew no strength from it. Just as she was about to put a foot onto the stoop of their flat she was struck by a heavy set man who shoved her out of his way and into the crowd. She almost fell to the ground. She caught her breath and held her temper. Jacques smiled at her restraint, relieved that she was unhurt and that no fuss was made over the incident. Their intent was to be discreet.

Their son Daniel was distracted during the instant his mother had been shoved into the crowd. Jacques had seen him a few steps behind helping a young woman with her market bag. The bag, made of net, was tattered and fruit had begun falling out. The young lady was unaware that Daniel had been following behind her picking up each apple that had fallen until he finally caught up with her to warn her. Daniel took her by the arm and brought her toward his parents, who looked stunned from both the rudeness of the man who had bumped Rebecca and now at the stranger whom Daniel had instantly befriended.

"This is..." Daniel said, not knowing her name. He was very much the polite gentleman. Through the years he'd developed the fine manners that originated long before his great-great-great-great-grandfather Monsieur Soeira walked these very same streets.

"Ruth," she said softly. Daniel looked knowingly at his mother, both of them acknowledging that the girl was a foreigner with a Jewish name. Daniel had seen and felt that distressed look at Akev. They'd frequently opened their home to relatives who'd come from Portugal to escape the persecution. He saw it now in Ruth, as did Jacques and Rebecca.

It was an uncomfortable silence while the three Akevians accessed the girl's situation. She appeared to have no coat, her dress was terribly worn and although her hair had been combed and her face washed, she honestly looked in need of a good soak. But when Rebecca reached up to scratch at her own dirty head of hair, she wondered when she, Jacques and Daniel could bath as well. Rebecca immediately went to Ruth's side and to the girl's surprise, motioned for her to go into their modest flat. Her smile broadened as they welcomed her and all quickly went into the cool brick ground floor sleeping quarters they'd recently acquired. When they closed the door behind them the brick building shut the commotion out so quickly the four were left in an awkward silence.

Ruth silently eyed the room. There was not much in it, just some hastily thrown mats and blankets for sleeping. She looked back up at them wondering who they were and they at her wondering the same.

"No need we be in the dark," Jacques said as he went for a candle at which Rebecca smiled and apologized to Ruth for the scarcity of things but Ruth just shook her head. All knew there was no need for apologies on anyone's part. Daniel was riveted and just stood staring at the girl with his mouth slightly open.

"Where are you from?" Jacques asked in French which she did not seem to understand.

"Where are you from?" he asked again in Portuguese. She grew embarrassed and frustrated at her inability to understand.

Finally Jacques tried piecing together a sentence in Yiddish he'd acquired through conducting business with the Ashkenazi community. "Where are you from ?"

"Ah," she said with a smile. "My parents are from Austria. I've become separated from them for a long time," her smile faded. Jacques thought about asking but the look from both Daniel and Rebecca forbade it and Jacques knew their hunches were probably right. If the girl wanted to divulge her latest unpleasant past he was sure she would. Until then, it didn't matter. But now what were they to do? They'd found themselves in a most intimate of situations inside this small room, further complicated by Daniel's inability to stop staring at her with his mouth agape. Jacques looked at Rebecca whom he could tell was thinking the same thing.

"Where are you staying?" Jacques asked again in Yiddish.

Unhappy with the question, she nervously traced circles on the floor with her right foot. It was obvious she didn't want to answer but no one else said anything so she finally spoke.

"I am staying with many people in a very small flat. It is a bit of a walk from this market where I bought my fruit."

"Are they family or friends?" Jacques asked.

"Aunts, uncles, cousins and friends. It was very difficult in Austria. We did not worship as most and..."

Rebecca had some knowledge of Yiddish and began to vaguely understand the conversation. "Ruth, we are only here temporarily. It's very small but you're welcome to stay. We can get you some blankets." Jacques repeated it to Ruth in Yiddish.

"I would love to stay. I must tell the others or they will worry about me. It is so crowded and there is not much food. I can work for you, I'm very domestic."

Daniel began to understand the conversation a bit more too as the girl began mixing her Yiddish with some Ladino she'd acquired in her travels. "I'll go with you," Daniel said. "I could use the walk."

Ruth was shy toward Daniel. As she looked around the small room she realized what she'd gotten herself into. But the living conditions of her current lodging must have been so unpleasant she was quick to smile at Daniel and say, thank you. "Where did you learn to speak Yiddish?" she asked.

"Perhaps the same way you acquired some Ladino," he said. They all nodded. Akev had such a diverse population, there weren't many languages they couldn't bluff their way through a simple conversation, especially Jacques.

As Daniel and Ruth headed out for the walk to retrieve Ruth's belongings and inform her family what she was up to, Rebecca grabbed Jacques hand. In their hearts they knew their son had just found himself a wife and under the unlikeliest of situations.

"Daniel always has been good at finding things, ever since he was a baby," Jacques said.

"Jacques! That sounds so..." Rebecca began to scold before her husband cut her off.

"Primitive?" Jacques laughed, with which Rebecca just shook her head and looked at the mess of beds. They'd left early that morning not knowing they would have a guest.

"I suppose it's all primitive. Have we been led to Paris to begin a new life or were we guided here so our son could find this girl Ruth?" she asked.

"We jump to conclusions. She might not come back. We may have to reassure him all night long," Jacques said.

"Jacques, you and I both know that look, that feeling. There is a fire growing between the two. She has the worst living conditions, she needs us."

"Yes, and you can see by her nature and her manners that she is from a fine family."

"She a stranger yet feels so familiar," Rebecca told him.

"Daniel has been good to us. Coming with us here has been a sacrifice. He'll make a good husband but we're worrying too much about the future and trying too hard to marry off our son. What shall we do?" Jacques asked her.

Rebecca was surprised at his insecurity.

"Well, I must confess I have been worried that the boy would never marry and now this nice young woman comes along. I love my son. I want what's best for him. I feel that in an instant everything has changed," Jacques confided.

"I feel we need to protect her. But here... in Paris... I can't even protect myself."

"We could return to Akev," he told her with a wry smile.

"We just got here. It took us..." she protested.

"Yes but wouldn't you love to show Ruth what a community we've built?"

Rebecca sighed and lay down upon her and Jacques's bedrolls. She knew she was going to need a lot of rest before the long trip back to Holland. It wasn't long before they could hear voices and rustling coming from the street outside the flat. The door opened and in walked Daniel with the biggest smile his parents had ever seen. And with him was Ruth with her sisters Rosa, Golda and Rachel.

"I believe Akev's population will grow larger than we'd anticipated," Jacques told Rebecca so only she could hear.

"My son will be forever indebted to me for this," Rebecca said in that same quiet voice.

"We do need a new Chronicler," Jacques reminded her loud enough so Daniel could hear. A perplexed look came over their son's face.

Rebecca repeated the hint. "Our community needs a new Chronicler. Jacques… it's time you had some rest."

"Rest?" Jacques looked at Rebecca then at the four radiant young women before him, "I don't see that in our future for quite some time. Our Daniel has seen to that."

As the carriage rumbled along, Jacques and Rebecca began to realize what they'd done.

"We've been warning everyone about the overcrowding of Akev, and here we come with four Ashkenazi girls," Rebecca said bleakly.

"With nothing but the clothes on their backs," Jacques added just as bleakly. "I've been sorting my thoughts since we left Paris. Thoughts that have been on my mind for quite some time but I have brushed them aside."

Rebecca was concerned that he was about to spring a past indiscretion, perhaps bedding with another, but she was relieved when he continued.

"It's plain to see. Akev has no land available for the younger generations. Where are they to go?" he asked his wife as they sat alone in the carriage.

Daniel and the girls followed behind in a crude wagon. The bright straw they sat upon was a clean and pleasant sight. The sisters were all smiles.

"Amsterdam is growing. The city fathers plan on adding soil to the wetlands and building homes on it," Rebecca said positively.

"Those of us with means can help one or two of our sons move into one of the older homes in Amsterdam, one that needs fixing, there are plenty of those. But what will become of the other young adults of Akev? Where will the children of the farmers go? And what of the Shochets? They are our relatives through my great-great-grandmother, Magdalena. They aren't wealthy. They're still the ritual slaughterers."

"The Shochets do a fine job. Though I'm not so certain they are performing the rituals correctly," Rebecca said then added, "but we all do the best we can. Many of us have not had a true synagogue nor the best-trained rabbis. We're an interesting community."

"Yes we are," he said and confidently put his hand on her knee.

She leaned into him. They were both in their forty-first year and had been together most of their entire lives. Never tiring of one another. There was a special bond between them. One they had developed when they needed to trust one another. When they would meet in barns to kiss and bring each other comfort, especially during difficult times. When the news from Spain and Portugal was anything but reassuring.

Jacques continued on with what he'd been thinking for quite some time. "I'm convinced that Akev's youth will immigrate to the New World."

"The Americas?" She turned and stretched her neck to look directly at him, not quite sure she had heard him correctly.

"Yes, the Americas. There are opportunities for land. Big pieces of land. There will be such expansion in the Americas, every conceivable occupation will be needed. A man will be able to take his family and live well on the abundance the land provides. I hear it is beautiful Rebecca, just beautiful."

"Will we ever see it?"

He gave her an honest answer. "No, but I imagine that one of our sons will consider making the trip."

She was quiet. She didn't like the thought of being without her sons. She turned and looked at the wagon behind them. Two big black horses pulled it along. She could tell that the youngsters were curled up in the hay. She wondered what stories they had to tell one another and what dreams they spoke of.

"Please sit down," Jacques told the small group of close friends and family he had called together once they had arrived home to Akev. "I have called you here today because if you look around the room you will see we are all members of the old families. Over here we have a descendant of Abraham. Abraham was a dear friend of one of my ancestors, Jacob, the first Chronicler of Amsterdam's

Sephardim. Today the man we know as our friend calls himself Abram, but we all know he is from the family of Abraham. His ancestor, Abraham gently tended grape root stocks in a small dwelling in Amsterdam and old Abraham's son, Stephen had his dreams shattered in Portugal, his family narrowly escaping with only their lives and a few crates of wine and some grape root stocks. Our children and grandchildren will soon be dreaming of moving to the Americas. I will not blame them for wanting to leave. Akev has become very crowded. It will be even more so when they become adults. Also, to my left is a descendant of Jean La Roz. Jean was a well-established merchant in Amsterdam, always one of us. And way in the back is a descendant of Rabbi Samuel. Oh there is a great story about Rabbi Samuel in my family. If you have not heard it you should."

There were chuckles. Many had heard the hilarious story about Jacque's ancestor Jacob and how he had thought he overheard Rabbi Samuel saying he was the father of Marie Belle's child, who was Jacob's love whom he married. It was a delightful story and one each generation enjoyed retelling. Jacob, Amsterdam's first Sephardic Chronicler had been a character and there were many stories told about his adventures. Thinking of Jacob reminded him about another issue but he would wait until towards the end of the meeting.

Jacques continued with his message. "We must see to it that we stick together as much as possible. Let your children and grandchildren socialize with the children and grandchildren of those in this room. If we stay together and keep the bond strong, it will be easier for our children and their children for generations to come. Most of the families in this room have been in Holland for almost one-hundred-and-fifty-years. I'm not saying your daughter should not marry a man from Zeeland. Of course that is acceptable. But what I am saying is… remember who we are. We trust one another. We know how to do business with one another. We have our own rules and we abide by them. We've had our own schools and we've grouped together to send our brightest to some of the finest Universities in Europe. There is strength in that. We needed one another and we still do. I don't see things getting easier. Yes… there's been more freedom granted to Holland's Jews but we are still persecuted. Everyone in this room knows this."

Jacques could see his words had made them nervous. Several stared blankly out the window but returned their attention to hear him finish.

Jacques cleared his voice and spoke with authority. "There are many outside of Akev who know I am a Jew. But I do not flaunt it for fear of trouble. We continue to assume the outward appearance of a Calvinist community and wisely so. We must remember that as our ancient forefathers wandered in the desert, our children will be wandering to new lands. They will need every advantage we can provide, including the trust we have for one another. By continuing to bond together, pooling our resources, wedding our families together and sharing our business dealings, we provide a safe foundation for their future."

Andries Le Sueur, a descendant of Peter Le Sueur who risked his safety to hold nightly meetings in his home in Amsterdam in 1450, stood up and began slowly clapping. His large hands smacked together securely as did all the other hands in the room, men and women. They rose from their seats and the solid sound of their clapping was reassuring to Jacques who said thank you and humbly asked them to return to their seats as he had one more issue.

"I'm also here tonight to formerly name my son Daniel to the post of Chronicler of Akev."

There was a noticeable hesitation in the room but all were very polite and shook their heads affirmatively that they would accept Jacques's choice. But it was obvious that Daniel had made himself a bit of a reputation for being soft and childlike. Not the type to keep watch for the community in an intellectual way.

Jacques spoke to their doubts. "I believe with all my heart that Daniel will fill the void that will come when I leave. Antwerp is a bustle and Amsterdam is growing. The shipping industry is booming. I see opportunities to advance my family and I suggest all of you seize these opportunities. It is time for us to work with the rest of the world."

Jacques stared at the group. Through the windows he could see their children and grandchildren playing outside while they waited for the meeting to adjourn. They played the same games that other children play. Hiding and finding, king of the mountain, laughing and smiling and getting dirty as all children do. Jacques knew the children of Akev should be treated no differently when they went into the world. But he knew that they would be. It was for them and for the children of the future that he had held this meeting.

Daniel waded into the swampy water directly in front of he and Ruth's fishing cabin. It was what they called home. Though Akev was overcrowded, they'd received a much better welcome than Jacques and Rebecca had anticipated. The four sisters were downtrodden and each held their own unique blend of mystery and beauty. They were not Sephardim as were most of Akev; they'd been Ashkenazi Jews all their lives and it was not easy adjusting to different ways of worship. Most of the Akevians had either lived in one of the Latin countries or had ancestry that did and they all were extremely proud of their roots. The sisters did not speak up nor argue their differences, instead chose to keep quiet. But when the four sisters were alone together they had much to speak of.

Ruth stood and watched Daniel wade into the water and check his fishing nets. He was content to be a great distance away from the other dwellings and because he provided fish to the community, he was well liked and none thought less of him. But there was gossip regarding his duties as Chronicler. He came up with stories only when truly pressed, by his father and mother. They nagged at him continually, which only made him retreat deeper into his world in the marshes.

Ruth loved her husband. As she stood watching Daniel, fishing, knee deep in the chilly waters, she wiped her cooking hands on a towel she'd slung over her left shoulder. She'd heard through her sisters that it was not only Daniel's parents but a majority of the adults who were missing the news that Jacques had always brought from near and far. Ruth was surprised that no other young man in the community had challenged Daniel's role. In the world where she came from, another fellow would have quickly snatched up the opportunity to be the hamlet's Chronicler. She had yet to understand the depth of Daniel's family line and how indebted the community was to the line of Monsieur Soeira. Still, the sharp-witted young Ashkenazi girl from Austria began to wonder if she might somehow fill the void.

"Daniel!" Ruth shouted loudly against the howling wind. "Come speak with me. The food is warm but grows colder. Must I call you a third time?"

Daniel turned and smiled. Seeing his handsome, nature-contented face sent chills throughout her slender frame. His perfectly straight teeth, his dark hazel eyes and dusky skin were perfection in her eyes. Just after he smiled, seabirds blew overhead with a haunting squawk, the sound of their wings in unison added to the drama she felt as she watched him.

As they sat cozily at the little wooden table, he asked, "Do I detect a different flavor in the soup? Have you added something new?"

"Yes. When I went to Amsterdam with my sisters they had spices from the Orient. They came through Antwerp. I was able to trade fish for them."

He smiled. She hated to break the pleasant mood but she'd heard that his lack of reporting for weeks was wearing thin on the adults and some of the older children were beginning to ask questions.

In the softest way she could, she asked, "Do you plan to venture out and find out what's going on in the world?"

Daniel was slow to anger. She was much more likely to lose her temper. He shrugged his left shoulder slightly and Ruth could see that he was contemplating the question. But he had an emptiness and a lack of ambition toward the topic. She stared at him with raised eyebrows. She held her breath, begging for his response but Daniel still hesitated.

"This issue cannot wait!" she exploded. "The whole community is talking about it. You must at least go to Amsterdam or Antwerp and come back with a story, you must!"

Daniel found himself amused at Ruth's emotional outburst. "I could go to Damstraat and speak with the ladies there."

Ruth cracked a smile. She knew Daniel would no more go to Damstraat to talk to the prostitutes than would the new rabbi who had arrived from London.

"Daniel," Ruth said as she moved in closer.

He knew exactly what she was going to say. He knew his wife was quite the storyteller but it would be out of the question.

"No."

Ruth pulled her lovely head back in surprise. She was a beauty. Her skin was also dusky yet her hair was lighter. She had big brown eyes and hair so curly she had a tough time getting it combed and usually chose to wrap some kind of colorful cloth around or through it, giving the lovely girl a disheveled look but still quite strong of beauty.

"You were so shy when we first met. Where is that shy girl?"

"All girls are shy when they're in new surroundings. We'd been through an ordeal. I hadn't been eating as well as I should have; my stomach was ablaze with new fruits I'd gathered in the markets of Paris. My emotions were heightened and I was afraid of what may happen next. You came along and your mother and father quickly gathered my sisters and myself up and swept us away. I feel welcome here, as do my sisters. I'm comfortable and secure. Though it is not always easy being an Ashkenazi girl amongst a Sephardic community pretending to be Calvinists.

Daniel laughed and grabbed at her aggressively. She'd called him for food and her soup had warmed him but just being next to her, smelling her and watching her confidently try to challenge him was titillating and he wanted to draw her away from the conversation and down onto their low-lying rustic bed.

She would not budge. She'd heard the talk grow stronger and was afraid something unpleasant might happen, not just to them for Daniel's negligence toward the community but to the community itself, for they had grown accustomed to the watchful eye of the Chronicler.

"Daniel, we can go places together. We have no children. We can take a stout and hearty pony and a well-made wagon. Spring is here and summer will soon be upon us. We could cover a lot of ground and find out what's going on out there. We can go to the docks and ask the skippers, in both Amsterdam and Antwerp. I'll even go to Daamstraat and speak with the girls there. If it worked before it will work again. We'll attend church in Leiden and get to know people of the community. We'll hear their beliefs and the stories they have to tell and we'll bring them back to the community. We must Daniel. It is your duty." She shook her head and Daniel saw her eyes were tearing up. They were large but different than the almond shaped eyes of most of the other women of Akev. Ruth's were big and round.

Daniel turned his head and looked at the peaceful swamp outside the door. He could see the water beyond. The dried marsh grasses were bent and smashed down from his constant wading into the waters to retrieve his net. Ruth had strung a clothesline from the roof to the ground and a strong breeze wildly danced their heavy under garments.

"I can't leave here," he told her. "I didn't choose to be Chronicler. My father chose it. He gave it to me. I didn't think much of it at the time, I thought I could do it. I've done a lot for my mother and father. My father was away... often... chasing stories. As a boy, I did a man's work. While he was gone, I filled his shoes. Why do you think I was an unwed man when we met in Paris? All the other men my age had long since wed. I was too busy caring for my mother when my father was away. I used to hate it when he returned and I would revert back to being just the son. I love my father and would do anything for him but I have grown to love fishing. I want nothing but to be a fisherman."

"You can't." Ruth said stubbornly.

"Nor can you," Daniel said rudely. He knew what she was up to. "You want to take me away from here, you don't like to stay put but I do!"

Ruth put her hand on his. They sat facing one another at their humble table where they ate meal after meal together in the quiet surroundings away from everything except the seabirds and mammals that came to drink at the water's edge.

"I don't see any other way. I've heard the talk. You'll shame your family. How many Chroniclers has your family had?"

"My family is fair. My father has always been kind to me, as has my mother. Yes, they push and yes sometimes I have been very angry with them. But what child hasn't? I'll go to my father and tell him that he must choose someone else to be Chronicler."

168

Ruth sighed and looked through the open door. She too loved the beauty before her. She loved Daniel and tried daily to enjoy their peaceful life. She had her sisters to take her away from time to time but she would never leave him. She would never leave Akev. But she worried about what the community would do to them when Daniel relinquished his position.

"Will they think less of us?" she asked.

"Who? My mother and father?" he said, not seeming angry in the least, more amused at how quickly Ruth's composure had changed. "No, they're kind."

Ruth tottered against a chair before finally sitting down. "They've been patient with me and my sisters. And they treat you gently. My concern is the rest of Akev. How will the hamlet react to this? Someday we'll have children. Your family brings us status. I would hate to lose that prestige."

Daniel laughed and leaned forward, "Who cares?"

She could see that he wasn't worried about what the community would think. "Your attitude reveals your strong standing in the community, that which your family has brought. I don't have that Daniel. I'm a newcomer, an outsider. Even our synagogues were different. I..."

Daniel rose from the wooden chair where he had been sipping the warm broth made of mutton the community had raised and vegetables Ruth had grown and prepared. He stood behind her as she wept. His hands gently massaged her shoulders. He looked down into her mess of thick curls that in the morning he'd watched her wrap and twist up with a colorful blue cloth. Relieved she was clearing the passages of her heart and expressing the emotions of her past, his body absorbed her shaking and trembling. They had spoken very little of the suffering her family had endured. He had never asked Ruth to reflect on her former days.

Daniel would much rather have spent his time fishing but he knew Ruth was right. He must confront his father with the truth. He was not suitable as the Chronicler. Taking his time, he wandered through the mucky wetlands that led into the hamlet. He arrived at his parent's home to find his father reading. He found comfort in his father's warm smile, especially since Ruth had said the whole community was talking, his father was sure to have heard it all as well.

"Daniel, my son. What brings your visit?" Jacques said, rising to embrace his son.

"Father... I... ah..." Daniel stammered.

Rebecca stood staring at her handsome son. She'd always known this day would come. She'd never thought Daniel would make a good traveler. Yes, he'd gone with them to Paris but that was because he was a devoted son. Rebecca knew her son loved the quiet and beauty that he'd found at the water's edge and always pondered how he could possibly mix that with gathering stories as a Chronicler.

"Yes, Daniel, roll the words son," Jacques said, not making it easy.

Daniel sat down on the chair next to his father. It was a solid chair, rather sparse in wood but his mother had made the most comfortable duck feathered pillow for it. At least he would be comfortable. He may have to sit for a long while.

"Father I have failed as Akev's Chronicler," Daniel conceded.

"Failed?" Jacques challenged.

"Yes Father, I've written few stories and as Ruth tells it, Akev is full of talk."

Jacques questioned him further. "What reasons do you have for not bringing the world's stories to Akev's doorstep?"

"I just don't like to be away from home. I love the quiet. I'm a fisherman, not a city dweller. You must find someone else. What about one of my brothers?"

Jacques was patient but stubborn. He shook his head no.

"But you must father. I can't do it." Daniel said, speaking like a child.

Jacques put his hand upon his son's shoulder. "Try this. Go about the community and gather stories from within the hamlet. You can go three mornings a week and..." Jacques became stern, "show up at the Synagogue on the Shabbat. There are plenty of stories there to be heard."

Finding an opportunity to change the subject and for the sake of an argument Daniel jumped on his father's words, "The synagogue? Since when did Akev have a synagogue? It looks like a Church. The only real synagogue is in the Cornelisz home."

Jacques smiled, "And there you have your story. We did not educate you so you could fish. You can fish every day but on those days when you deliver your fish you must collect the stories. If you have to stay up late into the night to write them, well, so be it. So did I and all the other Chroniclers in this family. It's a tradition and one that is not to be broken. It means too much to this community. If there are but few things that are constant, this must be one of them."

Daniel fought back. "The community demands more than what they already know about the false Church and the synagogue at the Cornelisz home."

His father was not to be dissuaded. "The people of Akev love stories that help them deal with confrontations. Write the story of Queen Elizabeth sending soldiers to Holland when Spain attacked. That will oblige them to forgive your idleness."

Daniel was thoughtful. "Great power the Queen displayed."

The tension in Jacques's voice eased. "Let the old and the young share what they've heard and piece it together like a puzzle. As our ancestor Jacob used to do. He liked fish too, did you know that?"

"Father, the way I heard the story was that he liked to eat fish," Daniel corrected.

"Ah," Jacques threw up his hand, "Fish is fish, and freedom is freedom. Let the stories be collected. Those were days when the sea was no longer the Spanish Sea and the Low Countries became independent and united in rebellion. Did not Holland and Zeeland earn the right to be free in regards to religion? Did we not gain the right to be free from molestation or questioning on the subject of divine worship?"

"Yes father, these words were spoken. Yet here we sit. A patchwork of a community with its Calvinist church and all," Daniel said angrily.

Jacques leaned forward aggressively. "There is your story Daniel. There is your passion. Go tell it."

Not exactly content that his son would stay close to home as Akev's Chronicler, Jacques decided he would keep his eyes open for another promising candidate. Their oldest son Francois was out of the question, he'd been keenly interested in becoming a rabbi and marrying young to keep his mind off the ladies and devote his time to studies. It was expensive to send Francois away to study and difficult when an extra pair of hands and a strong back were needed. There were resentments over the issue but no tempers ever flared because all knew that it had been Monsieur Soeira's original wealth that enabled Soeira's grandson David, to create the community in the first place.

Today Jacques had to sneak away. He would be away from Akev for weeks while he handled paperwork for the courts. Most of his political connections had died, having been in his family and handed down, father to son, for close to two-hundred-years. Now he had become not much more than a messenger boy for the courts. Yes, he still owned several fine homes in Amsterdam and thanks to the wealthy Sephardic merchants who leased them from him, financially, he was in fine shape. But the Monsieur Soeira wealth was dwindling fast. It wouldn't be long before he'd need to sell many of the family assets. His sons and grandsons would need financing for their court assignments. They'd need to continue funneling money into Akev, for the Soeira finances had always provided for the hamlet. So it was without major enthusiasm that Jacques tired body stumbled along uncomfortably while performing his duties as Brenger for the courts. If it brought revenue until he could repair his lucrative war-torn connections, it would prevent the draining of the Soeira wealth.

NINE

Spring arrived forcefully and the sun lit up the hamlet in a way that Jacques had not seen before. After the cold winters, the springs came upon them too soon, reminding him that another season had passed. How many more did he have left? He stepped up his pace anxious to see his wife Rebecca and find out what he had missed during the month he was gone. As he walked through the pastures and the open gates, he passed the animal husbandry sheds where the men and women smiled, nodded or waved from a distance. Nothing new there. He walked toward the crowded, original development where he and his family had lived for many years. Cottages were closer together and small homes for aging parents had been built next to larger ones. He shook out his arms, stretched his shoulders, puffed up his chest and let out a deep sigh. As always there were a great many children and grandchildren playing about and today they had shed their winter clothes due to the pleasant weather. Attentive young mothers, older sisters, brothers and fathers smiled broadly in the afternoon sun. A mild breeze blew through, just enough to clean the air of the rotting animal manures that were in piles waiting to be plowed into the grain fields.

Jacques hoped to catch Rebecca by surprise but all the loud friendly greetings of "Welcome home Jacques," brought her to the front steps. Her brunette strands of long hair had faded and streaked with thick gray bunches that hung down without much curl. Her eyes squinted into the sun. She wore the adoring smile he loved. Akev's prosperity, abundance of food and her fondness for baking had grown her body round.

"My love is home!" Rebecca believed in making a show of their love in front of the children gathered.

"Rebecca!"

"Jacques! You're here in time for the special event this evening."

Jacques clowned in front of the children who smiled and waved at him as he briskly jumped up the stairs and into the house. Rebecca quickly set the table. The lamb stew made his mouth water and the dark greens that lay stretched neatly beside large bright red radishes looked inviting.

"I'm delighted to be home to my wife and her fine feasts but please do not make me wait, tell me of this special event."

"Daniel is holding a meeting tonight in the large barn."

Jacques was surprised taken back. "Daniel? What's prompted the change?"

She shook her head. "I heard from Ruth early this morning. She was poking her head in everywhere. She said Daniel wanted as many to come to the meeting as possible.

"Very good. We now have our Chronicler."

They'd waited for years and it had not come easily. It was a bad reflection upon Jacques for not choosing correctly, so today was a day of vindication and celebration.

Jacques hoped to rest once returning home but the excitement was too much for them both and they lay next to one another engaging in stimulating conversation.

"What do you think he'll say?" Jacques asked.

"Don't know," she looked at him suspiciously.

"Rebecca, don't give me that look."

She leaned back into her feathered pillow. "I thought perhaps you and Daniel had a plan."

"Why would you think that? I've been gone for a month."

"You arrived just in time to eat supper and attend Daniel's first meeting as Chronicler," she said eyeing him, watching his facial expressions.

"And a good thing I did. I had no hunch the boy was planning this."

"He is not a boy," Rebecca reminded him.

"You're right. Today he is our man of Akev."

Jacques and Rebecca stayed off to the side in the barn where Daniel was to hold his meeting. He was late but that did not quell the group. They knew Daniel to be reliable and the anticipation only grew stronger with the wait. The children, picking up on the excitement, were happily running about as if it were a holiday and they would each be receiving a gift. Older girls danced arm in arm and many of the teens gathered in groups and sang songs.

"Why are they so joyous?" Jacques asked Rebecca. "I'm afraid they may be disappointed. No one seems to know what he's going to say."

"I had the same thought," she said, looking at the stage that had been set up. "Look how they've erected a platform for our Daniel to rise above the crowd."

"Akev is becoming a little city," Jacques uttered lightly.

Rebecca elbowed Jacques. "Look, here he comes."

Jacques turned around to see his son walking proudly into the barn and right behind him, very seriously following him was his older brother Francois. "Look there's Francois!" Jacques shouted.

Rebecca's mouth was agape. "What could he being doing with Daniel?"

Jacques was now just as excited as the rest of the crowd that had grown more excited when they saw Daniel's brother, the soon to be rabbi, following closely behind. Daniel hopped upon a sack of animal feed, propped up to use as a step. He turned and faced the crowd of Akevians.

"Friends, neighbors, family members. Shalom. Thank you for coming at such short notice. I am delighted that my dear father Jacques, returned home in time for this gathering."

"As you see I've asked my brother Francois to be with me here tonight. Most of you know Francois is studying to be a rabbi and he is very close to becoming one. While I've spent my time fishing and enjoying nature, going to Paris and returning with not just one, but four beautiful women," Daniel said jokingly, "my brother Francois has been studying the ancient scriptures of our ancestors."

Francois stood proudly. He'd been blessed with a fine wife and children. Francois's choosing to spend his days studying Judaism was just what the community needed. It had become too much of a patchwork of families piecing together what they vaguely remembered about Judaism and presenting it to their families. Visiting Jews had snickered at them for their incorrect ways of worship and ritual, but all had done the best they could. The dispersal of the Jews throughout the world and the ensuing persecution that led them to practice their faith in secret was a fact of life in Akev.

"I've consulted with Akevians who travel to Amsterdam regularly," Daniel began again. "Their concerns have brought me here this evening. It is their understanding that in Amsterdam, there are many who have a fondness for the Jews. It is almost an obsession with them. There are hours of conversation in the cafes. The women in the churches speak of the Jews regularly and from the pulpit there is not an easier topic to speak of than the Jews."

"What do they say?" a teenaged boy asked.

"The Christians talk of making a Hebrew translation of the Bible," Daniel responded to the boy's question at which point the crowd seemed like Daniel's answer was a good one and perhaps not a bad idea.

Daniel's tone of voice was sober. "A Hebrew translation of the Bible would include their New Testament. They want us to accept their messiah as our own. We believe the messiah has not yet come. We pretend to be Calvinists. We've set up a church for all the world to see, yet worship as Jews in the secret of our homes."

An angry young man called out. "Why do we continue that with that lie if Holland will accept us as Jews?"

Daniel quickly answered. "That day will come but it is not today. The Hebrew translation of the Bible could be a trap. They're seeking those fluent in Hebrew. Be careful! You'll be exposing yourself and the rest of us. Do not act in a hasty manner, nor one that will endanger your families. Francois, do you have something to tell us?"

Francois stepped to the front. He was clean and sharp in his dress and desirably handsome.

"Yes, thank you my brother. I don't know if many of you know this but I travel regularly and meet with other young men aspiring to be rabbis. I've studied in Europe and I often go to Amsterdam homes where Shabbat services are held. Some of the homes are very secretive but some of the other synagogue homes are known to the Christian community. We work together and hope to someday build a true synagogue in Amsterdam to serve the needs of that wonderful city, and the country that has embraced us in its own way. We urge you to take seriously our religion, the religion of Moses and Aaron. There is a great movement underway, a new movement to convince us of a messiah we believe has not yet come! I fear that we will lose some of you to the Calvinists. We do not want our children to be confused. We are Jewish. We are not Christians. Martin Luther died a very disappointed man knowing that we would not be converted. This is who we are. We are proud of our past. We head into the future with our heads held high. We will wait for our own messiah."

Exhausted, Francois sat down. He had turned the mood of the crowd. What Francois had not said was that he had sources who told him that for months, many of the Akevians had been seen in Amsterdam worshipping amongst the Calvinists and had been light of heart and full of song. These sources also told Francois that many of these Akevians had converted all the way to Calvinism and had begun to whole-heartedly embrace it. This he worried could be very dangerous to the community. Francois had begun to believe that the secrecy of Akev had been compromised but he believed that Holland's liberal government would not bother them.

Daniel thanked everyone for coming and added that he hoped he had, "Given everyone food for thought." There was no singing and dancing on the way out. Children looked to their parents for answers but received silence. The warm early spring day had turned chilly and the hands that reached for their children's to walk them back to their cozy homes had turned icy.

TEN

Old, tired and once again feeling lonely while her husband was away, Rebecca busied herself helping anyone with anything that needed fixing, cooking, mended, milked or mopped. But nothing took her mind away from Jacques. She'd never grown used to his long stretches away, especially as they grew older. Each time they hugged goodbye, she feared it would be their last. When the children started calling out her name, heralding Jacques return, she walked through the pastures and down the lane to welcome him.

She planted a kiss on his weathered cheek and pulled his thin hair back from his eyes. He wore an unusual expression, one that she didn't like. Taking a deep inhale she plunged right in and asked. "What bad news do you bring us now Jacques?"

He was irritable and didn't like her placing blame. "The news is not from my heart nor is it of my planning. I only have knowledge of it. Would you rather I not say?"

"Will it endanger Akev if you don't?" she asked.

He sighed just as loudly as she had, stopped right in the road and faced her. "You may as well know, the whole world will know eventually. England's King Henry has converted."

They both continued facing one another, Rebecca not sure she'd heard him correctly. Jacques grew impatient with the wait and sat down on his luggage.

"Converted to what?" she asked.

His stare was at first blank then his look was that of disgust. "King Henry IV is now a Catholic," Jacques said, not sure he could believe it himself.

"Will it have that much of an impact on us?"

Jacques told her firmly. "He's setting up the Royal Court in Paris. And do you know what old Henry said about that?"

Rebecca shook her head no.

"He said... *Paris is well worth a mass.*"

She wrinkled up her nose and sat down on his luggage with him. He wrapped his arm around her and they sat there for quite some time in the middle of the road with their heads hung low. It was Jacques who finally stood up and used all his strength to pull Rebecca's emotionally exhausted body back up again.

"Hello Father," Daniel said when he entered his family's home several days after Jacques return. Daniel wanted to discuss some stories he was working on. He'd developed a sense for how much information the community needed and he tried to come up with three or four stories a week. He'd begun to enjoy walking through the farms, workshops, barns and spiritual meeting houses and chatting up the folks. He'd become interested in the news each had to divulge and realized how important it was to have an informed community. Today he wanted to know what his father knew of the *Company of Far Lands*. Daniel had heard that this new company from Amsterdam was planning to send ships to the East Indies for spices.

Jacques looked dryly at Daniel before speaking. "Yes, that's my understanding as well son. The commander will be Cornelis de Houtman. There's another company that will operate very similar to Far Lands but it's based out of Rotterdam and there are two new companies in Zeeland. You've just learned of this?" Jacques patted his son on the back and Daniel stiffened. He'd been proud that he was doing his job as Akev's Chronicler and still able to fish most days and keep an eye on Ruth, whose first pregnancy had ended in a depressing and painful stillbirth. Daniel worried about her while he was away.

Rebecca stepped into the conversation. "Ruth's pregnant again," she told Jacques who looked at Daniel who nodded.

"This is wonderful," Jacques said to his son. "The next Chronicler?"

Daniel shrugged. He was still smarting from his father's insult. "Back to the shipping companies," he said impatiently.

Jacques noticed his son's shortness but chose to ignore it. "Yes, you should visit with the merchants in Amsterdam," he said before Daniel quickly interrupted him.

"Are they Portuguese?" Daniel queried.

Jacques raised an eyebrow. "If you mean are they fellow Sephardim then yes," Jacques told him. "There are a good many Portuguese merchants working with the shippers."

Daniel turned his back on his father then spun around facing him. In a domineering tone he spoke his thoughts. "I think I may travel to Zeeland. I'd like to make connections, it's less populated and I think I should enjoy the trip."

Jacques began to speak in hushed tones. "There's a skipper in Amsterdam...."

Rebecca drew near to hear.

"He is a very shrewd Sephardic skipper. He has sailed both the Roode Leeuw, and the Witte Leeuw," Jacques told them.

"Both ships? The Red and the White Lion?" Rebecca asked. She was impressed.

"He's a master of the seas but not just a skipper. He goes by the name of Manuel da Silva. I don't know if he owns any ship now but in the past he and five other Portuguese Sephardim owned a ship. When his ship was not loading and unloading cargos of figs, sugar and wine, he kept an office on his ship where he met with merchants that dealt heavily in diamonds."

"Jacques... don't tempt your son with riches," Rebecca preached. "All of us know the stories of families that are growing their wealth through the diamond mines but..."

"Rebecca please," Jacques said firmly, obviously disturbed by his wife's interruption, "Manuel da Silva is full of stories. He knows all that goes on amongst the Sephardim in both the shipping and quite a bit in the diamond polishing. What that man can tell you," Jacques said focusing entirely on his son, "the politics of Amsterdam are often bought and sold, do you understand Daniel?"

"Yes I do father. Unfortunately I do. Am I interested in Amsterdam's politics regarding the Sephardic and Ashkenazi diamond merchants? Does it have anything to do with our security here at Akev?"

Jacques raised his voice impatiently. "Of course, it has everything to do with our security. We need wealth too, don't we?"

"Are you asking me father, to become friendly with Manuel da Silva so that Akevians can somehow benefit from the diamond trade?" Daniel asked.

"The municipalities forbid Jews from forming guilds. Diamonds are an endeavor open to us. Too many professions are illegal for Jews. But diamonds..." Jacques said with a vengeance Daniel had not seen in years. "Diamonds are regulated by Jewish merchants. Our children need livelihoods if Akev is to prosper. And pay when the municipalities come asking for their share! We cannot all be farmers, ritual slaughterers and sea merchants."

"It's true," Rebecca agreed. "Nor can we all be rabbis. But it would be a more pleasant world."

Daniel thought constantly about what his father proposed. *Get the community involved in the diamond business?* His head spun from the contemplation. After a quiet afternoon fishing he broached the subject with Ruth.

"My father is encouraging me to be a liaison for the community," he paused. "With the diamond industry."

She looked at him with little expression. Daniel felt Ruth didn't understand what he meant.

"You know what diamonds are don't you?" he asked.

Her innocent face nodded that she did. Her big brown eyes were sad, as had been the case for months after losing her first baby. But with a child growing inside her womb, they were both hopeful.

"My father believes I should learn who's in charge and see if I can't stir young Akevians toward diamonds. When they come from India's mines they need to be polished. It's a skill that takes years of practice. There's a fortune to be made. If the young men start early they'd do well. My father feels we would be a welcome addition, although the workers would need move to Antwerp. They would bring prosperity to Akev."

Ruth nodded, still expressionless.

Daniel was patient. "We can go to the diamond merchants in Antwerp and select stones for the European Royals. Men who do this are called *purchasing agents*."

"*Hoffuden*," Ruth said solemnly.

"Yes, that's right," Daniel said, surprised that Ruth knew about them. "They are often referred to as *Court Jews*. Do you find this unpleasant?"

She didn't answer but continued to stare at him expressionless.

Daniel went on to explain. "Besides buying diamonds they bring messages to the Imperial Court."

Daniel was relieved when Ruth finally spoke. "My family knew a Brengerhof family. Some of the other Jewish families didn't like them. They were jealous of their wealth and their business connections with the Christians," she told him, then leaned forward, her eyebrows furrowing and her eyes squinting. "It became dangerous at times."

"It did?"

She nodded again returning to her solemn face.

Daniel was thoughtful about his inexperience of worldly matters. He'd been very sheltered. First growing up in Akev and then when he studied in Europe he was lost in his books and then after that it was his fishing. Now, he was forced to make honest and crucial decisions that would affect the whole community, especially the new generation. He looked at his beautiful wife and reached across the table to grab her hand.

Ruth accepted his hand but asked him honestly, "Do you want this for our child?"

He leaned back in his narrow, high-backed dining chair and contemplated what she'd asked and then repeated the question. "Do I want this for our child? I suppose I would have to think for a long time to know the answer."

"I suggest you do," she leaned forward and grabbed his hand. Her deep, dark eyes stared into his. "Stay here and fish for a few days.

Consider the path that Akev will take if you not only encourage but educate young men on the ways of the Hofjuden."

Daniel averted her eyes, for he was the son of a long line of Hofjuden, but in Holland their title was *Brenger*. His father had kept it quiet but his great-great-great-grandfather, Monsieur Soeira had rather flaunted his connections to Europe's Christian Royals. Daniel realized, as he sat gazing at his beautiful wife, that they had better have a long talk. She'd grown up speaking Yiddish. Though it had sometimes made communication difficult, he assumed she understood his family's past.

He watched Ruth as she looked down at the table. He could see that she was still depressed from losing her child. His heart ached over the loss and they'd cried together again and again. His eyes welled each time he remembered the burial. Ruth wrapped her fingers around the lifeless finger of their stillborn child and would not let go. As the shovels of dirt slowly covered the baby's body you could hear Ruth's mournful cries. But now, as he looked at her beauty he wanted nothing more than to feel close to her, physically close to her. She began to arouse him as her breasts pressed against the table she was slipping down onto. He reached for her hand. She looked surprised but slightly smiled. She knew what he wanted and Daniel was pleased that her smile revealed she wanted it too. He came and stood behind her and she rose from her chair. Her abdomen was only slightly protruding; most would never recognize she was in the second trimester of a pregnancy. The woolen sweater she wore, she unbuttoned and let slide over her shoulder. Daniel kissed her neck. Reaching his hand inside he was able to feel her breast and her expanding nipple. She stared at him. It made him uncomfortable the way she stared when they were in the act of loving one another. Her stare dove deeply into him. He wondered what she saw or what past she relived. He had not been sexually inexperienced when they first wed. He had had numerous playful affairs with young men while away at school and he had found the early experiences fun. At one point he had succumbed to a boyish affair and it had been most unpleasant when Daniel broke it off, the lad threatening to harm himself if Daniel did not return to their former sleeping arrangement. Daniel was relieved when one of the other male students took a fondness for Daniel's former sexual partner and the two young men were delighted to have found one another and the three became study partners and all was amicable. Daniel found no reason to tell Ruth, nor anyone else for that matter, nor did Daniel feel any need to know of any experiences Ruth had partaken. It had been a long ordeal for Ruth and her sisters. Their looks were stunning and during times of war, to have a warm companion to share your heart and body brought great comfort. He understood that.

As he stood behind her, he reached under her dress. Pleased that the weather had warmed and his wife wore less clothing, it made it easier for him to move the cloth aside and with his very stiff erection gently slid it into Ruth as she rested her palms upon the table. His organ was unusually moist, as was hers. It reached an awkward point when Ruth's position at the table grew uncomfortable and necessitated her shifting her weight. But they regained their rhythm and both were soon lost in the pleasure of the simplicity of his sliding in and out. Daniel's breathing became heavy and his panting into her ear heightened the sensation. She pulled away from him and he slipped out. She rushed to their sleeping mat and uncharacteristically, lifted her dress to reveal the thick, dark hair that nature had bestowed upon her, but that society had made her keep hidden. She brushed her hand across it and gently spread her legs. He smiled at the invitation and would have loved to be rough with her as he had been able to be with the young men in his school. But he knew better, so he slowly and carefully bent to his knees and with her help, plunged into Ruth. He began pumping himself into her and she delighted in his quickened pace. He pushed her breasts together and pulled at the bodice hoping to release them. Their refusal to be easily removed only enhanced the tension. She too was much more aroused and seemed to welcome a little roughness. Their sudden frenzy became their unspoken confession of their pasts and they began tearing at each other's bodies. When they finished they would go on as if nothing had changed until their hormones began to speak to them once more, the two lovers delighting in the secrets that were theirs.

"Father, I believe I will visit the Portuguese merchants in both Amsterdam and Zeeland but I would rather stay away from the diamonds," Daniel told his father after a calm day of fishing and enjoying Ruth's company.

Jacques raised an eyebrow. He'd changed over the years. If one could see him next to his great-great-grandfather, David Soeira, it would have been difficult to tell the two apart. Not that they looked similar, more an aura about them, an attitude and an ambitiousness that they both held. They understood what it took to provide for others, make compromises and sometimes do business with those who held beliefs completely removed from yours.

"Father?" Daniel brought Jacques from his trance.

"Sorry. I was lost in thought. I was thinking of the Chroniclers that have come before us. Have you ever paid a visit to the women of Damstraat?"

"No, I can't say that I've been to Damstraat father," Daniel said impatiently, wondering what criticism the man would come up with today.

"You should. That is all I intend to say but Daniel you should. There has not been one Chronicler that did not befriend the women of Damstraat. They've saved lives and many wars were averted due to their bits of information."

"I hardly think," Daniel started but Jacques would not let him be so snub.

"Daniel... you live a splendid life. You've not had to fight a war. You've seen better times than your ancestors. You're unappreciative. If we had known..."

Daniel put his hand on his father's wrist. Jacques looked surprised. It was an aggressive gesture but Daniel wanted his father's attention before he spoke. "If it will please you, I will attempt to establish a contact with the women on Damstraat but I am quite sure that I will not be instructing Akev's youth to polish diamonds nor go as liaisons between the merchants and the Royals."

"Fine Daniel. But I must warn you. It would be very offensive to others if you treat the diamond merchants with disdain. There is nothing to be ashamed of in the diamond profession."

"Ruth was not pleased with it."

"Ah, Ruth. I see," Jacques was thoughtful. "There are a few families here who work within the industry and the numbers will grow. The diamond industry is here to stay Daniel. We are fortunate this occupation is available to us as Jews. What more are we to do? We need livelihoods to care for our families."

"I understand. But Ruth has seen the other side, she has heard talk..."

"No need to further this conversation. Although I do predict that it will be diamonds that help the Sephardim branch out someday to the New World." He waved his arm exhibiting a wide expanse. "There are diamonds in India. And there are diamonds yet to be found..."

"I understand that father, but my desire is to keep my family on a different path," Daniel said firmly.

Jacques looked at Daniel with resignation. "Perhaps this is good news. We will keep the Chronicler in the Soeira family. Though someone must continue meeting with outsiders or this family will one day be only inn keepers, millers and farmers."

Daniel put his hand upon his father's shoulder, this time lovingly. "We will always have a Chronicler."

"Yes I suppose so," Jacques said. "But tell the stories well son, tell the stories well."

It was early in the morning when Ruth came to her mother-in-law's door. She'd wanted to pass the time with some familiarity. She enjoyed Rebecca and always found her home warm and hospitable, especially the kitchen. Ruth had not had the best success with her cooking, so enjoyed asking questions of her husband's mother.

"Where did you learn to cook with all these flavorings?" she asked Rebecca.

"My father was a farmer from Gelderland but originally his family was in Spain. My father's name was Isaac. He always managed to supply the bitter herb for Passover, he was known for that. As Passover drew near, people would come looking for him. In Gelderland everyone called him Isaac Har Hune," Rebecca turned, stopped what she was doing, spoon in hand and began reliving the past.

"Horehound? That bitter herb?"

"That's the one."

"I've heard that name before, Har Hune" Ruth absent-mindedly told Rebecca.

"You have?" Rebecca asked eagerly.

"Well," Ruth said, still absent mindedly, as if she had something she wished to discuss with Rebecca but couldn't get the strength to broach it. "I have met men with the name Hune."

"I see," Rebecca began to notice Ruth's dreamy disposition. "Is something on your mind child?"

With a shock, Ruth looked up quickly. "No," she lied.

Rebecca returned to stirring her soup and talking about the different greens and herbs that she included to make it more palatable.

"I must admit our connections to the Sephardic merchants and their connections to the Mediterranean provide me with plenty to season with. Jacques usually brings me a bag of some kind of spice. They're so easy to tuck in his pocket, so light. The merchants are forever giving him samples," Rebecca chattered on.

Ruth absent-mindedly traced her finger upon the wooden counter top. There were cracks and grooves that had been created through every day use and the wood had grown interesting over the years. As Rebecca watched her young daughter-in-law she wondered if she should worry about her nature. She had not grown to know her all that well. She and Daniel chose to live away from the rest of the group. Rebecca thought it odd that Ruth was so far from her sisters. But Akev was not all that large, so a short walk to visit was not out of the question. Finally Rebecca could stand Ruth's other-worldliness no more and spoke to her.

"Ruth, your mind seems to be someplace else this morning."

Ruth's startled expression gave Rebecca at least the impression she was somewhere in that head of hers. Ruth slowly walked from the kitchen toward the table that was set nearby. Rebecca could tell that the girl was very selective about what she was going to say.

"What is it Ruth?" Rebecca pleaded.

Ruth looked straight into Rebecca's eyes and finally found her voice. "I have begun to question all that I have been taught."

Rebecca's chubby, elderly body slouched into a relaxed position as she joined her at the table. "We all question what we've been taught. That's the process of becoming an adult."

Ruth stared at her, disappointed that she had not understood.

"It's about being a Jew. It's so confusing." Ruth started using her hands, trying to express herself and rambling on about the Christians and the empty church at Akev and the lack of consistency regarding the holy days.

Rebecca placed her hand on top of Ruth's. "I often feel the same. It's been hard to hide my beliefs. It's humiliating to pretend. It angers us all. It's important that we do the best we can. We must maintain our heritage and teach our children. We must never stray."

Ruth was not pleased with Rebecca's response. "I envy the Christians. The young women I see in Amsterdam, they know all about John Calvin. They know exactly how to pray and when all their holidays are. And what to wear and what to eat. They know these things. I'm so confused. I am Ashkenazi. Our songs are different and our synagogues are different that yours. Our language is different as well," she pleaded angrily at Rebecca.

"These things are difficult Ruth, all the elders know this. It becomes more complicated when we hide and never know from one day to the next who will be holding Shabbat. We try to preserve what we can of our Judaism. I've heard they do much better in Amsterdam and that soon many Jews will come to Holland and openly practice our religion."

Ruth gave Rebecca a hopeful look.

"What do your sisters say?" Rebecca asked, afraid of the answer.

Ruth put her head down and that was all Rebecca needed. The older woman put her hand upon the young woman who carried her unborn grandchild. "Be patient, please Ruth. We must endure. It will not bring goodness to abandon the faith of our ancestors. Nor why should we?"

"I suppose this is true. Why should we?" Ruth agreed.

They sat contemplating while children gathered outside to play in the morning sun. Outside of Rebecca and Jacques home, the crowd of children was often larger because Rebecca was known to come out from time to time with a warm basket of spicy cookies. Word traveled fast in Akev.

Daniel took longer to return than anyone had expected. They'd begun to worry until one day he marched into his parent's home and eagerly shared the knowledge he'd accumulated.

"You're right father. The wealth of the Sephardim is impressive. The shipping contracts are lucrative and yes, there are some who have pooled resources and purchased ships. Whole ships Father! They've built a network far superior to anything we have here at Akev. Sephardic bankers trust them and loan them money. They all speak Hebrew. They have contracts to gather spices, diamonds and the most beautiful cloth I have ever seen. Zeeland is alive with activity and our brothers in Amsterdam, what wealth! They're building some very impressive homes. What courage these merchants have to go to sea and return to Portugal where they're not welcome as Jews."

Jacques was pleased until Daniel brought up the Portuguese authorities. For years, he'd endured the gruesome details of persecution and could stomach no more. "Daniel, they're Portuguese Jews and proud of it. Their ancestors built strong networks. Returning to Portugal as merchants maintains these connections."

Daniel was growing overconfident. "In Amsterdam, it has become more relaxed for the Jews. Most still hide behind their Calvinist pretensions but some are openly practicing Judaism and growing secure in it."

Rebecca shook her head in disbelief and Jacques was also cautious. "Not yet son, not yet."

"Why not!" Daniel raged. "I am so sick of hiding who we are. There is no shame in it. We are Jews father. We should stand and be counted as all the others."

"Son, most of the others that stood to be counted are dead or exiled. They were forced to leave their land and possessions behind. I know the Nobles. I trade with the Nobles. I bring contracts from Sephardic hands and put them into the hands of the Nobles and others in powerful positions. Do not be fooled. Yes, they love our prosperity and what we can do for them, but they despise our religious beliefs and many of our customs. The cries from the pulpit to convert the Jews grow louder by the day. Theologians spend days, weeks, months, and years debating the conversion of the Jews. We will not convert, nor will we be ignorant and give them the chance to arrest us, breaking up our families and community. We must remain strong. Our defiance will be our secret worshiping and the strong brotherhood we've created."

Daniel's eyes were enormous after his father's forceful opinions and when he looked at his mother her face he saw pride.

"It's confusing and grows more so by the day," Daniel said softly. "I'm afraid we're losing the cohesiveness that this community needs. I know that many in our community have begun to enjoy Sunday church services in Amsterdam. Look around Akev on Sunday. There's no one here!"

"I hadn't noticed," Jacques admitted sadly.

"Nor have I," his mother agreed.

"What can *we* do? What can *I* do to pull our brothers and sisters back to the faith?" Daniel asked his parents.

Rebecca and Jacques gave no reply. Their wrinkled, weathered faces looked gravely at him in silence.

It was Sunday morning and Jacques and Rebecca made an effort to walk around Akev to see if Daniel was correct that many were leaving to attend Calvinist churches in Amsterdam. Their hearts were heavy when they recognized the wagon that belonged to Ruth's sister, Rachel. Rachel's husband was driving and their hearts sunk further, when in the back of the wagon they saw their own daughter-in-law, Ruth, who did not look their way.

ELEVEN

1591 *December*

"Jacques you're too old to be traveling in this weather," his elderly wife Rebecca told him. "The wind could not howl louder and a storm is coming."

"I'm going to Amsterdam. I'll be treated well in the homes of our brothers. I'll find truth and solutions."

"Do as you will. I have never been able to control you. I have known you as a child and a young man. And now a stubborn old fool!" Rebecca chided him.

Jacques was caught by her words and stopped to look at the woman he'd known most of his life. The memories of their afternoons spent in barns, hiding and telling stories, touching each other's bodies, and the late afternoons they lay outside in fields, waiting for the sun to retire so they could see the stars. He turned his face toward her, understanding it could be the last time they saw one another. He tried to explain his insensitivity.

"Our duty to our fellows must sometimes go beyond the love of our own families." He put his hand on her check. Her eyes welled. She had a dimple on one side of her face, the side she favored. The side that always showed strength. It reminded him of the soft, rosy skin of her youth. "I wish I could tell you I will return safely. I'm much too old. Let's trust our faith." He held out his hand for hers. "You will most likely see me in a week. I'll return for the beginning of Shabbat. Prepare a feast for I shall be hungry for the love of my family and my wife's cooking."

Through tears Rebecca nodded and smiled, drawing comfort from Jacques's determination to return safely. As she watched Jacques walk toward the stables, several of Akev's well-fed and joyful children ran by. They were a new generation of children. Sprouted from the succession of toddlers she'd watched reach adulthood. Each group becoming more confident. She knew that Jacques trip to Amsterdam would seal the bond within the Sephardic merchants and provide a future for the children. She remembered how proud she'd been when Jacques was a boy and stood on a crate to see the elders speak in the big barn. He'd drawn attention to himself with his brilliant ideas. He'd been an excellent Chronicler, as had his fathers before him. Daniel had not done so well. It would be Rebecca's job to speak to Daniel and tell him of his father's trip to network with the merchants. She knew Jacques would be embarrassing Daniel to some extent, but it needed to be done. Long ago, in Amsterdam's secret Jewish quarter, the Chronicler's words inspired the community. It was important that the Chronicler kept that bond alive. Through several wars and small skirmishes, through persecution and insecurity, through feast and through famine, the Chronicler had manipulated and cajoled Imperialists. He had connived and sometimes lied to local magistrates. Now the community was losing members to the Calvinist Church and Jews were accepting Jesus as their Redeemer. If Jacques didn't do something to stop their curiosity, the community would be dissolved and her son Daniel would be partly to blame.

"We're on unfair ground with the Calvinists!" Miguel Dorta told Jacques, and the almost sixty other men who'd come to meet. Word spread quickly through Amsterdam's Jewish quarter that Jacques, the former Chronicler of Akev, had requested a large gathering of minds.

"Miguel, state the reasons you feel we are standing on unfair ground," Jacques encouraged him.

Miguel hadn't a problem catching the eye and ear of the room of about fifty Sephardim and seven Ashkenazi men who were the leaders of their community. He was an interesting man to watch. He had thick, wavy, greasy, jet-black hair and large, round, black eyes. His nose was quite large but handsome and when he glanced sideways his profile was impressive. Because of his popularity with the girls, he had a dubious reputation amongst the women of Amsterdam. He enjoyed courting not one, but many. He was strong in his beliefs about community. His ancestors had come from Catholic Spain and had been one of the lucky few who wisely sold their hacienda and fled to northern lands, *before* the Inquisition, leaving their fortunes intact. Further wise choices the family patriarch made, led to their prosperity in Holland.

Miguel looked at the men earnestly. "The Calvinists speak from the pulpit, every Sunday. They're free to tell their congregation that when the Jews are converted, Christ will return, bringing a thousand years of peace to Jerusalem. For this prophesy to come about, the Jews must first accept Christ as their Savior."

The men shuffled their feet, stroked their beards, scratched their heads and bit the sides of their mouths, nodding and agreeing with Miguel, but none spoke.

"I can see by your mannerisms that you're uncomfortable with this situation, yet I hear no one offer a solution."

Jacques defended the men. "It's easy to talk boldly in the midst of our brothers, but there's not a man amongst us who does not know that if we dispute the Christians, we would draw attention to ourselves as Judaizers."

"And for that we'd be arrested!" a man shouted.

"Not in Leiden," another boasted. "They grow more lenient every day."

"We are not in Leiden," Miguel reminded him.

Jacques took to the center again and spoke practically. "The majority of us believe it's not wise to reveal our origins. What can we do to prevent the changes that will surely come? Have you noticed that the Calvinists have converted hundreds of Jews?"

A man off to the side laughed at the audacity of what he was hearing. "But we pose as Christians!" he said laughing again and shaking his head. Most did not laugh. They did not enjoy posing as Protestants. They were proud of their heritage. Jacques wondered if the direction of the mood was headed the wrong way and cleverly used an old trick. He changed the subject.

"Any new stories for my son Daniel? Have any of you been to Daamstraat and spoken with the women?" Jacques teased and the men laughed much more comfortably now, one even brave enough to speak back.

"We wouldn't tell you Jacques. You would tell your wife and she would tell ours," the man said, bringing soft laughter into the terse situation.

"Has anyone been to the docks this week? The weather's bad but has it prevented ships from sailing?" Jacques questioned.

A young man answered. "The seas are rough but the sailors are tough. The merchants have pooled their money and bought their own ships. They trade in precious gems, wood, spices and textiles. They grow rich while we sit contemplating our fate."

"Yes, the merchants do well pretending to be Christians," a fellow jabbed. Several men chuckled.

Jacques kept control of the situation. "Like our ancestors before us, we must stay together. Strengthen your business ties with your fellow Sephardim and the growing Ashkenazi community here in Amsterdam," he told them. "If we work within our own brotherhood we can work freely and we'll be strong. When we sit down with our families this Shabbat, speak to them of the importance of solidarity. We lost hundreds of thousands to the Inquisition. Encourage the young to have large families. Celebrate when our sons and daughters wed and rejoice in their having new children to fill the void we leave behind." Jacques lectured eloquently before tiring and nodding farewell and heading home. Where years ago, his great-grandmother found land and his great-grandfather did favors for wealthy Christian aristocrats to further his family's wealth and build the sanctuary, the community of Akev. It was time for Jacques to return to the security and warmth of his wife. It was time to help Daniel strengthen his family.

Jacques looked at the beauty of Amsterdam's elaborate architecture. He could smell the sea and felt it beckon. He headed to the docks where the first Chronicler, Jacob, used to pry the skippers for news. It was time Jacques instructed his son Daniel to follow in Jacob's footsteps. Though Daniel insisted on spending his days where the reeds grew by the water's edge, and the winds made percussive sounds on the leathery leaves of the riparian trees, that shaded the shanty he called home, he must learn the ways of a great Chronicler so that he may some day pass it on to his son. These thoughts reminded Jacques of Ruth, and how they had seen her leaving Sunday morning for what they feared was a church service in Amsterdam. He would speak to her and try to be more of a father to her and impress upon her the importance of learning the ways of the Chronicler so that she too may educate a son to pick up and take off where Daniel left off.

Jacques would no longer be *Brenger* of favors to the Nobles. He would find someone else to fill that position. There could be only one Chronicler, but Jacques believed he needed to school someone as *Brenger* for the Royals and their administrators.

As promised Jacques arrived on the Shabbat. It was chilly and the skies were darkening. As he walked down the lane towards his home, not many were about, and those that were either ran quickly to escape the cold breeze or were warmly bundled while they finished their industrial and agricultural work. Most of the animals had been tucked in for the evening and Jacques could hear the familiar contented noises they made. He was satisfied with the mission he'd accomplished and felt a sense of relief that he'd decided to stay close to home and make what remaining years he had left, go by very slowly. With his knowledge he could offer advice to young aspiring merchants. He could teach manners to the young men and school them on the ways of the European aristocrats, so that future generations of Akevians would continue doing business in the ways of Jacques's.

They're a mixed bunch, these Akevians, Jacques thought to himself, as he grew closer to his own bungalow and passed by those of his neighbors. There were residents who had Latin names and a distinct pride in their heritage. Their ancestors had fled Catholic Spain and Portugal. There were residents who had come from the Holy Land and settled in Spain only for a short while, before the Inquisition drove them away. He passed homes of neighbors who had tried to live in England but the experience had not been pleasant.

He passed two homes, very close together, that belonged to two Ashkenazi families that had come from the damp forests of Belarus. It had been a difficult transition for the Ashkenazi families, accustomed to forested land covered with lakes and rivers, always remarking how they missed the trees. Their harrowing stories through the swamps and traveling across northern Europe to arrive in Holland made the hairs rise on the back of Jacques neck just thinking of it. It hadn't been easy for them to join this community of Sephardim and having the two Ashkenazi families side by side had worked out well. Their children had adapted and had taught others their Ashkenazi songs and games. It was soon to be Chanukah and that would offer another unique opportunity for the Ashkenazi to share their cultural celebrating with other Akevians. Chanukah was dear to all the Jews and watching and listening to the sweet voices of children singing new songs would warm hearts and bring smiles.

Jacques finally reached the front of his cottage. It was dark and he could see Rebecca had lit the candles. He bowed his head in prayer to give thanks to that same power that delivered Moses from Egypt. Jacques put his hand on the cold latch and opened the door. The warm air blew in his face and carried the scent of lamb and root vegetables. He could hear the fire pop as it caught small pieces of damp moss and he heard Rebecca's hearty laughter. His had been a good life, despite all the horrific stories each generation of Chroniclers told. If he could spread his good fortune for another ten years, perhaps he would see a new generation grow strong in the faith of their ancestors and hold their heads proudly, as they worshipped. It would not be easy nor without suffering and loss. It would not be without a strong dose of patience and humility. It had never been easy for either the men or women to deny their heritage and pose as Protestants, but he knew that someday, not all but many of these toddlers would rise to prominence. Their names would be well-known throughout Europe. They would be known proudly as Jews who had led exemplary lives.

After Jacques knocked the mud from his boots and he and Rebecca exchanged affections they sat down to the meal she had prepared. His first business was to inquire about the family.

"How are Daniel and Ruth?"

Rebecca smiled and put her hand upon his that rested on the knife with which he cut his meat. "I was mistaken."

"Mistaken?"

"Yes. Ruth did go to Amsterdam with her sisters but it was not to attend the church services. She saw an opportunity for an outing and she took it," she told him as she ladled sauce over his lamb. "She has some interesting stories to tell. In Amsterdam she and her sisters met with other women." Rebecca shook her head as if she could not believe what Ruth had relayed to her.

"I was planning on a long visit with Daniel after the Shabbat. I will speak with them both. How is she feeling?"

"She feels well but she still carries that shadow. She and her family must have endured cold dark winters and sinister situations. I'm afraid to ask."

"It's not your place to ask. If she were to volunteer we would listen sympathetically, otherwise..." Jacques almost scolded her.

"I know I shouldn't pry but sometimes I feel she needs to talk about it. Perhaps if she did she would heal," Rebecca said in a tone that made him uncomfortable.

"As I said, it is not our place."

"I probably don't need to know, it would only bring sorrow."

"Indeed, which is why Ruth has kept it to herself," Jacques said, hoping the subject was over.

"So what news do we hear from Amsterdam?" she asked.

Jacques smiled. "Miguel Dorta has half the women in Amsterdam angry with him. If I heard about this once I heard it twenty times."

"Heard about what? And who is Miguel Dorta?"

"He's an extremely handsome man who takes advantage of his way with women. He not only has the women angry but their mothers, aunts and sisters. Rebecca, I've never heard a name bandied about as I have Miguel Dorta's."

"What does this Miguel do?"

"His family has resources and access to resources, they're prominent merchants. Miguel Dorta comes from a very large, well-to-do family. They've made a fortune with their shipping connections. At least that is what I have been told."

"How did you come to know him?" she asked.

"He was chosen to help me organize the meeting. He's well connected and highly concerned about losing brothers and sisters to the Calvinists."

"What will he do about it?"

"What will any of us do about it?" Jacques said angrily.

"We must make our Shabbat services more desirable and help them see the Calvinists as less so," Rebecca told him.

Jacques wished the conversation to lighten so he returned to making fun at the expense of Miguel Dorta. "Perhaps Miguel will bed all these beautiful young ladies and in this way he can expand the Sephardic community."

"Jacques! Your language is vulgar," she rebutted him but smiled at his humor.

"Perhaps I shall bed you and your joy will spread throughout Akev and all will be well," he said staring at her waiting for a response. Rebecca looked down. He could see her long eyelashes and the way they turned up just as her nose turned up, just a little. He could see he had embarrassed her and though she was looking down he could see she was smiling. The fire continued to glow. It brought much warmth and comfort into the small home. Jacques still had the desires of a young man and he looked across the table at the beauty of a woman who through the years continued to please him. This Shabbat would be no different than many of the others they had enjoyed together since the boys had grown and moved on. And on this cold winter's night, Jacques and Rebecca would find comfort and reunification through touch and relaxing into one another in the ancient act of coitus.

Jacques enjoyed the long tranquil walk down to the water's edge to visit Daniel and Ruth. As he neared the water, reeds sprang up forcefully. He understood how difficult it must be for his sensitive son to leave the little nest he'd created. A lump caught in Jacques throat with the knowing that he was coming to speak strongly to his son and interrogate Ruth about what she had found out in Amsterdam. This was an important day and with the wet and foggy weather, Jacques knew Daniel and Ruth would probably be indoors. It would be a good day to talk.

As he neared the rustic shack, Jacques was careful to watch where he stepped. The soil was muddy and slick and his son had not taken time to secure the trail for decent footing. *It is good that they are young,* he thought to himself, *they can walk through anything. They have good balance.* By the time Jacques reached the door, he clung tightly to the handle for fear he would lose his balance and slip. Irritated by the slipperiness of the path, Jacques grabbed the door handle to balance himself. When Daniel and Ruth saw him at the door with an angry look on his face, they were surprised. But Jacques turned it to humor. "Good morning!" he shouted.

The two returned the smile and welcomed him in. It was a very tiny living quarter and quite dusty inside. Daniel and Ruth frequently found themselves in a state of melancholy but Jacques could feel that the mood today was cheerful and that they truly were delighted to have his company.

"Father please come in," Daniel held the door open.

Ruth smiled and ran and puffed up a pillow on the one and only large comfortable chair in the room and welcomed him to sit.

"Would you like a hot cup of milk?" she asked.

Jacques smiled at her hospitality and graciously accepted her offer.

"What brings my dear father out alone on this dreary day?" Daniel asked, knowing it was probably for a lecture about his incompetence as Chronicler.

"How are you feeling Ruth?" Jacques asked, ignoring Daniel's question.

She smiled and rubbed her abdomen. "I feel happy as I anxiously await our son or daughter."

"I would be very pleased if it were a son Ruth. You know we are the line of Chroniclers and Daniel will need to be relieved of his duties one day."

Daniel sighed but knew it was coming. Ruth smiled and rubbed her abdomen again as Jacques continued. "Ruth, how do you feel about your son becoming Akev's Chronicler?"

"I would be proud to have my son as Akev's Chronicler. I would help him in every way I could."

Jacques raised his eyebrows. If Ruth would eagerly help her son be an efficient Chronicler, why had she not helped Daniel? Jacques wasted no time bending the situation to his advantage. "Do you advise Daniel with his reports?" he asked.

"Occasionally. I've not had much to offer, but we've been speaking about the discussions I overheard during my visit to Amsterdam," she said awkwardly.

Jacques turned eloquently toward her using all his charm. "Ruth we would be pleased with any assistance you give Daniel. Women have their stories too."

"Yes they do," she said and pulled up a chair right next to his and drew her face very near his. "I had all of Amsterdam's stories thrown at me in one afternoon at a friend of a friend of my sister's. Amsterdam is much different than Akev. It's a bustling city. There is so much activity, one could keep busy and not sleep, why..." Ruth carried on and then stopped to catch her breath and her thoughts.

"What did you find was the most interesting aspect of life in Amsterdam?" Jacques asked.

"The women enjoy clothing and they enjoy the influx of visitors that arrive daily. Their social lives revolve around the homes that hold Synagogue."

"What about the churches? Are Jews attending church?" he quizzed.

She put her head down but raised it again in confidence. "Yes, but neither I nor my sister have attended. She tells me she hasn't and I believe her but I also believe she's interested."

"Interested?"

"Well..." she said, thoughtfully biting her lower lip, "curious," she said confidently. "My sister is so curious about what goes on in the Calvinist churches."

"I see," Jacques said but before he could continue Ruth began again.

"But not near as curious as they are of us!" she told Jacques and Daniel who was glad to be part of the discussion.

"The Christian men are very curious about the Jews," Daniel joined in.

But Ruth was excited and continued blurting out what she'd discovered. "The Protestant women of Amsterdam want to know everything about the Jews."

"And why do you suppose that is?" Jacques asked.

She just shook her head but Daniel had an answer. "Perhaps their grandparents were among the Sephardim one hundred years ago and forced to convert. They heard little bits here and there over the years and want to know about the Jews."

Ruth shook her head as if she truly had no answer but Jacques questioned further.

"They must believe that there are a great many Jews in Amsterdam. And they must know of a home that holds Synagogue," Jacques said.

Daniel spoke up. "The Protestants are firm in their belief that the New Testament should be available to the Jews. They feel that if we were to read the New Testament in Hebrew we would embrace Christianity."

"I see," Jacques said, feigning ignorance.

Daniel spoke confidently, "It will be a good many years before the Protestants succeed in translating the New Testament into Hebrew, believe me Father."

"Yes, I'm sure you're right, besides, what Jew would wish to take on an endeavor such as that?" Jacques said with a short laugh.

"A Converso of course," Ruth said, surprised that Jacques would forget the thousands of Jews who'd accepted Christianity. "There are Conversos who truly believe that Jesus is the Messiah."

"Yes," Jacques said dryly as he took a sip of hot milk. "There are Conversos and then there are Conversos."

"There are indeed," Daniel said and walked to Ruth's side and delicately put his hand upon her shoulder.

It was with great sadness when a wagon carrying Rebecca's black-draped coffin lumbered down the path toward the cemetery. As much as possible, Jewish customs were observed but when Christian traditions worked their way into the burial, it was a painful reminder that the members of Akev were crypto-Jews. Jacques walked home slowly, his hat in his hand, letting the warm sun beat on the top of his head. His family tried to comfort him but he chose to walk alone. He still felt Rebecca's presence and wanted to speak silently with her as his feet put one in front of the other and meandered their way home.

Jacques could not eat nor drink much after the passing of his beloved wife. He laid in bed with his hand on the spot where Rebecca used to sleep. His family was deeply saddened to see his grief as they too grieved. They took turns staying with him but knew his days were few. One morning, after taking her turn watching him through the night, Ruth woke to find he had passed on in his sleep. Chills covered her arms and legs as she saw the smile upon his face and his hand still resting on the spot where Rebecca had lain.

TWELVE

1613 Amsterdam, twenty-two years have passed. Daniel and Ruth's son is twenty-one. His name is Seba

Seba shook his head quickly several times to set the thick unruly curls of sandy blonde hair he inherited from his mother's side of the family along with his average height. He was blessed with the perfectly straight teeth of his father Daniel, and had his father's dusky skin. But there was no mistaking he'd inherited his Grandmother Rebecca's transparent green eyes.

Seba's step was vigorous and confident. Earlier that morning, he'd made several profitable deals with diamond-traders who were financing a new shipping company. Holland's diamond merchants knew the British were on their heels, so in order to maintain a stronghold within the industry, deals like today would need to be made on an almost daily basis.

"I'm not sure I can keep up with this," Seba told his father Daniel several nights before, while in Akev visiting his family. Daniel's mother, Ruth had reminded him that his main commitment was as Akev's Chronicler.

"Your grandfather Jacques, rest his soul," Ruth lectured on the muggy, warm summer evening, "did not intend for you to be both a Brenger and a Chronicler."

Seba's father Daniel answered wryly, "He was an ambitious man. He torments me from the grave."

Seba enjoyed back room deals, the excitement of the *Exchange,* where money was investments in diamonds, precious stones, wood and textiles. And from the New World; tobacco and furs. There were also trading deals to be made with salt, sugar or Polish wheat. Profits brought quickly rising fortunes for the Sephardim and Ashkenazi merchants whose Dutch populations had increased significantly.

Seba tried to fulfill his roles as Chronicler, Brenger and Merchant, but it left him little time for much else. Amsterdam and the European world beckoned. Today, well dressed in a new coat and hat, he walked proudly down the same streets his ancestors had. He knew exactly where his ancestor Jacob, the first Chronicler, had met Marie Belle back in 1450, her dark eyes and bright wavy hair catching the eye of the optimistic free-spirit son of a cabinet maker. He frequently passed the home of Peter Le Sueur, the older more conservative man in Amsterdam who many years ago held nightly meetings in his home for Amsterdam's early Sephardic community. And when Seba went down to the dock, he thought of the stories he'd heard about Nicolaes, the rare gentle but stubborn sea captain who hated his time away from his family. The man who drew beautiful maps and knew how to follow the stars. And all the Chroniclers. Seba could recite and knew their history and style. Jacob, David, Akev, Solomon, Jacques, Daniel and now himself... Seba Soeira. He remembered what his great-great-grandfather had told his grandfather. "We want our children's children's children to know these stories and we can't always write them down. It's through the spoken word that the family history is kept alive. It's a flame we keep from going out."

Seba's remembering his grandfather's words brought him back to his old familiar self, the self that knew in his heart that above all else was his commitment to his people to keep that fire forever burning. All of Akev believed they were the children of the Lion, the tribe who had come from the Holy Land. Seba told himself that when he married and had a son he would name him Leeuw, the Lion. The name was Dutch enough to stave off persecution yet the child would be forever recognized as one from Judah. Who among the ancient tribe would not recognize Lion? Had not many signed documents with Lion after their name or as their name? Did these people not wish to be remembered as coming from the tribe that came from the desert so long ago?

Seba sighed at the thought that Akev depended on him to bring all the latest in conversation, politics, religious views and agriculture. And what were all the comings and goings from the Port of Amsterdam? What food crops were selling best? Should they plant them again next year? Who were the kosher food dealers? Were there rumors of war? Could they speak openly of their religion?

Each week questions needed answers but no one else in Akev had desired to accept the ceremonial task of Brenger, so he filled that role as well. Seba could not think of any other Akevian men, who had the wherewithal to act as a liaison between the authorities and his Sephardic community. But that was the important role of a

Brenger. And Seba believed he had enough respect, knowledge and education to hold a political office, even if it were in one of the smaller counties of Holland. Although Calvinists were considered the only legitimates who could hold a prominent place in politics, in some instances Jews were accepted to those positions and Seba felt he could be too, if he was openly a Jew. He knew all the important figures in Amsterdam, or at least knew of them. And he knew that when he walked down the street, they knew who he was, and it was with that pride that Seba stood tall. He was a Soeira. Two years before, civil war erupted between liberal and conservative Calvinists. The conservatives gained control of Holland. Seba felt his stories and a few private conversations with conservative Calvinist merchants, helped to bring Judaism into the light. Just as his grandfather, Jacques Soeira had said that one day it would. If only Grandfather Jacques had lived to see the day that Holland allowed Judaism in public. But Seba knew what his grandfather would say. "Not yet my boy, not yet. Make them believe you are a Calvinist."

Seba was proud of his religion and he would continue the strong line of Soeira men. He would be one of the best Chroniclers. He would continue to be a Brenger but he would also be a merchant trader at Amsterdam's Exchange. And as all the other Chroniclers before him, he would provide for Akev so it could continue as a sanctuary where Jewish families could relax and practice their beliefs.

Seba headed toward the administrative office of the United East India Company, *Verenigde Oost-Indische Compagnie*, the VOC. He wanted to find out the outcome, of a fleet liquidation he'd invested in. The venture was a high risk. The ship was to be liquidated upon return. A deep thinker, he had a habit of looking down at the street when he walked. It was not unusual for him to bump into things and today was no different when he rounded the corner and bumped right into a young woman. Shocked, embarrassed, flustered, and not knowing what to do, he politely touched the arm of the young lady who shyly would not look into his eyes.

"Dear lady, please accept my humble forgiveness. I was not looking where I was going."

When she finally looked into his eyes, he'd never before seen such beauty. He was frozen with an emotion that came from deep inside. No emotion so strong had ever revealed itself to him. In silence he stood and stared, frightened with the way he felt about this frail angelic creature. She was very tall and very thin. When Seba regained his thoughts he wondered how the winds did not blow the poor girl away. Her hair and skin were pure white, her eyes bright blue. Her cheeks were pink and she looked robust as if from a family with means.

"Pardon me..." Seba said, giving the girl the chance to state her name.

"Anabela," she said, her flashing eyes fixed upon his.

"Ah, Portuguese," he said.

"Yes, I'm named after my great-grandmother who came from Portugal."

"I would have mistaken you for a true Northerner," he smiled. Feeling more at ease, his personality came through.

"Yes, it is only my name that bears resemblance to our Latin roots. My family is all very..." she struggled for the words.

Seba helped her. "Dutch?" he laughed.

"Yes but what is Dutch?" she waved her arms about excitedly.

Seba could see she had a mind of her own and he let her continue.

"Holland is like a big pot," she said with a thick of accent.

He liked it. He liked her. He wished he could pick her up and whisk her away, all for himself. But time was not on his side. He needed to be at the administrative offices of the Verenigde Oost-Indische Compagnie and find out what had been the outcome of his investments.

Anabela noticed his distraction. She looked down and he was not quite sure whether she was being polite or irritated. An important point to differentiate. He was not one to become involved with another angry, young woman. There were plenty about Amsterdam and Akev was not without them either. Something about Seba's nature brought out confrontation in the girls he pursued; perhaps it was his unbreakable self-confidence. He stared at the top of her head, waiting to see her expression when she looked up.

She looked up and her blue eyes struck him in a place so deeply it hurt. Badly. Nothing that anyone had ever said or done to him had ever reached inside so painfully, to a spot he knew not existed. Again, twice within a few minutes, this young woman had reached dangerously inside of him. It made him consider theories he'd heard, about two souls who were meant to be together or who had been together in lives past. Two souls that had suffered a painful history, in another lifetime, finding one another... again.

"Seba?" She put her hand on his forearm. "Are you alright?"

He shook his head, realizing he had been lost in deep thought. He smiled softly and reassured her that yes, he was alright. "I feel as though I have met you before," he told her.

She was amused and smiled, looking down again shyly.

"I am sincere. But I do apologize for becoming personal with a young lady I've chanced to meet on the street. I hope our paths will cross again," he told her in his most respectable voice. "Soon."

She smiled cautiously, nodded and celestially walked away while he stood fixed upon the sidewalk staring at the back of the tall, wispy girl. Shaking his head again, to bring it from the clouds, he looked at his surroundings. He looked at the printing on the side of the building designating the street. He looked aghast at the familiar landmarks across the street. He had walked into his favorite neighborhood. This was the exact spot where his ancestor, Jacob, had first seen Marie Belle. Seba was not sure what to do with these emotions but knew he had two choices, faith or fear. As he began walking toward the business district of the Verenigde Oost-Indische Compagnie he was not sure which to choose.

Stimulated from the long day, infatuated over his encounter with Anabela, and excited about his financial successes at the Exchange, Seba was late to an evening meeting with Rabbi Jeremiah at the home of the young Portuguese Jewish merchant, Esteves Osorio. When he walked into the home, he was shocked at the opulence. Beautiful paintings adorned the walls. Greek statues made it hard to walk, and if common utensils or hardware could be gilded they were. Seba found the decor tasteless but he was not there for aesthetics and quickly found a wall to lean against in the filled room.

Rabbi Jeremiah spoke angrily to the men already seated. "The Christian leaders of Holland and Europe criticize the Talmud. Though some of the Talmud is compatible with the Bible, they do not consider it to be the true word of God."

Seba let out a deep sigh that didn't go unnoticed. And to the consternation of some of the attendees, he rolled his eyes. He recognized half of the men; a pious Sephardic crowd. The other half he recognized as Ashkenazi merchants from the diamond district. He determined that the meeting was designed to recruit those seeking more freedom in Dutch politics.

Seba was tired and fought his desire to escape back into the streets of Amsterdam. He pictured himself with his feet up, in one of the more rowdy taverns just outside the business district, not far from the administrative offices of the VOC, where men would be discussing European politics and the ebb and flow of the Exchange.

It would also give him a chance to sort his feelings regarding the agreeable young woman, Anabela, he'd encountered on the street.

Rabbi Jeremiah called to him. "Seba… Seba?" he called again. "Seba!" the rabbi shouted, waking Seba from his day dream. He straightened his body and drew his mind back to the room full of Sephardic and Ashkenazic men of Amsterdam and nearby counties.

"I see your mind is far removed. We hope that thy thoughts are pure," the rabbi scolded Seba.

But Seba was not to be disrespected, even if he was known to disassociate from time to time. "Yes," he spoke with confidence and composure. "Much in this world takes its place in the rooms of my mind. Forgive me. I am here in body but late to arrive in spirit."

The crowd laughed but Rabbi Jeremiah was not amused. "Is there a more interesting topic that Akev's Chronicler wishes to discuss? Would you like to lead the discussion?" the rabbi warned.

"We should discuss the New World," Seba volunteered, to the nods of many. "We want to draw Jews to the Netherlands but across the Atlantic, riches and promises of wealth beckon our finest men."

All the heads in the room turned to listen to the young man speak, and in unison they turned to hear the rabbi's response.

"The loss of our brothers to the New World will wait until that becomes a problem. We are gathered here today because we're losing young Jews to Calvinism," the rabbi said, trying humbly to regain his audience's attention.

Seba decided to back down and return to his daydream of the four-hundred-percent profit he hoped to reap when the ship he'd invested in, returned to Amsterdam's crowded harbor. In his imagination, he could smell Indonesian nutmegs and cloves from where he stood in that gaudy little room in Esteves Osorio's home. Now that Seba had drawn attention to himself he had no other choice but to stay. When an elderly gentleman rose and left his seat, Seba was relieved to rest in the chair and melt into the crowd.

Within Amsterdam society, Seba didn't discuss his Judaism, nor did he deny it. In the circles in which he mixed, most of his fellow businessmen were Jews, who did not flaunt it for fear of persecution. Holland had grown more liberal, but Seba kept his grandfather's warnings close to his heart. It was Sunday and the beginning of the week. he had enjoyed spending the Sabbath in Akev with his mother and father and had been delighted to see his uncle, Francois, who'd become a rabbi, settling in Akev with his family, complete with grandchildren.

So it was on a warm summer's Sunday morning that Seba kicked around Amsterdam in his casual clothes, waiting and wishing for something exciting to occupy his day. He stayed away from the docks and the business quarter, especially the business quarter. One of the nice things about being a Jew posing as a Christian, was that with the Jews celebrating the Shabbat on Saturday, and refraining from work, sometimes he could justify relaxing on Sunday as well, for it would be improper for him to be seen working on the Sabbath. So today he set about as he usually did on a day when he enjoyed the best of both worlds. He twirled a stick between his fingers and nervously fidgeted with his shirt. He'd left it partially unbuttoned, revealing his healthy chest and relaxed mood. The churches were soon to end their services and on Sunday mornings, he found it interesting to glimpse the lives of Christians. The churches were different than the synagogue homes he'd grown up with, or any of the larger synagogues he'd the occasion to visit while away with his grandfather Jacques. But there was something uniquely familiar about all religions. His grandfather had always told him that it was because the Christian religion had its roots in Judaism. But Seba could never understand how the split had caused so many wars and the division of families.

Anyone observing Seba's actions would have recognized that he was looking for someone. He made the rounds to all the churches but he did not see Anabela. And why did he assume she was attending a church? Was it her stark white skin and almost albino hair? And then again, maybe she didn't live in Amsterdam. These thoughts ran through his sub-conscious. After a frustrating morning not running into her, he brought his thoughts to the present. An ambitious young man, Seba focused intensely on all his projects. Finding Anabela was his new mission.

Seba made himself available on the streets. Even though he sometimes found disrespectable places delightfully fun, he stayed away because Anabela did not look the sort to spend time in Amsterdam's lower realms. The more he thought about it, the more he realized. She had that look of church about her. She did not look like a Jewish girl. This would be a problem. But at the moment he did not care. He only cared about seeing her again.

Seba peered into carriages that carried Amsterdam's elite, but did not expect to see her there either. Nor did he suspect that she came from an impoverished family. The more he analyzed her the more her social profile emerged. Though skinny as a sapling in a forest with no sun, she was well fed and healthy, with rosy checks and strong teeth. She could be from Zeeland. Or was she from Friesland in the north? Had she come from Utrecht? He leaned against stone pillars supporting a stairway that led to one of Amsterdam's new buildings.

He heard a voice call his name. "Seba? Son of Daniel?"

He looked up to see one of his grandfather's acquaintances, Miguel Dorta.

Seba straightened and came down from his daydream. "Yes, it's me, Seba. Son of Daniel. I recognize you as a friend of Jacques, my grandfather."

Miguel smiled, pleased with the recognition. "Jacques and I had some disputes. He was much older and wiser. When I was younger I was very angry."

Seba sensed Miguel was still a man who held a grudge. "And now?" he asked.

Miguel shrugged. "My family fled Spain when we had cattle and vast orchards. The children of my aunts and uncles all roamed freely..." Miguel looked at Seba but did not finish.

Through the years, Miguel had learned that anger helped no one. His fellow Sephardim had grown weary of his argumentative nature. Miguel eventually learned that his Jewish friends would never forget the atrocities of the past, but chose to live in the present. But if Seba were to prompt Miguel, he would rage on about the Inquisition. Instead, Seba only stared.

Miguel still took a moment to taunt him. "Please don't tell me that you're waiting for Christ to return?"

"No, but there's a beautiful Christian girl I'm waiting for. If she would walk by right now..."

Miguel froze. That was the last thing he wanted to hear. "You're waiting for a Christian girl? There are no beautiful Jewish girls who've captured your eye?" Miguel was seething.

Seba grew nervous, not understanding his present state of mind. He'd grown bored with the familiar. His business success had gone to his head. He wanted something new and different. He loved the feeling that meeting Anabela had generated.

"She has Portuguese ancestry," Seba said with a shrug.

"That's not good enough," the aging Miguel Dorta lectured.

Seba thought it odd. For years, he'd heard about Miguel's indiscretions. He had every woman in Amsterdam after him. The talk was always what a hypocrite he was. He would head to the front of the room during the Sephardic meetings, especially on Shabbats, and speak angrily about the unfairness of the Calvinists. Appalled that they insisted that Jews accept Christ as their Savior. Then Miguel would be seen caressing a beautiful woman, who all knew was a Christian.

"Who did you marry?" Seba asked him.

Miguel stared at him with furrowed brow. "I did not marry," he answered.

"What do you do with yourself? Where is your woman to keep you warm?" Seba asked him sarcastically. To which Miguel did not answer but looked off into the distance.

"If I find this beautiful girl I will ask that she become a Jew," Seba told him

"You don't know women!" Miguel shouted. "Do you know how many times I tried to convert a Calvinist?"

"Ah," Seba taunted him. "So now we hear the truth. You enjoy women who are..."

Before he could finish Miguel interrupted angrily. "Evil? Yes. I have loved evil women. They are all evil. Why do you think I haven't married?" Miguel said angrily.

Seba was surprised. "Surely you don't believe that all women are evil?"

Miguel would not answer but he had shaken Seba's emotions. Not regarding the danger of courting Christian women, but the danger of a woman's lure and the tendency a woman might have toward promiscuity. It had obviously made Miguel very bitter.

"What would your father say if I told him you spend your time in Amsterdam eyeing the Christian girls? You should be spending your time studying the Torah or searching for news. Aren't you Akev's Chronicler?" Miguel asked.

Seba stiffened. If there was anything that could get under his skin, it was any insinuation that he was not doing his job as Chronicler. He did an excellent job. He kept the community well informed. It was a position of pride in the Soeira family and had been for many generations. His father had not been the best Chronicler and Seba had all but made up for it. To criticize him was unfair. "I'm not sure that the religion of a wife is so important," Seba told him with a softening of his voice.

"It is everything!" Miguel roared. "You are a Jew! Jews do not marry Christians!"

"Miguel, this is Amsterdam. Look around you. I see it all the time. For over a hundred-and -fifty-years, Amsterdam's Sephardim have posed as Christians. Many are beginning to think they are."

"I can see that," Miguel told him. "I'll speak with the rabbi and with your father. We shall see to these matters. I can assure you."

Seba grabbed his arm. "Please don't trouble my father with our discussion, nor the rabbi. In Amsterdam we are free to worship as we please."

"If you marry a Christian it will not be tolerated," Miguel told him.

"But if they believe me to be a Christian how are they to know?" Seba asked him.

"Seba... I will not let this rest. This is the most important issue we speak of when we gather. We're losing young men like yourself, to Christian girls. And many Sephardic girls have married Christian men."

Seba shrugged.

"We are a brotherhood. We draw strength through that ancient bond."

"I believe I can love a beautiful Christian girl. She can go to church and I'll go to synagogue."

"What about the children?" Miguel asked. "What about the next generation and the next? All of Catholic Spain would love to absorb the Jews." Miguel shook his head in disbelief. "And you," he said, wanting Seba to feel guilty, "of all the Sephardim... you. Why you too?"

"I think it's in my blood."

"In your blood!" Miguel raged. "No, I cannot believe you tell me this," he shook his head disgusted.

Seba tried to explain. "You must remember that I come from the banker, Monsieur Soeira. Have you heard of him?"

Miguel rolled his eyes.

Seba continued bragging about the prosperity of his family, not unlike Miguel's wealthy family. "Monsieur Soeira was a Jew. He was one of the earliest to do business with non-Jews. He traveled throughout Europe; he acquired wealth and power. He enjoyed the company of Christian women and I desire to be like him," Seba said proudly. "If I did not know better, Miguel," Seba said, trying to look him straight in the eye, "I would say you are jealous."

Miguel was stunned and did not know how to respond. He retreated deep into his thoughts then turned and walked away.

Seba was shaking. He believed himself a thoughtful man, loyal to his family roots. But he felt disgust taking one side over the other, when sometimes he wasn't sure if there was a God. What could it matter if two people, a Christian and a Jew, loved as others do? Could they not make adjustments? Besides, Anabela had a Portuguese name. That was enough for him. He would build on that, if he could only find her.

Seba felt unnerved by the conversation with Miguel and guilty the more he thought about it. He'd not been to synagogue for quite some time, which had gone unnoticed because he lived in Amsterdam. Those in Amsterdam probably assumed he attended synagogue in Akev and the Akevians must have assumed he attended in Amsterdam. It was a clever arrangement but one which made Seba feel remorseful now that he had spoken too freely. In Amsterdam he'd even arranged to live on the edge of the Jewish Quarter right next to a Christian neighborhood. Was he ashamed of his community? No. He was proud to be a Jew. Was it wanting something that a man can't have? No, he did not think so. Seba believed that it was his youth and spontaneous way of understanding life. And now, a new understanding of his attraction to Anabela. Love felt no boundaries. Love was fluid and woven. Love was flexible and took form as needed, he was sure of that.

Seba walked into an unfamiliar tavern and looked around at the men. He studied their faces. As the alcohol relaxed him, he tried to discern for certain who the Christians were and who were the Jews. And though they would not volunteer that information, surely there must be a few Catholics in the mix. He wondered if some of the darker-skinned men had ancestry from Arabia or Africa and whether they might be Muslim. He speculated what their wives looked like. Were Muslim men married to only Muslim women? He knew that was not the case. If all men married within their ancient tribes, there would be no cities as welcoming and diverse as Amsterdam, Paris or London. It brought relief to think it through. He felt enlightened. He loved Anabela's look and the way he felt thinking of her. He would pursue her and sort out the formalities later.

"What! You want to return to Amsterdam to look for a boy?" Anabela's father shouted.

She nodded timidly. She was afraid of her father. Silvanus Camaroon was a demanding man. His family had come from the eastern forests and it had been a hard life. He claimed he had no knowledge of Jewish ancestry nor any interest in knowing.

Anabela's grandmother, on her mother's side, had been Jewish, but converted after marrying a Catholic. But religion was not for Silvanus, he abandoned the faith so he could "live in peace." An only child, Anabela had grown up with friends nearby who were Protestants and she'd attended services with them in Haarlem. Her mother and father had no problem with Anabela attending church. Her father was not interested in any church services and though her mother, Margarita would have enjoyed it, she had not the mind to argue with her husband and stayed home with him on Sundays.

Anabela had given her mother a Bible that she cherished and kept on her nightstand, often reading well into the night. As a miller, Silvanus kept busy supplying ground wheat and rye to the community as the demand was high for the ground grains and nearby ports brought constant shipments of the whole grains. Silvanus still had quite a bit of his stark white, wild hair for a middle-aged man, and a large bushy white beard and mustache that covered his face. He was kind but was one to reckon with when he wanted things to go his way, which is where Anabela got her strong personality. She'd also developed it by watching her mother's subservient nature. Margarita had come from a family that believed what the man of the family said was the final word and a woman was not to question him, even though time and time again Anabela begged her mother to stand up to him.

"You are like your father," her mother would say, and Anabela would just stare, unable to believe how timid her mother was.

"Yes Father, I met a handsome man on the streets of Amsterdam. He's the most beautiful man I've ever seen. I want to see him again," Anabela told her father. He scowled at her but she knew she could win him over. She usually did. He loved his daughter but he was a stern man and when it came to the boys he was overly protective. But now his daughter had become a woman of eighteen and Silvanus knew she would leave sooner or later. His only wish was to have some sort of control over it.

"We will see," he said trying to stall her.

"No, I must return to Amsterdam... soon. He may forget about me," she whined.

Her father glared at her and shook his head. He knew his daughter well enough to know that was not true. The boys never forgot about her, she usually forgot about them.

"Well?" she pushed.

"Well?" Silvanus pushed back while her mother in the background smiled at the whole scene. Margarita wanted her daughter to have any happiness she could and they had discussed the handsome young man who Anabela had met on the street.

"Silvanus, please," Margarita asked him gently. "Let her go with you when you go to the Exchange in Amsterdam. You'll be there for hours. It will be a nice journey for the two of you. Anabela will have time to look and see if fate will shine her way."

"Mother, I know it will," Anabela said sounding like a silly little girl. "It was as if a lightning bolt struck the two of us. We will meet again I'm sure of it. And taking me to the business quarter will be fine. He's a businessman of means. I'll find him there."

Silvanus knew he'd lost the battle and did not want to let his little girl down. He nodded his approval and waved them both off. Mother and daughter retreated to their clean, freshly-tiled kitchen to prepare an especially nice dinner for the man of the house.

Seba returned to the spot where he first met Anabela, the same spot where his ancestor Jacob laid eyes on Marie Belle, many years ago. It was still a residential neighborhood but many of the homes had been converted to storefronts, creating a lively business atmosphere. All the homes were several stories high making it a nice arrangement to have the family business on the ground floor leaving two or more floors for living quarters. There was the house on the corner owned by the Ashkenazi family that worked as diamond brokers. And from where Seba stood, he could see someone entering there today to talk the trade. Next to the diamond brokers was the headquarters of a small shipping enterprise and through the window Jacob could see several men inside. One of them was very demonstratively waving his arms about. It was a funny sight, one that Jacob had grown used to amidst the infernos of the city's active business climate. In the house next to that, a butcher had set up shop. He was one of a brave few who did not hide that he was a Jew, quite

238

the contrary, and to his benefit and the benefit of the whole of Amsterdam's Jews, he offered fine quality, fresh kosher meats. Customers from every persuasion did business with him. To Seba's knowledge, the butcher had no problems other than the usual bickering over prices, and squabbling over choice cuts of meat for the city's wealthier clients and their lavish dinner parties.

And then there was the home where Marie Belle had stood on the porch, brushing her bright long brown hair the first time Jacob laid eyes on her. The home had been sold many years hence, but Seba never failed to pay attention to it whenever he walked by, feeling that the home was sort of a good luck charm. Ever since he was a little boy, he would make a wish when he walked by. He'd heard wonderful stories about the tall, stately home where Monsieur Soeira lived with his beautiful daughter, Marie Belle and her son David. From Monsieur Soeira had come great wealth, prestige, manners, and charm. And above all… respect. Seba always knew that if he mentioned that he was the great-great-great-great-great-grandson of Monsieur Soeira, it opened doors and brought respect. And Seba found that occasionally, it worked outside the Sephardic community, especially when performing his role as liaison to European governments. On manners of great importance, he delivered papers to and from, usually not privy to what the contents held. He was paid handsomely for it and his expenses were paid when he traveled. He'd watched the development of *cash letters* and on occasion was able to predict small wars because he knew he'd delivered a large sum of money to a high-ranking public officer. The money had come from a wealthy source, a banker known to finance European monarchs and their bloody skirmishes.

When performing his duties as liaison, Seba kept his thoughts to himself. His grandfather Jacques had impressed it upon him that it was with only dignity that he was to perform his duties as a Brenger. He was not to discuss any manner of the transaction, nor that the transaction had occurred. It was all quite secretive and exciting, which Seba found helped to stimulate his days.

Recently, the old Monsieur Soeira home had been sold again. Conforming to the neighborhood the new owners had used the upstairs stories as living quarters and downstairs a baker set up shop. Seba had not yet tasted the baker and his wife's breads and pastries but had heard they were delicious. Feeling like a child again, he stood across the street from the home and closed his eyes, making his wish. Before he could open his eyes he felt a bump against his arm. Opening his eyes he saw a beautiful, jet-black haired woman, who he gauged was several years older than he. He presumed that she was Sephardic. She apologized and frowned at her friend who had swung her market basket around pushing her into Seba.

Her beauty caught him off guard. Chiseled features on sun-browned skin and eyes as raven as her hair. Her eyes spoke of kindness with a hint of mischievousness. He could discern that she was intelligent and something about her spoke of prominence. He'd known enough women to recognize wealth and status when he saw it. She oozed it.

"I am so sorry," she said in a thick, eastern European accent.

Seba smiled, "It's my pleasure to have felt the soft touch of a beautiful woman."

Amused, she motioned for her friend to wait but her friend would hear nothing of it and continued down the street leaving the two strangers alone.

"Are you from the neighborhood?" he asked her.

"Sometimes," she responded coyly.

"I detect an accent, Poland?" he asked.

"Belarus. My family is from Retske near Kurenets in Belarus."

"Are you visiting?"

She shook her head no and looked worried that her shopping companion had abandoned her and left her with the stranger. "My mother's family is from Belarus and I have taken on the accent but I have never been there. I live here in Amsterdam now, with my uncle."

"I see," Seba said glancing across the street at the stately, old ancestral home then back at the beauty that stood before him, wondering what he could do to keep her with him for as long as possible.

"I must be going, my friend..." she said

"I'm Seba," he said, bowing his head and introducing himself in the manners of his grandfather. "I would delight in escorting you home, if you would allow me. I have the highest of intentions and my reputation is stellar."

She smiled and looked again at the empty street where her friend had vanished. She had no particular plans for the day so smiled and agreed to the request of the conceited young man in front of her.

"Your name?" he asked.

"Kuerze," she told him, while he politely asked for her arm so he could escort her across the street.

The wind blew too much for Anabela. She kept herself covered up in blankets while she rode next to her father in the open wagon. The wooden seats were rough and her father's lectures and then long silences made the trip unpleasant. But the thought of finding the handsome Seba of Amsterdam, kept her spirits afloat. She curled up in the blanket next to the security of her father and the rollicking motions of the horse.

It was dark when Anabela and Silvanus Camaroon arrived in Amsterdam. They wasted no time checking into the inn. Anabela went upstairs to sleep for the night while her father retreated to the tables downstairs where there was a small pub for the guests.

Seba was up early and excited about the day ahead. He headed once again to the administrative office of the United East India Company, *Verenigde Oost-Indische Compagnie*, the VOC. He made some hasty decisions, and then walked toward the Exchange to check on the value of his shares. After tying up loose ends, he would then perform his duty as Chronicler and meet with his usual contacts and gather new stories. Today he hoped and prayed that his sources had only factual information because he'd had no time to verify or inquire with other sources. He was in a hurry to meet Kuerze, the raven-haired Sephardic beauty he'd met the day before. They would meet in front of the bakery at ten o'clock and purchase pastries. Then the plan was to take a stroll along the canals and get to know one another better.

Anabela and her father rose early. After checking out of the inn, Silvanus Camaroon insisted Anabela wait for him in the cart while he checked with some customers and made some deliveries of the freshly ground flour with which he was well known. He assured her they would be done by noon and that she would have all of the afternoon to search for her prince as Silvanus had begun calling him.

Seba stood alone in front of the bakery just before ten o'clock. He could see Kuerze just rounding the corner. His mouthful of straight, pearly teeth smiled at her from the distance and she waved. As he stood there by himself, a wagon pulled to the front. Commanding the wagon was a big, bushy-haired man with a beautiful distracted daughter, Anabela, who had not yet seen Seba, who looked at her and to the smiling Kuerze just feet away. Quickly racing across the street was Miguel Dorta, smiling pleasantly.

"Hello Uncle," Kuerze said to him.

"Uncle?" Seba said through a cringing smile.

"Yes," Kuerze said in a whispered tone, "but I suspect he is really my father."

THIRTEEN

Seba turned from Kuerze and walked into the bakery as if he didn't know her. She looked at him through the window, cocking her head to the side, wondering why he had walked away. He waved through the glass.

Anabela turned from her distraction. When she saw Seba waving from the bakery, where her father was to unload bags of freshly milled wheat, she smiled excitedly and waited for him to finish his business in the bakery and come and greet her properly as any gentleman would do.

Seba waved at Kuerze through the window. Warily she waved back having not seen the beautiful blonde in the wagon also waving at him. Seba stood frozen inside the warm bakery. The baker's wife was the first to see the young man's dilemma and quickly motioned for him to follow her.

"Out the back," the baker's wife said. "Quickly."

"I, ah ... I ah ..." he stammered.

"Young man you have gotten yourself into a predicament, one I would not wish on anyone. Go out the back, quickly. I will think of something," she said.

Without looking out the window again, Seba walked slowly around massive wooden chopping blocks. Once out of sight he dashed out the back. There was a lovely garden in back that held a statue of Jesus with vines draping around it. He paused but had no words and ran out into the adjoining streets not stopping until he had reached his home.

Throwing himself upon his bed his head pounding, his heart racing he wondered what had the baker's wife told Kuerze and Anabela? Had she been able to salvage the situation? Seba doubted it. Now all he could do was lay upon his bed and wait for hours for the sun to go down so that he could lay in the darkness where no thoughts could enter his mind. But it was not the case.

Miguel Dorta? Kuerze's father? She looked beautiful, with her jet-black hair and piercing eyes. And she's Jewish! My family would love her.

But ah, Anabela, she looked so lovely upon the cart, like an angel of the Lord. But a Christian? My family would scorn me and who was that wild-haired man she was with? Could that be her father?

Will Kuerze forgive me for abandoning her after I promised her a stroll through the canals? She is so beautiful and could be the mother of my children and she's Jewish! But Miguel Dorta? Her father?

Will Anabela forgive me for running off and will I ever see her again? She is beautiful and we would make beautiful children together. But she's a Christian, but I love her. But I love Kuerze too ... no, no, I do not love them, I do not know them ... I suffer over women I do not know. My pain is unbearable. I must go see the Baker's wife.

It was dark when Seba found himself rapping lightly on the door of the bakery. Before too long the baker's wife came downstairs in her nightclothes and cap and opened up the door.

With fretful lines upon his brow, Seba asked her, "What was the outcome?"

"It was not easy," the baker's wife said. "Silvanus Camaroon is our most reliable and important vendor."

"Silvanus Camaroon? Who is Silvanus Camaroon?" Seba asked, thinking she did not remember him.

"He is the father of the beautiful girl upon the cart, the one with the bright hair and sea blue eyes of an angel," she told him, obviously smitten by her beauty as well.

"Yes, she is an angel. Her name is Anabela. She has my heart," Seba said wistfully.

"Nor was it easy with Miguel Dorta, why he is our best customer. He's the buyer for the almshouses, he buys more pastries and bread than anyone in Amsterdam," she said.

"Oh," Seba groaned, "Miguel Dorta."

"You look as if you're ill child."

Seba nodded. "Miguel Dorta," he repeated again then nodded again, "a bit ill."

"Miguel is ill? I did not know," the baker's wife said to which Seba said nothing.

"What about the other one?" Seba asked, hoping for a positive answer.

"The beautiful one with raven hair and eyes of loyalty?" she asked to his wide eyes and nodding. "She left. She waited, you did not return, she was soon gone. She did not even come in."

"She didn't?" Seba asked with raised eyebrows. "Perhaps there is a chance."

"Yes, perhaps," she agreed.

"And what of Anabela?" Seba was anxious to know.

"That poor girl. Her father told me they came all the way from Haarlem through the wind and cold yesterday so she could search for you. Silvanus called you her prince," she told him with sympathetic eyes.

"Did you speak with her?" he asked.

"No, she did not come in either," she told him, her eyes now just as wide.

"Did either of the young ladies know about..." Seba asked.

"The other?" the baker's wife finished his question.

Seba nodded and she shrugged.

"I don't know. I told Silvanus that you remembered you had to feed a cat."

"A cat! Feed a cat? You told him that?" Seba hollered at her.

"I had no time to think. You should thank me, what was I to say?" she leaned in looking at him, her face uncomfortably close to his, Seba could smell her yeasty breath. "I do not even know you. You have only begun coming in here. Perhaps these women could do better," she said to him waiting for an apology.

Seba put his hand on the woman's shoulder. She felt that perhaps she had failed, after promising him she would try to salvage the situation. "You did well. It was the best you could do. It was my foolish behavior. One day I was in love with Anabela the next day it was Kuerze."

"Are you Jewish?" she asked, which frightened him. The words of his grandfather rang in his ears. *Not yet Seba, not yet.* He looked at her and did not answer.

"I would not answer either," she said fearfully. "We are not Jewish either. We are followers of the Dutch Church," she told him. He nodded in agreement as she looked warily at him. "But if you will excuse me for noticing… these two, they are both very beautiful and very different."

"Different?"

"Different from one another."

"Anabela is a Christian and Kuerze is..." he started to say Jewish but froze. It was not his place to reveal her as a Jew. Like most of the Sephardim, she was probably living under the pretension that she lived by the ways of the Dutch Church. "Yes… they are both different," he told her.

"What are you going to do?" the baker's wife asked.

Seba looked around the bakery. Here he was, long after dark, in the establishment of a stranger. Talking to an old woman in her nightclothes, about his love interests and their religions. And she stood staring with wide eyes, dying to know how the story would end.

"I don't know, I truly do not know," Seba said sadly.

"I know the location of Silvanus Camaroon's mill in Haarlem. You will go there and tell the girl of your poor cat," she said.

"I don't have a cat!" Seba shouted at the woman who was beginning to feel like a mother to him.

"Well you had better get one," she said.

Seba ran feverishly through the back streets of Amsterdam, in the dark of night, looking for a cat. He usually saw them every day, especially at night. Now, when he needed one desperately, they were elusive. Who kept a cat anyway he wondered? *Only the very wealthy with their abundant bowls of milk.* All the cats he saw were skinny, bony and scrounging for garbage. Would they believe he had cared so much for a cat that he would run off like that? Of course they wouldn't. He would tell them that their beauty frightened him. He would confess he was afraid of commitment. He would tell them anything to regain their trust. But why should they trust him when it was all lies? He needed to decide which of the two beautiful women to pursue. He would put all efforts into one. Just one. He should ask God. Talk to the man who he's been ignoring lately. His father talked to God and so did and his father and the father before him. They all trusted in God. But Seba wondered. Had Monsieur Soeira? He must have. No one could be that successful in life and that blessed with a beautiful family had he not had faith in the God of Moses. But Monsieur Soeira had lost his wife at a very early age. Was it punishment for a lack of belief?

As Seba thought of the wrath of God, he wondered not only what God would do with him for his lack of faith but what would he do with him if he took up with a Christian? Or made her his wife? He shuddered and decided he should pursue Kuerze. The Lord would show favor on him if he did but first, he must find a cat.

Seba was terribly scratched when he arrived back at his small home. Once inside he let the wild feline escape from his coat and doctored his wounds. He hadn't been able to decipher whether the cat was male or female and was not sure if it mattered. The sole purpose was so that he could make the best of a small lie and if need be show that he truly had a cat. He looked at the skinny thing and was convinced any sympathetic young girl would agree that this cat should not miss a feeding. Seba went to bed exhausted from the ordeal but peaceful that he had a plan.

Seba was awoken before daylight with the cat screeching eerily and jumping from location to location frantically looking for a way out. He looked at the poor creature. Trapped... just like him. "Is it worth it for me to tame you so that I may have an alibi?" he asked the warily looking cat. "Well I can see you are not too happy with me. You are not the only one. I am not too happy with myself. I cannot let you free but I will make a deal with you." The cat continued to glare at him and at one point raised an extended claw. "If you will help me to pull off this lie, or lies, depending on the circumstances, I promise you, I will take you myself to Akev where you will be free to live in the barn and catch mice all day long. Agree?" The cat jumped down from his bed and went to the floor and urinated. "I see this will not come easy," Seba acknowledged.

The weather was once again beautiful and the great businessman that Seba was, put his cares behind him and headed to Amsterdam's business quarter. He passed an odd spectacle and stopped to listen to a man propped upon a wooden crate preaching. Seba recognized him as an *Arminian*, a follower of the late Arminius Jacobus, a Dutch theologian who had died a few years back.

"We need greater religious tolerance," the man said, when Seba had stopped to listen. "We need not purge the Jews and Catholics from the country. Nor must we discriminate against other Protestants because they do not share the same beliefs. There is no absolute predestination," he argued. "The Holy Spirit's call won't be heeded by all and there will be no promises of salvation. Do you agree Sir?" the man asked Seba.

"I agree that we shall not purge the Jews from the land. The Catholics, I will pray about that," Seba laughed.

The man jumped from the box. He continued proselytizing ambitiously. "Those with orthodox Calvinistic views, say that

Arminianism will divide the Dutch. But I say… pay attention to us, among our ranks are Holland's best scholars."

"Sir," Seba asked him, "I respect your right to stand on this crate and preach. Is this not a grand city?"

"Yes it is," the man agreed and Seba continued on.

When Seba reached the cafe where he'd planned to have a late breakfast, he was approached by a business acquaintance wanting to discuss the advantages of merchants from outside Holland enlisting the services of Dutch ships. They were attractive to foreign shippers because of their efficient crews and quality engineering.

"Know anyone who has a cat?" Seba asked.

"A cat?"

"Yes, a cat," Seba told him seriously.

"No. Well, yes, I've seen families feed them. Yes, I've seen it," the man answered.

"What do they feed them?" Seba asked.

"Fish?" the man answered. "Holland has lots of herring when the boats come in. With all those tons of herring, what do we see down at the wharf?" he asked Seba.

"Cats?"

"Yes. You never noticed? Why if it were not for the cats we would have too many rats. The cats keep them down."

"Hmmm," Seba thought. "So a man could say he had a cat to keep the rats away?"

"Yes, I suppose he could," the man looked at Seba strangely. "Do you have a rat problem?"

"Not unless you call women rats," Seba answered at which the man laughed loudly and got up to pay for his food and left.

Seba finished his breakfast and left the cafe only to run into none other than Miguel Dorta. Seba was tired from the night before, not in a fighting spirit and was annoyed at seeing him. He was about the same age as Seba's father, Daniel, who to Seba was an old man. Miguel's silver hair was thick and wavy to which Seba felt the man had applied one too many layers of grease and Miguel's large, round almost black eyes seemed to peer into Seba's privacy. Seba didn't care how many women Miguel Dorta had enjoyed the company of when he was younger nor that his ancestors from Catholic Spain had sold their hacienda and large piece of land just before the Inquisition took it from them nor how well they had prospered once coming to Amsterdam. He had heard it all before. But what Seba did care about was the whereabouts of Miguel's lovely niece, or was it daughter?

"Where is she?" Seba asked rudely.

"Where is who?" Miguel answered Seba and looked at him as if the young man had lost his mind.

"Your beautiful daughter, uh, I mean, uh, your niece," Seba stammered suddenly realizing he had divulged what Kuerze had surely not wanted repeated.

Seba could see that there was weight behind his knowing the truth behind Miguel's masquerade as a flawless man whom Amsterdam had few of.

"I will pretend as though I did not hear that," Miguel said. "She is at the almshouse today. She has promised me she would help out. My regular assistant needed a day off."

"Almshouse? Where is this almshouse?" Seba asked.

"It is on the first side street off of Damstraat," he told him.

Seba did not thank him but headed on his way.

Just as Miguel had told him, Seba found Kuerze working at the almshouse. She was in a little office adding up cash letters when he walked in and stood coyly before her. She did not act surprised that he was there.

"Good morning," he said.

"Good morning Seba," she said, looking up only long enough to slightly smile then return to calculating the cash letters.

"I'm sorry I didn't fulfill my promise to walk with you along the canals. I have no explanation except a silly story about my cat. I am here today though, and I was hoping..." he said but she cut him off.

"No," she said still counting the cash letters.

"No? You can pass up a truly wonderful day that easily? With just... no?" he said.

"Yes," she answered back.

"Ah, I get a yes. I will come back in two hours," he said and quickly dashed out while she tried hollering back at him. She ran to the doorway to make sure he heard but couldn't help but smile as she watched him run down the street with his hands over his ears.

Between counting cash letters and doing paperwork, Kuerze spent the next two hours fussing with her hair. When Seba returned she had decided she would give him another chance to be the gentleman she believed he was.

"Can we start anew?" he asked.

She nodded.

"Do you have a cat?" he asked as they walked toward the canals. She laughed and held his arm tighter. Seba realized that she'd grown closer to him through the ordeal.

They spent the day watching birds that dove and squawked everywhere they went. They walked a great distance and talked about what was important in their lives. She told him how she had moved to Amsterdam in the last year, from Antwerp, and that after her mother died she came to live with her uncle. Over the years, she put bits and pieces together and was positive that Miguel Dorta was her father.

"He's your father?" Seba asked.

"I'm quite sure he is. It all fits," she said.

"I accidentally mentioned it. He did not deny it," Seba confessed.

"You said that? I wish you hadn't."

"After I said it I realized I shouldn't have. Sometimes, I open my mouth to speak and the wrong words come out," the look on his face was one of humility. "Do you have a cat?" he asked again to change the mood and she laughed. When they reached the edge of the city, Seba could see that they were alone. He stopped walking and turned toward her. He took a lock of her shimmering black hair and wrapped it carefully around his index finger. She heard his breath quicken and knew he was preparing to kiss her. The structure of his face was perfect, as was his skin, his straight teeth and his thick unruly curls of sandy blonde hair. His personality was so witty he had made her laugh throughout the day. And now he stood facing her with a lock of her hair wrapped around his finger while she looked into his transparent green eyes. And then he kissed her. It was a shy gentle kiss but one that stirred them both.

"I wish I hadn't done that," he said.

Kuerze raised an eyebrow then kissed him again. As she did, he felt her breast brush against his thin summer shirt. He felt a chill run across his chest and his nipples stood erect.

"I wish you hadn't done that," he said then looked down at his crotch. Kuerze put her hand over her mouth, appalled that he had been so bold to draw attention to the erection the kissing had brought. They both laughed and held tightly onto each other's hands as they walked their way back into the bustle of the city.

Kuerze found herself spending too much time at the Almshouse run by Miguel. His devoted young assistant had suddenly refused to show up. It was apparent the girl enjoyed helping the poor. Now Miguel had suddenly come up with plans to keep Kuerze busy, wanting her to sit in on the board meetings and help with fund raising. Miguel even insinuated to her that her beauty could be used to convince the wealthy to support their cause. He even went so far as to set up an appointment with an aristocrat whose mother was dying, and arrange for Kuerze to be alone with him and charm him into bequeathing part of his mother's wealth to the organization. It had been terribly uncomfortable for Kuerze. She'd been tricked into it. But to her surprise, Miguel's manipulation worked and the man not only gave generously but also convinced an associate, a local magistrate to donate a valuable work of art toward the Almshouse lottery. Miguel pulled tricks to keep Kuerze away from Seba but finally after several weeks of having to wave Seba off while she attended to her tasks she finally laid her pen down, looked at Miguel and said, "Bring her back."

"Bring who back?" he asked.

"Your assistant. I have other matters to attend to," she told him.

"Care to share?" Miguel pried.

"Love," she said standing him down. She gathered her full skirt and pulled her hair out from underneath her scarf. Her black silky strands fell quickly down her shoulders. Miguel stared at her and it caught Kuerze by surprise. She had never seen him look at her that way before. Her look of inquiry merited a response.

"It's just that..." he said and then looked away. It was easier for him to speak if he wasn't looking at her.

"Yes," she said expecting him to continue.

"You look so much like her."

"I know," she said. Knowing this was the moment when he confessed that he was her father. But Kuerze had no sympathy for his drama. She'd known for a very long time that Miguel Dorta was her father. His reputation was so scandalous, she was sure he had other children, probably in Amsterdam.

Kuerze and Miguel looked very much alike. There were few in Holland who shared their traits. Each time she saw someone with jet-black hair and dark, dark eyes and similar profile, she grew uncomfortable wondering if they were siblings. There was one young fellow whose resemblance to Miguel was undeniable. She and the young man had made eye contact one day. It was apparent that he knew as well, how could he not?

"Shall I call you father?" she asked sharply.

He turned and smiled softly. "No, you may continue to call me Miguel. I know you knew, I just couldn't confront the..."

"Hypocrisy?" she chided.

"I have lived with it and suffered remorse as long as I can remember. If it is of any consolation, I truly loved her. I loved her more than I have ever loved anyone. If I could turn back the hours I would. I should have stayed with her," he said sadly and Kuerze knew he was sincere.

Kuerze went to him and took his hand. She was not a hardened woman. Her heart was soft and her nature was forgiving but she was not always easy, nor the first to concede. "You've been extremely generous. And as an uncle I always thought you the best. It's now my turn for love, and I believe I have found it in Seba. He's a silly young man but that's what delights me about him. For too many years there's been an underlying sadness among the crypto-Jews. Seba is part of a new generation of Sephardim, who look forward to the future."

Miguel was humbled and spoke softly. "We've done well after coming north. One day we will walk the streets as Jews, not Portuguese merchants."

She didn't answer him. She wasn't usually the first to concede.

"Finally!" Seba called to Kuerze when he saw her waiting for him outside the Exchange. She walked up and took him by the arm, wrapping both of hers around his. She wondered how he had kept such taut muscles, considering he was neither a dockworker nor farmer.

"What shall we do today?" he asked.

"Walk?" she answered.

"Walk? Again? We'll wear out our shoes," he teased. "The lady wishes to walk, we shall. Which way?"

"I'd like to walk through the Jewish Quarter," she told him.

"But that's where we live. It's overly familiar," he complained.

"I want to walk arm in arm with you and enjoy our culture here in Amsterdam. They know us in the neighborhood and it will be our sort of coming out," she said, bending her face into his, her dark eyes looking to see his reaction.

"A man knows when a woman has won. The Quarter it is. Onward to Jodenbreestraat."

They walked slower than usual, both tired from the mental stresses of their work. She didn't tell him of her conversation with Miguel, nor had he mentioned that a shipload of grain he invested in, had become soaked and ruined. They spoke of nature as they passed flowering gardens. They both enjoyed being the first to spot a bird and identify it, Seba often knowing more than she. But when they neared the Jewish Quarter, Kuerze had him beat socially. She knew each and every artisan and vendor in the marketplace. It wasn't as sunny as it had been in previous days and Seba heard from the men at the Exchange that a storm was coming. It was late summer and the evenings had been warm and the days hot. He didn't say a word when they walked past his home but kept it as an option if they got caught in a downpour.

"I don't know where you live," he said.

"I live overlooking the river... Amstel Sluizen," she said with a smile, knowing that he would use the opportunity to poke fun of her.

"It must be lovely to see the lumber float through," he said, making her laugh.

"Would you like to see where I live?" she asked.

"Would you like to see where I live?" he asked.

"I asked you first," she teased. "But rethinking my proposal and being the refined lady that I am, it would not look proper to my neighbors to have a man alone with me in my home."

He pulled on her hand and held tightly, forcing her to stop. He turned and put his face into her thick hair and whispered into her ear, "I'd love to see where you live."

"You might become one of those peepers," she said, giddily.

But he did see where she lived and Seba was enchanted by her little place.

"Have you traveled and gathered these things yourself? You should design the interiors of the mansions being built in the city," he told her while looking around the room.

"Every chance I get to barter for something nice, I take it," she said, walking to an Oriental pillow. "I received this for caring for a set of twins. And this?" she said holding the end of an Arabic tapestry, I got down on my hands and knees and scrubbed a huge floor for this."

"You're a very nice girl aren't you?"

"It's difficult at times to judge oneself," she told him.

Seba could see she didn't like talking about herself so he abruptly announced it was time to see his residence and they walked back out into the street.

The trees were still fully leafed out, and they spoke about how different it was when they weren't. She told him how she wasn't crazy about the cold winters but that she loved to ice skate.

"Do you? I do too. There's nothing finer than when all of Amsterdam is dancing on the frozen canals." He stopped walking. "Isn't Amsterdam the grandest place?" he waved his hand, portraying a grand expanse. "What more could we wish for? Have you ever seen so many happy faces? There's plenty of work for those able and willing. There are theatrical performances, music and dancers. There are gardens and there is even a fellow with a fabulous butterfly collection. Have you heard of him?"

She loved listening to him talk. It felt so good to be near him, with his positive attitude toward life. "I'll bet you find joy in the depths of darkness," she tested him.

"You know, I do! My mother always said that," he dropped his head at the thought of her.

"Is she still alive?"

"Yes, both my mother and father are doing well. They live a very simple life in Akev."

"You speak of Akev so often, I would love to go."

"I'm surprised you've never been. It's a distance. It's farther than Haarlem," he said thinking of Anabela.

"Haarlem? Why do you say Haarlem?" she asked.

"No reason particularly, just Haarlem," he answered.

"Just Haarlem?" she asked.

Seba could not tell whether this was just one of their silly little banters, or if she had knowledge of the girl who was often in his thoughts.

"I was only saying that Haarlem is not as far as Akev."

Their awkward discussion was cut short by the banging of wind outside.

"Here comes that storm."

"Yes," he said apprehensively. "Here comes that storm."

Seba's rejection had infuriated Anabela. After avoiding her at the bakery, poor Silvanus had to listen to her all the way back to Haarlem. He looked at his beautiful daughter and wondered how she could be so sweet one moment and become unhinged the next. His wife was not like this nor had his mother, but his father's mother, he'd heard stories about her temper.

"Where are you going?" he asked his daughter.

"I've found a ride to Amsterdam, I'm going to find Seba," she told him.

"A ride? With who?" he asked gruffly.

"Two brothers are going to Amsterdam to lay tile in one of the new homes their building on the grandest canal. They said they'd be happy for me to come along," she told her father, who was incredulous.

"Have you neither seen nor heard? There's a storm brewing!"

"Not until tonight," she said looking straight through him with her bright-blue determined eyes.

Silvanus knew he could do nothing to stop her and instinctively knew she would be fine. It was true. The storm wasn't expected to arrive until much later in the evening. If they left immediately and rode quickly, they would arrive just before the storm breaks.

"Where will you stay?" he asked.

"It's a large house with many rooms. The brothers told me to bring a blanket and that I was free to stay."

"You think you are going to stay in a mansion in Amsterdam? With two men?" her father screamed, "No!"

"Yes Father. And do not immediately think ill of it. They will be enjoying the taverns. Leaving me alone to ponder life's difficult questions. Neither of them have an interest in me. They know me too well."

"I'm sure they do," he scoffed. "When will you return?"

"After the Sabbath. I'm excited about attending church in Amsterdam," she said, then gave him a delicate kiss. "You know how much I love you father, please don't worry. This is something I must do."

"I know," he sighed. "I know."

Seba embarrassed himself by taking Kuerze to see his flat. In his infatuation with her he had completely forgotten about the cat. When he opened the door, it was not a grand first impression. His curtains were ripped from the cat jumping and clawing, trying to get out. It smelled of cat urine and feces. And because he hadn't expected to bring her to his flat, he'd left his under-garments strewn on the floor and they were now adorned with a nice pile of kitty poo, caked on top.

Kuerze gagged when she walked in. Holding her hand over her mouth she looked at him not knowing what to think.

"Did I say I had a cat?" he asked. She nodded with wide eyes and her hand over her mouth. He walked over and kicked his underwear away from sight and tried to catch the cat. Kuerze looked on, her image of Seba not a little tarnished.

"You can always tell a little something about a man by his home," he said trying to make a joke but Kuerze thought him serious.

"I understand that you women are very clean. All that business of not wanting the world's dust to enter the threshold of the home," he said to her while her eyes roamed his domain.

"It would look better if the cat hadn't been in here," he said. "I wish you didn't look so horrified. I'm still the same man."

She nodded and appeared to be thinking about giving him the benefit of the doubt. "Why do you have this wild cat in here?"

"I made a promise to him," he said without thinking.

"A promise? You made a promise to a cat?" she asked, unconvinced of his sanity.

"Oh dear," he said, thinking of the promise he'd made to the cat about helping unravel his mess at the bakery between the two lovely ladies, she and Anabela.

Luckily she did not wait for his answer and posed another question. "Where did you get this wild cat?"

"Out in the streets. The poor cat was out in the streets," he said, reaching out affectionately to the cat, who hissed and jumped at him, scratching his hand and drawing bright red blood.

"Why did you bring a cat from the streets?"

"Um," he said, stalling, while trying to remember what he'd discussed with a friend. "Rats."

"You have rats in here?" she asked as she walked to the door. "I can't stay in here, I can't breathe. It's too vulgar. I don't like wild cats that tear curtains and defecate on the floor, I'm much too clean for that."

"Then it's back to your flat?" he asked with raised eyebrows.

Kuerze took one last look around and then looked at Seba. She was much too bright a woman to not understand something was amiss. "You did say you had some kind of cat story. Is this why you ran off at the bakery?"

"Why yes. This is exactly why I ran off. You see," he said waving his arms about. "You see what this cat does to my dwelling when I don't return on time."

"I do," she said, looking at him dubiously. "You don't just have a cat story you have a cat problem."

Seba escorted Kuerze back to her flat. She'd been cool toward him on the walk home. She pulled away when he tried to grab her arm but after a few of his witty jokes, she was smiling and allowed him to give her a warm promising kiss before saying good-bye.

Seba was in no hurry to return to his smelly domain. It would be a job to clean up after the cat and he'd grown tired of it. The cat had cost him too, having ruined some of his things. Perhaps he would go to Akev tomorrow and take the cat with him as he'd promised. The afternoon sun was slowly lowering and Amsterdam's nightlife would be coming alive. It had been a stressful week. Unwinding in one of the taverns with a mug or two of ale sounded like a nice way to spend the evening. The walk would be relaxing and conversation with other merchants would be informative. His love interests had kept him from his duties as Chronicler. There was no better way for him to fudge and acquire news than to loiter at the pub.

"Evening," a gentleman greeted him.

"Evening," Seba said. "I've seen you at the office of Marcus De Luna and Sons Shipping Company."

"Yes, that's it. Of course. I've chartered with De Luna many times. I've had good luck with each venture. And you?"

"Yes, most have been fruitful. If I lost on an investment, it was no fault of De Luna's. Pirates was a problem once and the other loss I incurred was due to weather."

"I've not yet encountered pirates but the weather, can cause a lot of problems."

"Yes," Seba agreed. "There's a storm looming now."

"I hear it's a nasty one," the man said.

"Yeah?"

The man leaned into the big wooden table and spoke seriously in low tones. "This is expected to be a monster of a summer storm."

"Yeah?" Seba asked. "That's what you hear?"

"Many a man will be ruined by this storm."

"We should remove ourselves from harm's way," Seba told the man, who said nothing but stood firm in his premonition.

Anabela and the two brothers arrived in Amsterdam with just enough time to escape from the high winds and downpour.

"Wonder if the vendors are still at the market?" one of the brothers asked.

"Why would they? The storm is almost here," he shouted back against the growing winds.

"We need some food," the brother shouted back.

Anabela shouted out, her high voice barely audible, "I'll walk around and see what I can find."

The two brothers nodded but both shouted for her to be careful and be back swiftly or they would soon come looking for her.

Anabela was bundled up in a dark woolen cape. The softly lined hood kept her warm. She was excited about spending several days in Amsterdam and hoped to see Seba. But she hadn't expected to run into him immediately upon hopping into the street and only walking a few steps. They both gasped, startled by one another.

"Anabela!"

"Seba!"

"What are you doing out on a night like this?" he asked.

"Same as you I suppose," she answered.

Seba could tell by the inflection in her voice she was nervous. He was afraid to look her in the eyes. Afraid that one look would be all it took. He'd made progress with Kuerze and their romance was promising. With Kuerze he could have all he needed. A loving, caring, intelligent wife that was not only beautiful but also fun. His family would love her, she would be an asset to his business needs and there would be no conflicts of religion. With those thoughts in his head he drew strength and looked into Anabela's eyes.

He wished he'd not done that. Again, as before, he stood in a frozen emotion that came from deep inside. The feeling had returned but this time it was stronger than any he'd ever endured. It had frightened him the first time, his feelings for this frail angelic creature. He finally spoke.

"The first time I met you I wondered how the winds did not blow you away."

She smiled, pleased that he cared.

"Now here I stand, again facing you, another chance meeting and I know I must take you and protect you from this strong gale," he said, spellbound by her pink cheeks and her pale, pristine skin nestled within the hood of her dark woolen cape. Her bright blue eyes spoke that she too longed for him. He knew now there was truth in those romantic theories. There are two souls who are meant to be together as one.

"I'm staying across the street," she said.

Seba turned and looked at the huge home that was being built for a well-known Sephardic Merchant. "You're staying there?"

She nodded.

"It's the future home of Felipe Bento," he told her.

"Is it?"

"Why are you staying in Bento's unfinished house?"

She laughed. "Oh, I see your confusion. I have come from Haarlem with two brothers who are laying tile for Bento. They told me I was welcome to stay, provided I bring a bedroll."

He looked in front and behind to see if anyone had seen him, then Seba took a deep breath as he gathered the hand of Anabela and walked with her across the street with the thought of her small bedroll in his mind. The thunder clapped and a bright bolt of lightning lit up the tall narrow house. The storm had arrived. Seba could feel it in his gut.

"Where are the brothers?" he asked.

"They must have gone out, they said they were very hungry."

Seba admired the large expansive entry hall. "This is beautiful. Felipe Bento has been highly successful."

"Um hmm," she said mostly looking adoringly at Seba who turned to her as all the light through the windows was waning.

Seba did not... could not wait. "May I kiss you?" he asked.

Anabela answered with a wet kiss upon his lips. Seba had spent the day with Kuerze and her beauty and sexuality had aroused him all day. He was ready to explode. Anabela must have sensed his vulnerability. She spent the next two hours kissing and teasing Seba. He had never known such pain. When the two of them heard the painters returning Anabela grabbed Seba's hand and they both ran up the long expanse of steep stairs. She chose a bedroom and threw her bedroll down. She put her finger to her mouth for him to be quiet and she whispered.

"There is no need for them to know you are here." He nodded.

"Anabela!" one of the brothers shouted.

"Yes, I'm here," she answered sweetly. "I did not go out after all, it was too much a risk. I will retire now, goodnight."

"Goodnight," they called out.

In the darkness, the tall, wispy girl pulled Seba close. The room was growing dark but enough moonlight shining through the glass lit up her platinum blonde hair. She began removing her damp clothes. Her skin was very cold. Her lips, which she repeatedly pressed into his, were warm and reassuring. She stood in the nude, in front of him, while he, still clothed, ran his hands up and down her body, getting the feel of her height, the fullness of her firm breasts and her tight youthful backside. She began to help him remove all of his clothes. He was more than eager. He was in pain. He felt as if his erection had been up all day and when he turned her and gently laid her upon the bedroll he slid up and into her. The wind blew wildly outside but the strong home that Felipe Bento had built, withstood each blast. He could feel her bright blue eyes staring up into his. She smelled of lilacs and he sensed her joy in his entering her. The first day he met her he recognized Anabela had a mind of her own and she exhibited that as she rolled on top of him and took no shame in the ecstasy that his thrusting brought her. She squealed with pleasure. That they had to contain their vocal expressions brought poignancy to the act. When they both grew close to finishing, she bumped her body into his, squeezing out the last bit of gratification. Both their panting was strong, especially his. He had never before experienced anything like this, nor ever expected to again, with anyone but her. They had both finished, but the thrilling feeling of her tight cold nipples on his chest made him wish he had more. She sighed, rolled over and threw her head back, combing her hand through her hair. She took her finger, ran it down his tawny chest toward the wetness of his groin and then down into the curvatures of his well-muscled leg. He took his mouth, put it on hers, and kissed her deeply. He loved this girl. She moved him in ways he was sure no other woman could. He longed to possess her and prohibit other men from coming near her. He would care for her and protect her. The baker's wife had said Anabela called Seba her prince. She had just made him her king.

They lay in each other's arms quietly while their breathing returned to normal. Seba realized he needed to leave. The thought startled him. The realization of all that had happened woke him to his normal reality.

"I can hear them down there. The brothers are awake. I can't go out that way," he told her.

"Why must you leave so soon?" she pined.

"I can't be caught up here, it's inappropriate." He stared at her. For a moment he thought he was feeling remorse, but the strong feelings returned and he lay back down again and she rested her head upon his chest. Remembering again that he should not be caught with her, he moved over to rise and as he did felt wetness on the bedroll. In the flickering candlelight Seba could see it was blood. He took another look at Anabela. *So pristine.* He had not for a moment thought that he was engaging in a virgin. He lay back down again and ran his hand through her bright blonde hair.

"Am I your first?" he asked.

She nodded and was very shy about speaking of it.

"I hope I am your last," he whispered into her ear, sending shivers across her shoulders. "I must go, I must. If we're found together, like this, no one will understand. All of Amsterdam would hear of it," he warned her. He put his clothes back on and cringed when he heard the rain start back up again, beating loudly against the window.

"It's coming down in sheets," he said, standing in candlelight that reflected his bare, well-muscled torso.

"Why don't you stay and sneak out tomorrow?" she asked.

"No, I know that won't work. I have to leave soon. Are there any other doors besides the front?" Seba asked hopefully.

"Yes there are three doors but they are all downstairs. You would have to walk by the brothers and they are still awake. Can't you hear them?" she said, not sure what to make of the situation.

"Well then I will have to climb out this window," he said, walking toward it as water splashed up against the pane. He stood studying the situation.

She could tell by the way he moved his head that he was unable to see anything through the thick downpour. "You'll be drenched!" she protested.

He returned to give her a delicate, short kiss goodbye. "Where can we meet before you go home?"

"I'm leaving after church on Sunday," she told him in a dutiful voice.

"Church?" he asked.

She turned to him and in her most matter-of-fact voice said, "Why yes, I've become quite involved with the Dutch Reformed Church in Haarlem. I've heard that there is a beautiful church here in Amsterdam that I must see."

"I'm Jewish, did I tell you that before?"

"You did not need to. Your name is Seba. Only a Jew would name their son Seba," she told him.

He was not sure whether it was a compliment or an insult.

"You look Jewish as well," she said. "And I've heard plenty of talk about the olive-skinned Portuguese who came north, fleeing the Inquisition. Everyone knows you're not Christians."

"They do?" he asked incredulously.

"It does not bother me. I suppose one would consider me a Jew as well. After all… my great-grandmother was Jewish. Isn't that how it works?" she asked, while he grew impatient as the rain pounded against the window. "Through the Mother's line?" she asked.

Seba pulled at his thick curls and started pacing the floor. He looked at her wondering what had led to this outlandish discussion in the pitch of darkness with the rain pounding on the window and two brothers downstairs who he feared might walk in. Then he thought of leaving her and remembered.

"You will be at the church on Sunday? Of course I will not be there," he said.

"Not yet," she said.

Ignoring her, he continued. "The baker's wife will tell me where to find you in Haarlem. May I come see you at your home?"

Anabela jumped up and hugged him. He could see her tall, skinny body in what little light they had and it roused him again.

"I must go," he said, maneuvering the window open then closing it again after rain poured through. He stepped back into the room. "It's terribly windy out there. And wet. There is no ladder, how will I get down?" he asked, scratching his head.

"Are there any bricks that stick out that you could put your feet on and climb down, like you would a tree?" she asked naively.

"I suppose there are," he cocked his head, trying to see through the glass. "I can see there is a ledge. I was always good at climbing trees. I'll be fine," he said, and quickly braved the storm again, this time closing the window behind him. She could see through all the water pouring across the glass that he was smiling and gave her a wave. He quietly slithered down from the third story of Felipe Bento's half-finished mansion. Seba would never look at the wealthy merchant the same again.

By the time he made it down from the third story, Seba's clothes were soaked. Due to the storm, no one was out in the street to see him leave through the darkness, after sleeping with Haarlem's most beautiful virgin. He walked past several pubs where he heard the lively crowds inside. He had no interest in joining them. He ran through the streets and was pleased when he finally made it to his neighborhood. Until he opened the door to his flat... and saw her.

He froze when he saw Kuerze lying on his bed. She too was startled, for she had not wanted to give the wrong impression. She had waiting for him for hours and had grown tired. She sprang from the bed and stood up.

"I came to visit and found that the cat..." she said apologetically.

Seba looked down at the cat licking his paws.

"I brought him some fish heads," she said kindly. "I hope you don't mind."

Seba looked around the room. It was clean. "You did this?" he asked.

"Yes, I felt bad for you. You seemed to care deeply for this cat and he'd made such a mess."

He stared at the cat who looked up smugly.

"You truly do have a cat excuse," she said cheerfully.

He had to think a bit to remember what she was talking about. "Yes, the bakery, I ran off."

"Why are you wet?" she asked.

"I saw a ... a, ah ... friend and I should have, ah ... ah... I should have come home but I didn't and guess what? I got caught ... in the rain," he said waiting to see if she believed him.

She accepted his statement, having no reason to believe otherwise. But Seba was tired and cold and wanted to be alone and sort through his thoughts. He stared at her as she stood watching the cat. Her face was content and she had a calmness that he knew he would miss. He studied the line of her feminine body and knew he would miss that too. He looked again at her face and her delicate lips. Should he kiss her again one last time? She looked at him and knew something was wrong. Cocking her head and squinting her eyes she stared at him. He averted her look.

Kuerze took a deep breath, bent down and grabbed the cat. "You're a liar," she said and headed for the door.

"Where are you going with my cat?" he shouted out after her as she raced down the street in the rain.

"I'm going to set him free, right now," she said and let go of the cat. He ran off into the dark rain-washed street.

"I'm sorry," Seba hollered after her. "Kuerze, I really am sorry!" he yelled again but she did not turn around. He stood in the pouring rain until he could see her figure in the shadows no more. He stood long after she was gone. His heart pounded loudly in his chest. The rain poured on his face, hiding his tears. Kuerze would have brought him peaceful days and beautiful children. It had been within his reach but had not been his destiny. He didn't know what awaited him as he walked through the years with the choice he had just made. But as he stood in the pounding rain in-between two different neighborhoods, in-between the sobs, for the first time in a long time, he prayed.

Feeling secure that he'd made a wise choice for a wife who waited patiently for him in Haarlem, Seba dove back into his work. Many things were on his mind but the first chance he had, he would go to Akev to visit his mother and father. He would need to report all the latest Chronicling. He usually sent it along with one of several young boys who came to Amsterdam but he would go himself for he had some issues to discuss with his father before speaking openly about it to the Akevians. He would also have a long talk with his mother.

But today Seba planned on spending the afternoon in Amsterdam's finest meeting house, the tavern closest to the Exchange. He felt a little uneasy as he entered. He was not the same man he'd been a week ago, before he made love with Anabela in Felipe Bento's unfinished mansion. Seba was not sure that he'd not been seen shimmying down the side of the successful Portuguese merchant's extravagant new home. He was not surprised to see Felipe Bento inside. No one seemed to think twice about Seba so he relaxed and found a table. The storm had ended as quickly as it had arrived, and today a delightful ocean breeze blew through several large open windows. The front door was propped open with a massive iron anchor that probably took three men to move.

"Don't forget what happened in ninety-six," Seba overheard a man storytelling at another table. "De Houtman's expedition reached Banten. He had a fight on his hands with the natives and the Portuguese."

A young investor spoke up. "And lost a crew of twelve! But they made it home and they made a profit."

"De Houtman suffered great losses but brought back a shipload of spices," another man added.

"To the Dutch East India Company!" a man with blood-shot eyes held up his mug. Seba wondered if the poor man had received any sleep in the last week.

"Once our government gave us a monopoly over Asian trade," the younger investor said. "Enabling us to establish forts and defend ourselves," he said confidently. "We've all prospered."

"The Company has a grand arrangement," another investor said. "Not until the end of the decade is the East India Company expected to present financial records to the Dutch government. What a deal."

Seba could see the three had been sitting there drinking for quite some time. He wondered if they would be able to make it home.

"We need only fear the English," the young investor reminded them. "They are building trading posts and threatening our East Indies trade."

Seba was growing tired of hearing inebriated men ramble on about what was not news to anyone in the pub.

"We should push the natives back," the blood-shot eyed man spoke and slobbered.

"Let's run them off," a young man said.

"They can be starved off," the blood-shot eyed man laughed. "Better yet, we should make slaves of them. They will help us build splendid plantations!"

Seba knew that the money he made was tainted with the blood of innocent natives but he didn't need to hear the intricacies from drunken fools on such a gorgeous day. He decided to postpone his trip to Akev no longer. The Exchange could wait.

It was evening when Seba arrived at Akev. He had ridden with a group of several others who co-opted the carriage ride from Amsterdam. He always welcomed the walk of the extra two miles that the carriage would not take him. He remembered walking to greet his grandfather, Jacques, returning from business. It was the old familiar, well-traveled path to Akev and as he grew closer, Seba could hear some of the residents singing old familiar Hebrew tunes and playing musical instruments. He recognized the tune and sang along as he walked into the hamlet he would always call home. The closer he drew, the more children he saw enjoying the last bit of light. The days would be growing shorter and colder, not that the children instinctively knew that, but their parents did and grew lenient about their coming in for the evening. Seba wondered what life would be like if he were to return to the simplicity of Akev. He thought about Anabela and wondered if she would oblige him and return to the Sephardic roots of her great-grandmother. Would she enjoy living here? Would he enjoy living here after all the excitement in Amsterdam? He thought not. He had changed too much. He was no longer simple and innocent. That saddened him. When he made it to his parent's home down by the water, his mother, Ruth immediately recognized his despair.

"Daniel! It's Seba and I can see our son is distraught," she said calling her husband from his wooden seat on the water's edge, where he usually sat most evenings, either fishing or watching the sun retire.

"Mother... I am not distraught," Seba told her.

"What is it then? Why such a long face?" she demanded to know.

"Doesn't a mother ask her son if he needs something to drink or if he is hungry?"

"Yes, yes," she said and brought forth a wheel of cheese, a cutting board and huge knife. "Now... tell me what is troubling you."

"I have grown accustomed to Amsterdam. The city is full of activity. Hundreds of people are out walking the streets. The docks are loaded with elaborately rigged ships. Their sails blow in the wind. The smell of spices permeates the sea air while sailors unload tons of grain. One could spend the day admiring it all."

"That does not sound sad," she said.

"I've come to visit because I missed you and father. I felt a sadness when I entered Akev," he put his head down. "I would miss Amsterdam. I've grown to love the excitement. But I would love to raise a family, here in Akev, as we Soeiras have for generations. Mother... this is our community. We built this community."

"Yes, but it would not be built if you and your grandfathers had not ventured away to provide for us as you continue to do today. Don't tell your father I said that. He wasn't the best at leaving to Chronicle," she told him with a look that said, *let's not bring that back up again.*

"Yes Mother. We Soeiras have been one of the wheels that have helped turn Holland but it's all changing."

"Changing?"

"Yes, we venture further into the seas. We travel to the ends of the world to enrich ourselves. But the men who lead the expeditions are not as thoughtful as they've been in the past. They're crueler and more dependent on human trafficking. In this new era, our children will eat well but Mother… it's all very unkind."

Ruth looked down. His words brought back harsh memories of when she was a girl living in Austria. It had been hard as a child and she'd not spoken of it to anyone since arriving at Akev. Her silence prompted Seba to speak out about what was foremost on his mind. His hands were shaking. Knowing no other way but to speak directly and honestly, he began.

"I have fallen in love with a Christian."

Ruth was slow to look at her son but when she did he could detect a twinkle in her eye, "My son has fallen in love?"

"Her name is Anabela. Her great-grandmother was Jewish from Portugal but Anabela follows the Dutch Reformed Church," he told his mother, hoping for acceptance.

"I see," was all she could say, but Seba still saw that gleam in her eye.

"Shall I tell father?" he asked.

"Yes. Otherwise he will hear it from someone else. He's been speaking with some of our community members who have taken fondly to the Reformed Church. They reassure him they are still proud of their ancestral roots and continue with their Jewish faith but he is afraid they will one day abandon our faith and that their children are vulnerable."

"Mother… you know I understand that."

"In Akev we have a good many households who celebrate both the Christian and Jewish holidays, especially Chanukah and Christmas," she said sympathetically. She turned her head, lost in thought. When she turned back again he saw her sadness but Seba was quite sure it was not anything that he'd just said to her but something that had happened long ago. He rose and faced the doorway and was about to walk down to the swampy area they called the water's edge where Daniel had been fishing all his life. Ruth stopped him.

"I'll tell him. Please, Seba, I know your father. I must be the one to tell him."

Seba nodded. Suddenly he missed his lively city of Amsterdam but he could not leave until tomorrow. He dreaded the idea of spending the night with the secret he and his mother held.

Seba walked back into the world of Amsterdam with renewed gusto. After a few days off he was more determined to make accomplishments in his work. His first task would be to stop by the Dutch Court and check in with an official. Seba's family had worked as liaisons with them for over one-hundred-and-fifty years. He ran his fingers through his wet hair and ran the flat of his hand down the front of his shirt, easing the wrinkles. The only apprehension he had was the lingering stench of cat he had been unable to remove from his clothes.

Seba greeted each person he passed with a smile and a nod. He could not remember ever feeling this friendly. He hopped up the stairs of the court, pressed his hand into the brass handle and pulled. He walked down the long hallway to the small office in the back where behind closed doors he would discuss what would be needed of him.

"Good day," Seba said to the official who looked up and then back down to his work.

"I'm checking on the business that needs my attention," he said to the distracted man.

"It's all taken care of," the official said, finally giving him eye contact. "We've enlisted the services of Monsieur de Brebon."

"Monsieur de Brebon?" Seba asked.

"Yes, David de Brebon. Monsieur de Brebon brings us European connections from within highly affluent circles."

"And I ..." Seba was about to say.

"Higher," the official told him but could see that Seba did not understand what he meant. The man tried again, "wealthier... more affluent circles than those you bring us."

"Wealthier than my connections through the Exchange and the VOC?"

"Much wealthier," the official said with a wry smile. "The decision was made without my knowledge otherwise I would have told them that your work has been satisfactory."

Seba was stunned. He'd just lost his family's position that they'd held for over one-hundred-and-fifty-years.

"I do have a few little things," he said handing Seba a receipt to pick up a pair of boots from the cobbler for one of the judges. Seba took the receipt and looked at it and with a sick twist in his intestines politely set it back on the desk, turned and left.

"What have I done?" Seba asked himself aloud as he walked out the door of the courthouse and down the steps. He headed straight to the tavern by the Exchange. After settling in at a table and trying desperately to act as if nothing had happened, an acquaintance Seba recognized as a fellow Sephardim came and sat down.

"Mind if I join you?" he asked.

"Please do. I was hoping for conversation," Seba told him in a sincere, friendly voice.

"Converse," the acquaintance said with a smile.

"Any new faces in Amsterdam that we should know of?" Seba asked, intending to prod as many new names from the acquaintance as possible. When finally the fellow mentioned Monsieur de Brebon, it was taxing for Seba to keep prodding him, so he would not know it was de Brebon with whom he desired knowledge. After slowly asking questions about the last few names, Seba remained composed and asked his acquaintance. "Monsieur de Brebon, a Frenchman? What's his business?"

The man sat up. "What business does he not have a hand in? If there is anything in Amsterdam that is sweet... Monsieur de Brebon will have his finger or his nose in it. *He is everywhere*. I am surprised he's not here. I've heard he's part owner of a ship at the Middleburg harbor and partakes heavily in their wine and cloth trade. He owns and rents out several large homes along the canal in Amsterdam. Lucky would we be if one day we are invited to his home when he entertains, I hear he provides well for his guests," the acquaintance carried on. "The talk is that he is a Jew who poses as a French Huguenot," he said in whispered tones.

Seba had heard enough and finished his ale, bade the gentleman good day and headed back outside into the late summer's morning. He headed to the Exchange.

"Good day," Seba said, returning the greeting to those who spoke to him. He looked up at the chart of names showing the rise and fall of the month's investments. David de Brebon's name was all over the board. Seba could see that the man who'd taken his court job as Brenger for the Nobles, had his hand in many ventures. Why had he not noticed this man's name before? Who was this strange Frenchman?

Seba continued with the day's business and invested in futures of herring and wheat through shares in the Dutch East India Company. He also invested heavily in some unusual tulips that had become all the rage. As the building grew more and more crowded with ambitious men eager to make their fortunes, after being pushed and shoved, Seba squeezed himself out of the crowd and back outside into the light and fresh air. Wanting something familiar he headed toward his flat. When he reached his home, he walked past it and ventured deep into the markets of the Jewish Quarter. Everyone there knew him, but today he noticed several of the once friendly vendors casually turned their back on him, pretending they didn't see him.

"Hello," he said to the produce vendor. The man turned around and nodded but in an unfriendly manner. Seba walked to the woman who sold knitted socks. They usually engaged in friendly conversation but today she too snubbed him. He walked further and smiled at the potter who usually spoke with him, but today pretended not to know Seba, who bewilderedly bought a few things then walked back to his flat. Could the knowledge of his romance with a Christian girl have reached Amsterdam's Jewish Quarter's gossips?

What had started as an upbeat day for Seba turned into a surreal afternoon. But nothing surprised him more than when he got home and saw what was waiting for him outside his flat. The cat.

Happy to see the cat, Seba reached down to pick him up but the cat revealed his fangs then extended his claws and scratched Seba's hand drawing blood.

"Hey, why are you here? To give me a bad time like everyone else? Don't you come in friendship?" The cat answered by rubbing up against his leg.

"You're just here because you think you'll see the beautiful raven-haired woman who cared for you, but she does not live here nor will she ever return," Seba spoke to the cat outside his doorway while the man next door looked at him as if he were mad.

"See, I am in trouble again. I wish the baker's wife had never suggested to anyone that I had a cat," he said to the cat as he held the door open, "come in."

Seba cringed when he entered. The combination of the cat's lingering smell of former defecations and Seba's fish that he hadn't thrown out soon enough, had taken the opportunity on the warm summer's day to become nauseatingly odiferous. He was relieved that no one would be coming by to visit. He lay on his back on his bed while the cat cried for something to eat.

Seba wondered why he continued to live the way he did. He questioned his motives for all that he'd accomplished at the age of twenty-one. He'd completed his university work. He'd traveled wherever his position as Brenger had required. Taking him to Paris, the Rhineland, Brussels, all over the Netherlands and once into England. It was expected of him to be a large part of Akev's financial support but in the last several weeks his life had changed dramatically. The tide had changed for him and he could do nothing to change that nor would he. This next era of his life would require an expenditure of personal strength he'd never expected. He would need to either convert Anabela or be a man with two religions. Thinking of it was very tiring. He fell into a deep sleep. The cat jumped on his chest, curled up and fell asleep in his arms.

FOURTEEN

The day Seba headed for Haarlem to see Anabela had started as most of his mornings did. But when he walked into the fresh air and heard little birds singing he became intoxicated. The chemicals in his body had changed. His brain behaved peculiarly and his body was filled with adrenaline. He welcomed the trip but was not thrilled at the prospect of seeing her strange father. But he would give him a chance and he hoped the father would do likewise.

Seba shared the carriage with two men and one woman. They kept to themselves the entire ride, except for a few cordial exchanges. They all wondered privately what each would be doing once arriving in Haarlem, but none were rude enough to ask. Seba didn't know how to find Anabela but he came equipped to spend several days looking for her and assumed he would find her swiftly because her father operated a popular wheat mill. Seba took the time to ask the carriage driver if he knew of just such a mill and the driver responded with hand gestures and affirmative nods and smiles. He knew just of the white-haired, bearded miller with the beautiful blonde daughter.

"Down that lane. Go all the way down to the end. It's across the lane from the ironworker. Watch for the forge."

Seba stood on the lane and could see it was a long walk to the mill. His stomach was in knots. Luckily his shirt absorbed the sweat that collected on his chest and under his arms but he had no cure for his racing heart. Did he look all right? Was his hair combed enough?

Had he gained weight since last seeing her? Would his mouth smell fresh when he spoke to her?

He walked for several miles carrying a small satchel. Having no intention of imposing on her family, the Camaroons, for lodging, he looked for an inn but sensed he was going in the opposite direction. He also got the eerie feeling that he was being watched or followed. Not wanting to be obvious about it, he did not turn around until his curiosity forced him. There in the shadows was Anabela. Her hair was a mess of tangles as if she hadn't combed it in days and the clothes she wore surprised Seba. He smiled at her and she shyly hesitated. Walking toward one another they both wore the crimson face of embarrassment. They had known each other's body too early in the game. Now they would need to know each other's mind. When they had taken enough steps to face each other, neither spoke. Anabela lifted her shoulders, rolled her eyes left and then to the right, then giggled uncomfortably. Seba nervously grabbed at the thick curls at the top of his head, twirling them in his index finger. Without looking into her eyes he finally spoke.

"I thought I would come and see you."

She did not answer so he looked up. She was confident and smiling, obviously happy to see him but not quite sure what to do with the young man.

"Do you have a place to stay tonight?" she asked.

"Where can I find an inn?"

Ababela pointed a long slender finger in the opposite direction, "down there."

"Down there?" he asked.

"Yes," she nodded playfully. "Way down there."

He paused and his green eyes squinted slightly, as if attempting to read her thoughts or felt some sense of guilt remembering their rendezvous in Felipe Bento's home. "I would never ask you to accompany me to the inn."

Anabela's wide-eyed, frozen response told Seba more about the girl. She was confident when away from her usual surroundings but in the vicinity of her family and community she was reserved. That was reassuring.

He grew comfortable with her again. "Last time I saw you it was very stormy."

She looked around to see if anyone was near. "I'm glad you made it down safely."

"Yes, I made it down safely. I have had an unusual course of events since I last saw you. It's good to get away."

She didn't ask what had befallen him. She struggled with the uneasy situation of her parents but remembered that in their own ways they were supportive of her chasing after Seba.

"Let me take you to meet my family."

He would have loved to grab her hand but held back. Instead, they made small talk as they walked in unison all the way to the Camaroon Mill. She stopped when they reached the front and by that time Seba had recognized the forge landmark the carriage driver mentioned. There was a sturdy but graying boardwalk at the front of the mill and a large barn across the lane. Silvanus Camaroon kept the large sacks of un-ground wheat in the barn and the canal that ran along the backside spun an enormous waterwheel that turned the massive stone that ground the wheat. Their home stood adjacent to the little gray wooden building across from the barn. Their residence served as the office where customers came in to discuss orders. Anabela took Seba into the office where they found Silvanus covered from head to toe in flour dust including his wild white hair and beard.

"Hello father, this is Seba."

Silvanus looked up but did not smile. Seba was depleted from the look her father gave him but seeing Anabela smile and whisper something to him though he didn't understand, made him relax.

"Your prince is here," Silvanus said sarcastically. Anabela seemed to smile all that much brighter. She was not afraid of her father. He loved her very much Seba could see that.

"It's a pleasure to make your acquaintance," Seba told him and reached out to shake his flour dusted hand.

"I suppose," Silvanus said, extending the gesture and giving him a firm handshake. "You going to take good care of my daughter?" he asked.

"Yes sir, excellent care, if you'll permit me," Seba said, just before losing control of himself. "I'd like to marry her."

Anabela's eyes were huge. She opened her mouth widely and looked to both of the men who sounded as if they were bartering her.

"You would, would you?" her father questioned but Seba did not answer, his eyes were also huge and his mouth also somewhat open in disbelief. Her father was old and wise enough to understand what had transpired. He was kind under all the gruff and spoke comfortably to Seba. "You look a hearty fellow. She will not be easy but she will be a good wife and will make a fine mother."

Seba looked at Anabela who looked at him then to her father then toward the door that led into their home where Seba assumed she wanted to run.

"I'm sure she will Sir," Seba said, then turned to Anabela, who just shook her head, grabbed his hand and pulled him through the door she opened that led into their home.

The first thing Seba noticed in their home was a mechanical clock powered by falling weights. The clock was very well cared for and he sensed it held sentimental value. The second thing he noticed was that there were many paintings upon the wall. There were two portraits of Anabela and no other children so Seba reckoned she was an only child. There was a portrait of the three of them and then there were numerous scenes of the sea, a windmill and nature paintings of marshes, swamps and seabirds. Eventually, Anabela's mother came out, embarrassed by her unkempt appearance. Seba had to refrain from laughing at her full head of fluffy curls that had been wrapped and braided but it must have been days ago and she too was covered in wheat dust.

"I'm Margarita," she said touching her hair as if her stubby little fingers could hide it. "I did not know we would be having company," she said sadly.

"I'm sorry I intruded but I so wished to see Anabela again," Seba said politely.

She smiled and nodded. "Anabela has told me she has not known you long but she has quickly grown fond of you."

"Yes, we are fond of one another. I don't mean to be so abrupt Margarita but as I told your husband I wish to marry Anabela."

Margarita was shocked at his statement. She looked at Anabela who had grown comfortable with it. "Married? You wish to be married? I believe I need to sit down."

Seba winked at Anabela who put her head down shyly. "Since we're acting so quickly on this manner," Seba said changing into his business voice, "there is an issue that we need to resolve." He looked to Anabela for reassurance but she became distracted as the door opened and Silvanus walked in. He looked disappointed that they were still talking about the marriage; he was hungry and would have loved a good meal. Seba sensed that, as did Anabela.

"An issue?" Margarita asked and looked at Anabela who was also surprised.

"Yes, may I sit down?" he asked.

"Yes please," Margarita said and once again nervously began fiddling with her wheat-dusted curls and constantly looking to read her husband's thoughts.

Seba found a comfortable chair and also one for Anabela. Margarita had already sat down on a bench.

"I am a Jew and Anabela is a Christian," Seba began.

Margarita nodded. "My grandmother was Sephardim. From Portugal."

Seba smiled. "As you know Amsterdam has progressed but not when it comes to Jews and their freedom to worship. It is forbidden for a Jew to marry a Christian."

Margarita looked down while Anabela's body posture grew obstinate but Seba did not allow Anabela to protest. "We must share our religions. It will not be easy but it will be necessary. There are many that are fully aware I am Sephardim but most in Amsterdam believe I am a Christian. In my family, that has been the situation for almost two-hundred-years. I would like to have a ceremony, a nice ceremony," he said looking affectionately at Anabela who had calmed down. "We could have it at Akev."

"Akev?" Margarita asked.

"Yes, that's where I'm from. It is a wonderful little hamlet south of Amsterdam. My great-great-great-grandfather created it as a farming community where the Sephardim could come and live unmolested. It is named after their son, Akev, which means Jacob."

"It all sounds very nice Seba," Margarita said, then looked wistfully at her only daughter and then to Silvanus who remained silent.

"That is very nice of you Seba, will we have a Christian or a Jewish ceremony?" Anabela asked and Seba could see he had better answer it correctly.

"It will be both. We have a church in Akev where we can have the ceremony. Then we can go to one of the homes that are used as a synagogue and receive our blessings there. I have seen it many times in Akev," he said, uncomfortable divulging such private information to strangers.

"Would you mind if your daughter escorted me to the inn?" Seba asked Anabela's father.

"Certainly not," Silvanus said, happy to be alone with his wife who smiled her approval.

Seba shook again the dusty hand of Anabela's father and nodded politely to Margarita. "It has been a pleasure to meet you both."

"Watch out for the wine. In Haarlem it flows rather freely after dark," Silvanus cautioned Seba as he and his wife Margarita looked gravely at one another.

As soon as the door closed and Silvanus could hear his daughter's laughter further down the street he turned to Margarita.

"Our daughter is to soon become a Jew," he said to his wife.

"No. Seba is soon to become a Christian."

"Pfff...," Silvanus scoffed, looking his wife square in the eyes. She could see the blood veins in them were inflamed. Even though much of his white hair and beard was covered in wheat dust, it sparkled in the late afternoon sunlight that came through the small window. "Do you believe the Jews will let their namesake's son go to church? What's the name of that community the young man said he was a part of? Akap?"

"I believe it was Akev," Margarita said amused that her husband had so quickly become emotionally involved in the issue.

Silvanus's twisting in his chair was no match for his twisted face. "Church! Pfff..." he said again. "He will not go to church. The Jews would never hear of it. Never! Margarita my words are genuine. Anabela will become a Jew. Her Christian days are over."

"But she enjoys her church so much," Margarita said, while her hands nervously twisted her apron string.

"Well her church days are over. Over!" Silvanus shouted. "I'm hungry. Please, let me eat."

"We can't," not here Anabela told Seba as he pulled her between the darkness of two buildings.

"No one will see us, I must kiss you. I must," he said passionately. "I wish to hold your body again. I ache for it."

"I have lived here all my life. My image will be tarnished if we're seen like this," she pleaded with him.

"Is there not somewhere, a barn, a hay loft?" he pleaded back.

"My uncle has a boat," she said thoughtfully.

"Where is your uncle?"

"He is away. I know for certain he is away and no one will find us there."

She giggled as they grabbed hands and ran behind the buildings and down to the water. There was an abundance of boats and many people were about tending to them. Seba and Anabela slithered carefully around until she led him down a pier that held a smaller than usual wooden ship. It was a miniature of the largest ships Seba had seen, the ones owned by the Verenigde Oost-Indische Compagnie.

"It must have taken someone years to build this. Wow! A bowsprit and three masts."

"My uncle and his son built it. Yes… it took them many years. It is beautiful isn't it?"

They looked around to see if anyone had paid them any heed and none had so they both snuck aboard. The boat rocked with the tide but a massive rope and anchor kept it from floating back out to sea.

"This is gorgeous! Your uncle is an artist," Seba said, admiring the polished woods from faraway lands. "His woodworking skills are superb. He lived down here until it was finished, I can see that. Look at these little brass fixtures," he said while fumbling them, temporarily forgetting his lust for Anabela who stood passionately waiting.

"Your hair," he said teasing her. "What has happened to your hair?" he said to her, in the dark, after she shut them in.

"I slept on it wrong, it will return to normal after I put water on it," she said standing femininely with one shoulder cocked and her head thrown back. Seba could hear her breathing had accelerated. He leaned her against a short wall. She slid down and sat herself on the floor. Her bright blue eyes and pink cheeks reminded him of the other two times he'd seen her.

"I didn't know you were a virgin," he whispered heavily into her ear.

"Of course, I have waited until the man I knew I would marry. My mother and grandmother taught me a nice girl is to wait."

"How did you know I would not leave you for someone else?"

"I'm good at knowing. I knew from the beginning." Her eyes rolled back from the pleasure of his male voice speaking softly into her ear.

"What is that smell?" she asked, suddenly changing her demeanor.
"Smell?"

"Yes, your shirt, it smells strange. Seba it smells foul."

"Oh, it's my cat."

"Your cat?" she asked incredulously. He nodded and was relieved that she appeared to not know of his cat. That would mean that her father had not mentioned anything to the baker's wife.

"I never imagined that love could act so swiftly," he said to her.

"Nor I," she said reaching her hand inside his shirt, feeling his soft warm skin.

He felt relaxed and alone with her in the small ship. He began removing his clothes and she hers. The two stood naked with the only light coming through a small round window that faced out to the sea. The sun was receding and it would mean that Anabela would return home later than expected but she didn't care as Seba kissed her neck and shoulders, his warm breath reaching down her back. He knew they could not stay long so he quickly entered her and she winced, behaving more like the virgin she'd been that stormy night. Her change of personality surprised him. He would need to grow accustomed to her many faces. Again he could feel the absoluteness of their destiny and now as they mated within the darkness of the ship that rocked with the tides, their bodies rocked in unison and it was with a soft, sweet whimper from them both and tears they hid that revealed their vulnerability.

"The English are establishing trading posts in Java and Sumatra," Esteves Osorio told several other men as they stood in front of the tavern smoking tobacco from the New World.

"There goes our monopoly," the other Portuguese merchant answered back.

"Someone needs to rustle our diplomats into writing up a mandate," Esteves said gruffly.

"And hold the English to the sword until they sign it. We can't lose our hold on the East Indies trade," the merchant said in his most contentious voice.

"They'll cooperate," Esteves told him. "They must. We can't lose what our grandfathers labored for all these years."

"And theirs before them. Would they believe their eyes today? Behold Amsterdam! This is the age of prosperity, such as the world has never seen," the merchant boasted.

"Miguel!" Esteves said jovially when he saw the familiar figure walk towards them.

"Good day gentlemen," Miguel Dorta replied.

"Is life good?" a smiling Esteves asked him.

"Life is good Esteves, life is good. Well, I was about to enjoy an ale with you boys but I see someone I don't wish to see," Miguel told them when he saw Seba coming up the steps to the tavern. Seba was easily in hearing range and he scowled when he saw Miguel but greeted him politely.

"Miguel," Seba said nodding respectfully then turning to the other gentleman, "Esteves," he said greeting the vaguely familiar merchant whose gaudy home Seba had been to for a meeting. "I believe we have not met," Seba said politely to the other merchant who told him his name was Jorge and shook Seba's hand.

"How's your cat?" Miguel asked confrontationally.

Seba didn't know how to respond so he ignored the question preferring to discuss the day's commerce. "What do we hear of the pepper shipment that got held up by pirates?"

"The pirates took more than half but the investors still made a profit," Esteves told him.

"Not a windfall but a nice profit I understand," the merchant agreed.

"I saw you in stormy weather Seba," Miguel said antagonizing him again. Seba did not know what Miguel was speaking of so just looked at him.

"You. I saw you standing with the tall girl with the very white hair. Did you enjoy the luxury of Felipe Bento's home?" Miguel said, with the intention of shattering Seba's confidence but the young man held strong, acting unaffected.

"Have you heard the outcome of the disagreement between the widow of Cornelius Vega and Denis Rodrigues over the glass bottles of civet?" Seba asked the men who all seemed interested.

"Fighting over a bottle of perfume? Esteves asked between chuckles.

"Healing perfume," Seba told them, laughing along with Esteves in an attempt to hide his nervousness.

"I will not tell Kuerze I saw you, she is damaged enough by your fraudulent nature," Miguel persisted while the other two men looked sympathetically toward Seba while Miguel badgered him. "She has another to entertain her. Have you not heard of David de Brebon?" Miguel said, finally capturing Seba's attention.

"The name sounds vaguely familiar," Seba answered. "Your niece…" he paused, "is a wonderful woman. I have enjoyed her friendship," Seba said averting Miguel's eyes. "If you will excuse me gentlemen," Seba said to the men and then he finally turned to Miguel and in his nastiest voice said to him, "I have a cat to tend to."

All the way back to his flat, Seba ran Miguel's words through his head. *Have you not heard of David de Brebon?*

Heard of him? He wished he hadn't. The man stole his position as Brenger and now he'll have to see him strutting around Amsterdam with Kuerze. *I love Kuerze!* Seba's mind reeled. *But I love Anabela more and I will marry her.* To hear Kuerze's name shot pangs through his heart and pains to his gut. He was glad that when he got home the cat was not waiting for him. Perhaps the cat was finally gone from his life and he could put that episode behind him. He would have to forget Kuerze and devote himself to just one woman. It was not hard to love Anabela. Just thinking of her made him smile.

"Mother!" Seba greeted Ruth. She was cleaning out the small shed where his father kept his fishing equipment. She was excited to see her son and Seba was relieved to see her in good spirits.

"Just in time to enjoy fresh bread and cheese," she said reassuringly.

"Have you told father?" Seba asked, looking around for his father.

"Yes. He was very angry. Not like him to scream so loudly. I was able to calm him but only on the condition that you would not *ever* abandon your Jewish faith."

Seba nodded. "I had no intention of that. Anabela has agreed to have two ceremonies, a Christian and a Jewish." His voice was worried but lightened when he remembered. "And she has agreed to be married here at Akev."

"I can think of nothing that would make a mother more proud. I will do all I can. We'll have the pretentious Christian ceremony by the light of day and we'll hide and have the Jewish ceremony in the secret synagogue," she said. And with a mischievous look asked, "Has Anabela agreed to the Jewish ceremony as the first?"

"We didn't talk about any of that Mother but I'll ask," he said seriously. "Is it wrong of me to want to marry a girl I have only known a short while? I feel rushed but it is a grand feeling."

"Your father and I knew immediately the day we met in Paris. We knew we would be together for all these years," she said then paused, "About the Christian wedding, your Uncle Francois..."

"Yes, Uncle Francois, Rabbi Uncle Francois," Seba said to her and they both looked at each other wondering.

"He has spent his life trying to save the Jews from what he calls the great movement," she said to her son. "We have all been concerned. But Seba," he knew by the change of her tone of voice she was going to confide in him. "I almost went to the Calvinist church one day in Amsterdam. I was outside planning on going in but when I thought of how much it would hurt your grandparents, especially Jacques, I couldn't do it. I would have had to lie to them."

Seba nodded. Her youthful divulging didn't help, it only increased the guilt beginning to build.

"It's no wonder people strayed and went into the churches. It was bound to happen. It was confusing to the children. Either they are or they aren't Christians," she rambled absent-mindedly.

"Did you tell Father that Anabela's great grandmother was a Portuguese Jew?" he asked hopefully.

"Yes, and that helped, though your father will not rest until you get that girl to convert." Her eyes were still big and brown, her hair thinner but still very curly like his.

Seba let out a deep sigh. "You see Mother, this is why I need to get this behind us. I want to be a happily married man and enjoy life. I want to have a son, maybe two or three and of course a beautiful daughter. Mother, Anabela is so beautiful. You will love her."

"What does her family do in Haarlem?"

"Her mother and father own a grinding mill," Seba said, laughing about it. "They were covered in flour when I met them. Her father, whew," Seba fanned himself. "I have never seen a man who looks as frightening as her father. He has wild white hair and a wild white beard but he is very kind, amidst his gruffness."

"Well then, he shares the belief with us that the messiah has yet to come?" she asked.

He laughed heartily. "Her father looks as if he doesn't believe a messiah will ever come!"

"I see," she said looking down, thinking heavily. "And her mother?"

"I believe her mother has only the mind of her husband, Silvanus Camaroon."

"Silvanus Camaroon? Did you say Silvanus Camaroon?" his mother was shocked and darkness came over her. She sat down. "Oh Seba, I know this man you speak of."

"No," Seba reassured her. "You don't know Silvanus Camaroon."

"Oh yes, but I do. He was in Austria," she said frantically and began to cry.

"What is it mother? Did he hurt you?"

Between the tears she shook her head no. Seba slowly began to understand the feel of his mother's emotions. If anyone should know the allure that a Camaroon had, it was he. Had he not committed the worst of sins that night in the storm? Had he not tarnished the home of Felipe Bento with his carnal lust for Anabela? If a magistrate were to have found them that night, a Jew with a Christian virgin he would be the scorn of Amsterdam. Then Seba remembered Miguel Dorta's taunting him about that night and suddenly it all came together. He *was* the scorn of Amsterdam. Amsterdam's *Jewish Quarter*. No wonder the vendors who had usually been kind, were so cold. He shook his head to bring his thoughts back to his mother. How could he say to his mother that he knew that Silvanus Camaroon had taken her virginity? Seba looked at her pathetic posture and tried.

"Mother, none of us should ever be ashamed of love. Hold your head high. Your secret will be kept close to my heart. I would never tell Father nor anyone."

She smiled, "I feel bad but I feel better." She put her hand on Seba's and that mischievous look returned to her eyes.

"He is a Jew," she whispered.

Seba and Anabela's weddings were beautiful. Those close to the family were concerned that the Jewish ceremony would be discovered because the women couldn't stop talking about it.

"Is she not the most beautiful girl you have seen?" one woman asked another who responded with, "No. I saw him with just as beautiful a girl in Amsterdam. A black-haired raven beauty, not that long ago."

"Really?" the first woman asked, her mouth agape.

"Yes, and they were kissing. It was at the edges of the city, on the road to Leiden," the second woman gossiped.

"Tsk, tsk, tsk," the first woman said. "Seba rushed quickly into this one."

"Yes he did, didn't he," the second said. "Shall we watch for an expanding waistline?"

The first woman giggled. "Only if you shan't tire of counting on your fingers."

Seba was the fifth generation Soeira to settle in Akev if one wished to call it settling, as the two newlyweds were usually missing from community events and constantly on the go elsewhere. As an only child, Anabela promised her parents she would come home frequently, which she did. And as a lively young woman intoxicated by Amsterdam's golden age, she was always in the city.

The prestige of marrying a Soeira had Anabela holding her head highly but not as highly as was held the head of another beautiful woman, Kuerze Dorta, whom Anabela had heard fragments of rumors. Kuerze was frequently seen arm and arm with Monsieur de Brebon, the wealthy Jewish Frenchman who overtook Seba as Brenger. To Anabela's understanding, Monsieur de Brebon was the owner of several lavish mansions along Amsterdam's wealthiest canal and lived in a mansion where he entertained the world's dignitaries. She heard that he was part owner of a ship at the port in Middleburg, and that he was a respected, high-ranking representative of the Dutch East India Company. Exactly who Kuerze was, Anabela was not sure. But what she did know, was that Seba had not long ago had a fondness for her. He never spoke of Kuerze, but often spoke of his dislike for Monsieur de Brebon.

"That man," Seba growled one day after returning to the flat that he continued to keep in between Amsterdam's Christian and Jewish Quarters. "Everywhere I go he has been there first. He has superlative business skills. I don't know where he learned them but it's as if I had taught him myself. He knows all that I do and a whole lot more," he said to Anabela who sat in a chair by the door. As was usually the case, Anabela was dressed in finery from head to toe. She had to have the latest fashions made from Calcutta's textile factories. Seba assumed she would tire of it, as would he, and they would one day spend more time in Akev raising children. Once he'd married Anabela, a new world opened. She went every Sunday to the Dutch Reformed Church and usually dragged him along. They would make penance for it on Saturdays, when they were in Akev to attend the lovely hidden synagogue. Holy days were difficult, but so far they managed. Seba's father Daniel, was disappointed whenever Anabela didn't show up for her Hebrew lessons, but a reassuring, sincere apology from his new daughter-in-law kept him hopeful that one day she would finish all her lessons and be a fully converted Jew. Daniel understood that Anabela was still young. He was well aware of the cultural opportunities Amsterdam offered a young couple, especially those with means, like the Soeira family, now that Seba was spending more time at the Exchange and the VOC. No one at Akev was complaining. The storehouses were full. Flemish sheep grazed in the fields. Their wool kept the farmers busy. Several new barns were erected after freshly cut lumber made its way to the hamlet. The opulence of Amsterdam flowed to Akev as freely as the wine at one of David de Brebon's receptions, to which Seba and Anabela had not yet been invited.

"Why are we never invited to Monsieur de Brebon's gatherings?" Anabela asked Seba one night in Akev, where they stayed in the old home that many years ago Seba's grandparents, Jacques and Rebecca built.

Seba frowned. He was reading and the light was growing dim, he did not look up.

"And you always frown when his name is mentioned. What is it?" she asked sweetly.

He put the book down, knowing she deserved an answer.

"You know he stole my position as Brenger?" he said to her, hoping that would suffice.

She nodded but he could tell by her expression she waited more of the story. He remained silent.

"I've heard bits and pieces," she said cuddling up with him. "I would love to put them all together. Is it true that you and David's favorite female used to spend time together?"

Seba was surprised.

"You're not frowning anymore," she teased.

"Yes, we spent time together, but for a very short while," he reassured her. He rose and walked to her. He put his hand on her long, slender leg that lay dangling out of the bedcovers. Wishing to be distracted by her beauty he began stroking the length of her leg before she abruptly put her hand on his to stop.

"Continue. You used to spend time with... what is her name?" she asked, and she could see it was painful for him.

313

"Kuerze," he said thinking deeply. He looked once again at Anabela's long, slender leg hanging from underneath the bedcovers. "You see," he whispered as she cuddled more with him, "I used to have this cat..."

1619 *May*

Six years passed and Seba and Anabela were never once invited to the extravagant soirees hosted by David de Brebon and his new wife Kuerze. Anabela and Seba had seen the birth of not one or two children, but three little Soeiras now ran around their home in Akev where Anabela spent most of her time. A fully-converted Jew, the young mother and wife of Seba, retained her youth and beauty but on many a day it could have gone unnoticed. She loved her children and let them grab onto her hair so it usually resembled dried briars. Her lack of sleep left telltale signs of dark rings under her eyes. Yet no one had reason to pity her, for she was never without a smile. Climbing on the floor to play with her children, walking with them along the river's edge to absorb nature's beauty, fishing with Seba's father, Daniel and sharing the preparation of the Shabbat meals with Ruth kept Anabela fulfilled.

Anabela had complete trust in Seba, who was every bit the wonderful father as she the mother. And though he was often in Amsterdam, the Flemish and French countrysides and occasionally England, Seba kept his promise to his ancestors. He continued to hear the echo of their voices. Many of Amsterdam's successes could be attributed to the continued old-world bond that the Chronicler kept alive.

Seba had been away tending to business when Anabela heard her children calling out to him. She ran to the front stoop and sat while her children climbed on her back and twisted at her hair.

"Why do you let them do that?" a boy of about nine asked her.

"Do what?" she asked.

"Why do you let your children pull at your hair and climb all over you?"

She laughed. "It feels good. My children love me and they have an abundance of energy. If I can feel them tugging at my hair I know they're safe."

The boy shrugged. "Here comes Seba," he said as if she did not know.

"Thank you," Anabela told the boy, then walked several yards before the boy stopped her again.

"Why do you wear those?" he asked.

"What? Wear what?" she asked, this time annoyed at his peskiness.

"Everyone else wears shoes. Why do you wear those thick woolen slippers outside when everyone else wears shoes?"

This time Anabela laughed harder than the first. "I suppose I am strange to you," she just shook her head, "Everyone is not the same."

"Especially you!" he said with a mean tone. "Because you aren't really a Jew. You're really a Christian."

"I'm a Jew," she said to him. "Just like you. I am a Jew."

Anabela tried putting the uncomfortable encounter with the lad out of her mind but she thought of it during the evening while Seba spoke of the latest politics.

"Jan Pieterszoon Coen is the newly appointed Governor-General of the Verenigde Oost-Indische Compagnie," he told her as he elevated his feet and chewed on a warm chicken bone.

"Coen?" Anabela asked, "A Portuguese merchant?"

"Considering the Dutch East India Company was financed by the diamond merchants, I could not say whether this Coen is Sephardic or an Azkenazi but I would be willing to wager he is one of the two. But I would not be surprised to see him on the steps of the Dutch Reformed Church on Sunday," Seba told her. "I've known of him but I don't know his history. He's probably a member of the old network of Sephardim or the newly-arriving Ashkenazi who've gained strength the last few years. Both groups speak Hebrew. The bankers know and trust them and loan them money. They pool their resources and purchase ships. They have extensive shipping contracts and a tight bond with the diamond industry. I would say that without Sephardic or Azkenazic connections Coen would not have risen to the position of Governor-General."

"What do you think Leeuw?" Seba asked his oldest son, whose name meant Lion, fulfilling a promise to his grandfather to give his children names that would always trace back to the old tribe.

"He's only four," Anabela said. "He does not need to know Amsterdam's politics."

"Oh but he does! It's never too soon to teach Leeuw about politics. I hope he will be the next Chronicler," Seba said, lifting his boy onto his lap.

Anabela was pleased. "Chronicler? Yes, he will be Akev's next Chronicler. He already speaks to everyone in the hamlet. I think they expect him to be the next Chronicler. It's as if everyone in the community is tutoring him."

Seba smiled proudly and Anabela could see that he was falling into deep thought. His mother had warned her of that but she didn't mind. She enjoyed watching him sit and think. He was beautiful lost in that deep thought, with his dusky skin and thick unruly curls of sandy blonde hair with one streak of gray. He soon fell out of his trance and with his transparent green eyes he continued relaying more of the world's news.

"There's trouble brewing in the Palatinate," he told her.

"Trouble?" she asked, a lump thick in her throat.

"Yes, mercenary soldiers roaming the countryside are stirring things up. They're not being paid so they go to the farms and help themselves to what's available," he said, then spoke quietly so the children wouldn't hear. "They've been helping themselves to the women as well. It's all very cruel," he told her sadly.

"More violence?" Anabela was dismayed.

"It's what I hear," he said gravely. "North German barons detest Ferdinand's Catholic rule."

"All very familiar," she said. "Protestants in the north fighting the Catholics coming from the south. Will there ever be peace? I find it more interesting to hear of the new Governor-General of the VOC," she told him, deciding not to mention her own trouble brewing right there in Akev when a lad had spoken rudely to her about her Christian roots.

Even on issues of business, Seba spoke from deep within his heart. "Coen sees new directions for the Company. He's not afraid to take risks. He's a man who craves power, and to be the head of the VOC is a way to obtain it. He is not a gentle man. Talk is that he's taking many ships to the Banda Islands. It will decimate the natives. They will not stand a chance."

"Coen wants to kill all the natives?" Anabela asked.

"Or make slaves of them so the Dutch can have plantations and grow wealthier with a monopoly on cloves and nutmeg," he told her.

"Slaves and war? Over nutmeg and cloves?" she said holding her other son and daughter close while Seba held firmly to little Leeuw.

"Men profit from the misfortunes of others. It has always been this way."

"Men must always have their wars," she said sadly.

Seba sat up, startling Leeuw. "And who is it that wants nutmeg and cloves? It's the women! Men go to war not just for themselves. Men may do horrid acts but the women reap the rewards. Do not expect women to walk innocently through the pages of time Anabela."

She curled up and clutched her children tighter. Leeuw began to cry.

FIFTEEN

1635

Leeuw Soeira grew from a strapping lad into a striking adult. At twenty, the handsome, well-educated young man and new Chronicler of Akev had not only the brains for politics but the heart of his namesake, *the Lion*. Leeuw inherited his father's thick unruly curls but they were not sandy blonde like Seba's, but the bright blonde of his mother, Anabela. He also inherited his mother's bright blue eyes and pink cheeks but there was no mistaking his Portuguese Sephardic origins when one laid eyes on his beautiful dusky skin. When he smiled he could convince anyone of anything and the very few still alive that remembered his great-grandmother, Rebecca, never failed to remark on the twinkle in his eye, just like hers.

Like his father, Leeuw was drawn to Amsterdam and the cultural, financial and social opportunities it promised. But Leeuw's biggest magnetic attraction was to seventeen-year-old Hanna de Brebon, the lovely daughter of Monsieur de Brebon, although he never dared mention it to his parents. Through the years, he'd more than once heard his mother bring up Monsieur de Brebon and his wife Kuerze. They'd never been invited to any of the Monsieur's parties and it forever hampered his parent's social, political and financial opportunities, not being able to mingle with Amsterdam's wealthiest. Leeuw though, was not going to let his parent's resentment stand in his way.

Hanna de Brebon had everything a young Jew, pretending to be a Christian, could want. Leeuw was sure that her father, French Huguenot Monsieur de Brebon and his wife Kuerze, descended from Sephardic families. Time had made it harder to trace familial lines, but Leeuw was Akev's Chronicler and he knew exactly who to go to and how to dig up the past. How to catch the attention of young Hanna would not be without some clever wrangling. For reasons unknown to Leeuw, Hanna's parents would clutch their daughter when he was anywhere near. Leeuw was certain that their actions were triggering a rebellion in young Hanna, for on each occasion in the last month that they had done that, Hanna was aware of it. Leeuw wasn't sure, but the last time he thought he caught a smile on her face, which was more than enough to keep him open to the possibility of making her his wife.

"One day soon I will find a wife," Leeuw promised his parents.

"And grandchildren?" his mother Anabela asked.

"Yes of course, many grandchildren."

"Father," Leeuw said changing the subject. "Did you gather information from the women of Damstraat?"

"Leeuw, I think my father Daniel was the only Chronicler to not gather information from the women of Damstraat."

"I'm concerned about my reputation," Leeuw said, bending down closer to his father and speaking in lower tones.

"Your reputation? Why?" his mother asked.

Leeuw laughed, "Don't worry Mother. What I mean is that, it concerns me if someone were to see me in Amsterdam's unsavory quarter."

Seba told Leeuw, "Make your quill pen visible and look like a man conducting business only."

Leeuw laughed at his father's remark. "All of Damstraat has businessmen."

"Yes, this is true Son, but all who know you understand that you are the Chronicler. The women of Damstraat have the widest breadth of information for hundreds of miles. They spend time with the sailors and the skippers."

"And many a magistrate from what I'm told," Leeuw added.

The next day Leeuw took his father's advice and in his best suit of clothes walked into the jurisdiction of the ladies of Damstraat. He'd been there before, only briefly, when he and two other lads had wandered curiously into the quarter. It was early in the morning and beautiful women were out doing chores. The girls were free with their smiles and Leeuw wondered how a pretty girl could wake up one morning and find herself living on Damstraat. Today he saw it differently. Further discussions with his father had led him to understand that the women of Damstraat were an intelligent lot and usually eager to help a Chronicler in any way they could. He had no idea what he would ask them and practiced different opening statements as he walked closer to the brothel.

"Excuse me," he said, popping his handsome head inside the door left slightly ajar.

"We're closed," a gruff woman's voice called out.

Leeuw stammered, "The door was open and..."

"We're trying to air it out. We're closed," she said again in a deep hoarse voice.

"I'm a Chronicler," Leeuw said, not wanting to give up.

"A what?" The woman came to the door. Leeuw was surprised that she was young. Her voice had him believing she was a woman well advanced in years. He was severely taken back at her youth. There was a kindness in her eye and he immediately took pity on her. He looked at the clothes she wore. They were beautiful and his imagination told him that one of the sailors or perhaps a skipper brought them to her as a gift. He'd heard of men falling in love with the women of Damstraat. The longer they stood staring at one another the more she softened. She smiled in amusement and leaned against the doorway. "You're a what?"

"I'm a Chronicler."

"What's a Chronicler?" she asked, looking over her shoulder to see if anyone was watching her digress from her work.

"A Chronicler is one who records the events of time," he said, not sure those words would suffice. She gave him a look that he interpreted to mean she thought she'd just been fooled so before she turned away he tried again.

"It's my understanding that with all the activity here on Damstraat, information flows freely," he told her with raised eyebrows while he waited for her response.

"Strong drink is what flows freely here, what's your name?"

"Leeuw Soeira," he said, reaching for her hand to kiss it. She extended it, he did.

"You'll have to come back when it gets dark. And you'll have to pay like everyone else," she told him with the softness leaving her eyes. "If you bring enough money, I'll give you a story you'll never forget."

Leeuw was stunned. Suddenly he did not pity her, nor felt she would be a reputable source of information. He wondered how men could come here and violate themselves with such women. The longer he stood staring, the more he noticed the painful look in her eyes and where her eyes should have been white they were yellowing. *Disease,* he thought.

"Thank you for your time. I'll not trouble you this evening, nor any evening," he said, as he turned to walk away, down the dark, urine and alcohol-stained cobblestones.

Leeuw's home in Amsterdam was finer than the Chroniclers before him. They'd lived in flats, fashionable for their time. But in this era, a man of Leeuw Soeira's standing could easily afford to live in one of the homes his family owned. Not lease them out as his ancestors had done. Not situated in front of a dazzling canal as the

324

de Brebon residence was, Leeuw's home sat in the heart of Jodenbuurt, on a quiet street known for its well-tended gardens, not far from one of the canals that circled Amsterdam. Most of his neighbors were elderly members of the old Sephardic families who'd come north from Spain or Portugal. Several of the neighborhood's widows had been the wives of prosperous merchants or sailors who knew Leeuw's family well and kept an eye on him. Besides being intertwined with Haarlem, Middleburg and other Dutch settlements, Jodenbuurt was intertwined with Akev. Though most of the old families still postured as Christians, especially the younger generation, both the Sephardim and Ashkenazi were becoming confident that one day they would build a synagogue. But there was always the constant fear that religious tides would change. Until then, most felt secure holding services in private homes. Just such a private home used for a synagogue was across the street from Leeuw and every Friday evening he attended Shabbat services. It was at one of those Friday evening services when Leeuw met Mademoiselle de Brebon. He knew exactly who she was and found that she was still an attractive woman, especially her dark eyes. Her head was covered with a jeweled cap, below which flowed six inches of thick silver hair. He found her beauty seductive. After recognizing her, he made his way across the room.

"Shalom," he said catching her by surprise.

Her smile was faint. "Shalom," she said, looking around the room for someone to rescue her. But he was too quick and too eager to make headway with her daughter.

"I'm Leeuw Soeira," he said reaching for her hand. He kissed it lightly.

"I am..." she started to say, but before she could finish Leeuw interrupted.

"Mademoiselle de Brebon," he said.

"Kuerze," she volunteered. "Please, call me Kuerze."

"I've seen you many times but we've never had the pleasure to meet," he told her.

"Yes, my husband is very busy and we attend many functions," she told him coolly.

Leeuw had the old Soeira charm and felt confident that she would warm to him, though perhaps not today. "It was a pleasure to make your acquaintance," he said, nodding and backing away.

"Aren't you Seba's son?" she asked, catching him by surprise.

"Why yes, how did you know?"

"I knew your father when we were young," she said, not wanting to delve into the past. But Leeuw did not sense that.

"The two of you cared for a cat together? Is that correct?" he asked, while scanning the room for familiar faces.

Kuerze was shocked at the audacity of Seba that he would have mentioned the cat to his son. She let her guard down. "No, we did not care for a cat together. Your father..."

Leeuw realized he should not have mentioned the cat. "I'm sorry Mademoiselle de Brebon, I did not know that the cat brought such strong emotions..." he said, before she interrupted him.

"Your father had strong emotions over the cat who," she looked at him in amazement, "we..." she tried to finish but Leeuw had to finish it for her.

"Cared for together? Yes," he said, wishing he'd not broached the subject. But when he saw tears in her eyes he was mortified that he'd been foolish enough to mention the cat.

Embarrassed, Kuerze tried to remedy the situation. "I loved that cat."

"Yes, I can see that."

"But please," she asked him in such a warm voice, Leeuw instantly grew fond of her. "Don't mention the cat to your father. If you would keep it private, our meeting, I would appreciate it. Speaking of your father..." she said... again unable to finish.

"Seba," Leeuw helped.

She smiled softly and laughed gently and then reached her hand to his, "It opens old wounds."

"Yes, I understand," he said, embarrassed for her.

"Leeuw..." she paused.

"Yes."

"You should call at our home some evening," she told him genuinely.

"I would find that very enjoyable," he answered.

"Our home is to the right of the curve in the River Amstel, next to the home of the diamond polisher, are you familiar with that area?"

He paused and pretended to think about the area, knowing full well where the spectacular home of Monsieur de Brebon sat, as did all of Amsterdam. "Yes, I know the diamond polisher. I would be delighted to come calling some evening, I look forward to it."

"It was very nice to meet you," she said, surprised to have been so delighted with him.

"Yes, Madam... uh..."

"Kuerze," she said with a smile.

Leeuw had no intention of running up the stairway to the entrance of Monsieur de Brebon's home, like an anxious fool. He would though, take a daily inspection of who came and went. He had to make his rounds as Chronicler so why not stroll through the neighborhood and find a quiet, hidden place where he might analyze the competition for the affections of Hanna de Brebon? Leeuw wanted to know who came and went from the de Brebon residence.

After a week of watching, Leeuw was surprised at how quiet it was. Early each morning in a long, dark cloak, Monsieur de Brebon would walk out the door and methodically turn and close the solid door of his towering, wide brick home, brush down the front of his clothes with the back of his fingers, stroke his cropped beard and look carefully around. As if he were concerned about being followed. The only other visitor was an unknown man who Leeuw discovered later, was Rabbi Maronne, a new rabbi from France, who would do the same looking around before he went into the home, as Monsieur de Brebon did on the way out. Leeuw stood looking at the situation, knowing that as a Chronicler, there was a story to tell here at the de Brebon residence.

Feeling conflicted, he sought the advice of a new friend, Antonio Vas Porta.

Leeuw told Antonio, "My original intentions were to make the acquaintance of Hanna de Brebon."

Antonio was from the same community of mostly Portuguese merchants, excluding of course Leeuw's great-great-great-great-great-great grandfather, Monsieur Soeira who had always considered himself a French Jew. Antonio's father was a familiar sight at the VOC as he invested heavily in Baltic imports, especially grain and timber. The family had also amassed considerable wealth through their investments in Swedish mines and the metal they exported.

"How do you know she's not betrothed to someone else?" his round-faced friend with gleaming brown skin asked him. "In our community the parents try desperately to find mates for their children, sometimes from birth."

Leeuw scoffed at the notion. "My parents and I believe most of my ancestors fell in love."

Antonio laughed. "You're such a sentimentalist. I've heard the rumors about your grandfather, Daniel. His wife, your grandmother

Ruth, may have been Ashkenazi but she was still a Jew. We stick together more than you realize. Monsieur de Brebon must have a suitor all picked out for his daughter."

"Hanna's mother extended the invitation," Leeuw told him. "Which brings up another issue."

Antonio smiled again. "How many issues do you have my friend?"

"There are several," Leeuw told him. "Be patient Antonio and I will relay them all. My father and Hanna's mother were at one point in their young lives, very close."

"How close?" Antonio asked with a laugh, which he loved to do. He was popular with other young Sephardic men because of his wonderful sense of humor and keen intelligence. When young men relaxed in the taverns with Antonio, little by little, a small crowd would grow around him, which is how Leeuw met him late one afternoon after a hard day at the Exchange.

"I don't know how close my father was to Kuerze de Brebon," Leeuw told Antonio. "And Kuerze requested I not mention our meeting to my father, Seba."

"Kuerze? She has you call her by her first name?" Antonio teased. "You have several issues at hand, your father's old love..."

"No! That is not one of the issues. I have spoken with her and have been invited to their home. My father and mother are offended that they have never been invited to one of the de Brebon's exceptional soirees. I believe it's because my father and Hanna's mother were at one time..." Leeuw paused, having difficulty saying it, "in love."

Antonio looked at him thoughtfully. "Yes, that's an issue but a small one. The most important issue would have been that your father was from a nice Sephardic family, which he was."

"Yes, the politics of Jews," Leeuw lamented. "After all these years..."

Antonio laughed heartily.

"I'm curious about the new rabbi who visits the house."

"Is it your business?" Antonio scolded, "Your parents named you *the lion* because they wanted you to be ferocious?"

Leeuw smiled. "They wanted all to know that I was from the tribe of Judah. That is of course if our origins are lost," he said with trepidation.

Antonio wasted no time in making a joke of it. "Do they really believe that five-hundred-years from now someone will see your name as some sort of clue and trace you back to Judah?"

"That's what they had in mind," Leeuw answered, a little embarrassed. "What will they trace about you?"

"Probably the Levy they placed in my name."

"Antonio Levy Vas Porta?" Leeuw asked. "That may be a good clue someday," he said laughing.

Antonio was contemplative. The two men had given each other plenty to reflect on but it was time they both carried on with the rest of the day's business. Antonio decided he would visit with his mother and ask her questions about the origins of his name. Leeuw decided he would sit by the water, watch birds and ponder. *Should he go by his gut instinct and see if he can find out why the wealthy Jewish Frenchman, David de Brebon and the strange Rabbi Maronne are acting so conspicuously insecure? Or should he ignore his suspicions and pursue a courtship with Hanna de Brebon? Would it be dishonorable to do both?*

Leeuw stood across the street from the staircase leading in and out of Monsieur de Brebon's home. He'd seen no one come or go. Suddenly from behind him, a deep man's voice spoke in an African accent. "They left early."

Startled, Leeuw turned around to see a statuesque dark-skinned man, about thirty years of age, dressed in fine clothes. The man stepped forward and stood next to Leeuw while they both faced the home in question.

"I don't know who you are or why you concern yourself with the de Brebons. Do you care to tell me?" the man asked angrily.

Leeuw knew if he revealed his interest in Hanna it would make him look too weak to pursue the young lady or that he was deranged. He was silent.

The man looked Leeuw up and down. "You're young enough to have interest in the daughter," his African accent grew more pronounced. "Your clothing is expensive. I don't suspect you a thief but the way you come here every morning and hide in the shadows while you observe the comings and goings..." he paused, "leaves me to think you are some sort of information gatherer."

His words gave Leeuw a heightened sense of ego and a blood rush. He'd chosen his duty as Chronicler over his desire for Hanna de Brebon and for that he felt proud.

"Do you report to the VOC?" the man asked.

Leeuw shook his head no.

"Do you represent the Reformed Church?"

Leeuw found that especially amusing. He chose his clothing to look like the other Dutchmen. He'd always wondered if he blended in, doubting that he did, assuming he'd not disguised that he was Jewish. He felt a sense of accomplishment. *Just another Dutchman.* But then immediately he spoke the truth, "I'm a member of the Sephardic Community. We're often referred to as Portuguese merchants."

"Ah, a Jew," the man was satisfied and in a rich African accent asked, "but why do you stand here every morning and observe who comes and goes?"

Leeuw believed he could confide in him but first he must know who he was. His squinted eyes and turned up lip must have asked the question.

"My name is Soetste," he said with a wry smile. "I'm the head of Monsieur de Brebon's housekeeping staff."

Leeuw gave the man his hand and shook it firmly. "I came here to get the feel of the de Brebon residence. Kuerze extended an invitation. I'm interested in meeting her daughter..."

"Hanna," Soetste interrupted.

"Yes. I wanted to take a measure of my competition and in the process, became intrigued with Monsieur de Brebon's suspicious nature. He has but one guest and the man behaves oddly as well. I feel something is unsettling Monsieur de Brebon *and* his guest.

The look on Soetste's face was grave. His skin was black, but he was of mixed blood, like those within the Dutch community who intermarried with native populations of Africa and the Indies. But Soetste's skin was dark enough for Leeuw to understand that most of this man's ancestry had remained constant. Soetste finally spoke. "I'm afraid there is a political issue that troubles the Monsieur. He requested the services of a new rabbi," he told Leeuw who nodded in fascination. "Your feelings were correct. Monsieur de Brebon and his new rabbi are facing a crisis. And so are you."

Leeuw realized he had not given Soetste his name, "Leeuw Soeira," he said nervously reaching out and shaking Soetste's hand again. Leeuw's love of a good story had him tapping his foot nervously and licking his lips anxiously awaiting the rest of the story and now this stranger was going to pull him into the climax.

Soetste looked around to see that no one was around who might overhear their conversation. "Are you aware that they have just completed a university at Utrecht?"

"Yes, of course."

"And there is a theologian, Voetius," Soetste told him, while looking around again.

"Gibertus Voetius," Leeuw grew excited.

But Soetste was not excited. He was disturbed. "He presided over a debate... *whether it's best to export the Jews or to kill them.*"

Leeuw's heart left his chest. The breakfast he'd eaten of cheese and bread grew heavy in his gut.

"Rabbi Maronne has a background in Christian rhetoric. He's French but resides in Utrecht as a visiting professor."

Feeling as if he'd been hit in the stomach, Leeuw asked Soetste, "Do they know Maronne is a Jew?"

Soetste shook his head no and the two of them stared into each other's eyes. Leeuw could see in Soetste's deep, dark eyes that he was gravely concerned, not just for his own situation if Monsieur de Brebon and his family were executed, but his understanding of a man's ability to control another man's destiny.

"What are they doing about it?" Leeuw asked.

"The rabbi comes every morning and spends the day in the study with Kuerze. He's composing a treatise against the threat."

"And Kuerze's role?" Leeuw asked.

"She's eloquent and writes with exceptional skill. She's a fine asset for the Monsieur."

The news that Christians were debating whether to kill the Jews spread like a fire on dry grass on a blazingly hot summer's day. It reached the Jewish Quarter as if a lightning strike had hit each and every resident, the young and the old. Meetings were planned. Every group or association came together including the burial societies.

Within three days of Leeuw's learning of the morose debate, there was not one Jew in the whole of Amsterdam and its surrounds that did not know, including every diamond polisher, all the Portuguese merchants at the VOC and the clerks at the Exchange Bank. It was on the lips of all the women. From inside their peaceful gardens behind their pristine brick homes they spread the story over one rock wall to another. By Sunday it had spread fear through the Dutch Reformed Church and the many members who lived double lives as both Christians and Jews. When the fury over the debate ended, and the Jewish Community of Amsterdam and beyond were still alive and well, they got back to normal as best they could and Leeuw decided it was time to finally pay a visit to the de Brebon household.

He was dressed in gray linen trousers and a vest over a light shirt. He walked briskly up the stairs to knock on Monsieur de Brebon's door. He was not surprised when Soetste opened it. The two had developed a friendship. Soetste was not a free man, so their relationship had been that brief meeting out on the street. But by the smiles on both their faces, it was apparent they hoped to meet again.

"Good afternoon Sir," Soetste went through his official routine, pretending the two had not yet met.

"Good afternoon to you as well," Leeuw said smiling. "I've come to pay my regards to Madame de Brebon," he paused and noticed Soetste was confused. "Kuerze," Leeuw whispered.

"Ah yes," Soetste said in the rich accent Leeuw had grown to enjoy, "Madame de Brebon? Come this way Sir."

Leeuw had been in many a fine home but none with such splendor. To his left and right were statues and paintings done with the finest of hands. The sun hit bits of stained glass and created a visual sensation of color that amazed him as he walked by. He smelled herbs and spices flavoring meat cooking in the kitchen. A hint of perfume caught his nostrils and he turned to find Kuerze behind him.

"Shalom," she said, not hiding her happiness at his coming.

The colored rays of light in Leeuw's peripheral vision and the potpourri of aromas in the warm home had been stimulating, but the beauty before him was most unbearable. *How could a woman this age be so enticing?*

Accustomed to the adoration, she casually continued. "Soetste, will you bring us something fresh and cool to drink, along with something to nibble?" she asked in a soft voice, quite pleasing to Leeuw.

My mother must have been something else to be chosen over this woman.

"Did you say something?" she asked.

"No, I didn't say anything," he said nervously.

Kuerze took him into a large room, full of what must have been Amsterdam's finest art. Most of the paintings were religious in nature, but there were a few portraits on the wall, unusual for a Jewish home. She sat him down at a brightly polished ornate table. He wondered what species of rare wood it was and how it must have taken craftsman a year to complete. His attention was diverted by the rustling sound of her dress. She wasn't wearing a head covering, enabling him to get a good whiff of a delightful scent she'd spritzed into her hair.

"I'm so pleased you came." She put her hand on his.

Words escaped him and any confidence had completely evaded him. He did manage to mumble a bit which didn't faze her.

She laughed at his shyness. "You remind me so much of your father when he was your age," she told him, her hand still on his.

He nodded.

She was talkative. "We had a brief but delightful few days. We may have married... your father and I... your mother seemed to have caught his eye."

It was clear she longed to know the whole story.

"I don't know how my parents met," Leeuw lied. He'd heard their love stories repeatedly. Nothing about their sexual experiences had been told but when Leeuw grew older he filled in the blanks. "My father sends his regards," he lied again.

Kuerze did not question his honesty. "I suppose we should speak of other things. Except the debate at Utrecht. My poor husband," she shook her head. "And Rabbi Maronne, we're relieved that he is no longer at the University. He works with me now."

"Oh?" Leeuw said, his Chronicler instincts aroused.

"I'm sure your father has told you of my charitable work. We've created an organization for displaced girls," she said, then looked down.

Leeuw detected her sadness. "I've noticed that Amsterdam has more and more displaced girls."

She looked into his bright blue eyes and saw that he genuinely cared. "Indeed it has. Over the years, Holland has amassed great wealth and culture, but with that growth comes higher populations of destitute youth. It is hard sometimes for me to go out. I feel so..." she looked up at him and could feel there was more than just a normal chemistry between the two. Whatever had been brewing between she and his father, now with his son that same spark was quickly growing to a flame. And she understood that he was fully aware of the fire that consumed them. Neither of them would nor could look away. Finding it difficult to breath brought Leeuw back to reality but not without deep guilt. He sensed in Kuerze that same confusion.

"It is a lovely afternoon, isn't it?" she asked, hoping to break the spell.

"Too lovely."

She smiled. "I believe we were speaking of my charitable work."

"Yes, we were. You're assisting displaced girls?" he asked, his breathing heavy, his voice low.

"We provide dowries for girls born out of wedlock to Portuguese merchants," she said delicately.

Leeuw thought quickly of all the skippers and sailors away from home for months at a time. "I've heard that it's become quite a problem. It's also my understanding that far too many of the men in our community bed their female servants, a practice common in their native Portugal. Amsterdam's rabbis are uncomfortable about it and speak to the men. But they don't always want to discontinue the practice."

"Yes, I see," she said, fidgeting with her napkin and biting her lip.

"It must be easy to find destitute girls. They're everywhere," Leeuw said wondering if he had said too much.

"Yes," she said, leaning forward and catching him glancing at her breasts flowing softly and respectfully from a tightly woven blouse. "But they must prove to us that they are the daughters of Sephardim, either from their mother or their father. Proving parentage is difficult. If their parents are deceased," she shrugged, "how can they prove they're Sephardic?"

"Yes, I see," he sympathized.

"Many are generous. It must ease the conscience of a man who suspects he fathered children with a native. Actually, we have more wealth than young women. If in your travels you know of any such young lady, please tell her that if she can prove to us, through acquaintances or otherwise, that she is the daughter of a Jew, we will provide a dowry so that she may marry within the Sephardic Community.

"Does this extend to the Conversos?" he asked.

"Of course... provided they have, or had in the case of death, returned to their Hebrew roots."

"I see," he brightened at the thought of such caring people. "Have you a long list of young women waiting to be legitimate brides?"

She smiled at his youthful exuberance. "I'm sorry that my daughter, Hanna, is not here this afternoon. She has gone out."

"Yes," Leeuw said, his breath beginning to race again. "But it has been one of the most delightful experiences, visiting with you here today," he took her hand and looked into her dark eyes. Her breath quickened. If no one had been around he would have loved to bring her lips to his and finish what his father had only started.

"I agree, it has been a pleasant visit," she said as she rose, the rustle of her skirts and the distribution of her perfume once again into the air, her hand still held in his.

"I shall tell my father that he was a lucky man to have spent those days with you, though they were few. Seeing you here today and our intimate discussion leaves me knowing it was not an easy decision he made."

Kuerze smiled. "You have no idea how reassuring your words are."

"I think I do."

"Why are you choosing her?" Kuerze asked Leeuw.

He stood with his hands in his pockets, feet flat on the floor, legs a bit apart and with a slight rocking motion, forward and then back, he smiled. "She's beautiful."

Kuerze knew there was more. She knew how to sense the depth of a man and Leeuw was not shallow. She waited for more.

"Did you see the way she stood alone in the corner?" he asked Kuerze who could see he'd already developed strong emotions for the girl.

"You know she's a Negress," she told him.

Leeuw looked at her as if she had no sense at all. The most dominant aspect of the young woman he'd seen at the social for displaced women, was that she was darker than any of the other girls. "Yes. It's very apparent she has Negro blood. It's what makes her..." he said trailing off wondering if he should sentimentalize with a woman of Kuerze's social standing and the ability to tell all of Amsterdam his deepest thoughts. But Leeuw was an open and honest man, excited about the prospect of a new wife and he could see by the look in Kuerze's eyes, that she would repeat all that he said. To whom she would repeat it to, he didn't know. But he decided that a few delightful comments could only help the poor girl's situation, and his for making her his choice for a bride.

"She looks..."

Kuerze's eyes grew larger. Leeuw pictured her around a table, with women she'd summoned for tea and gossip, her faithful servant Soetste, bringing tea and treats. Understanding this, Leeuw felt he should give them something to talk about.

"Strong," he said, a little embarrassed.

"Strong?"

"Yes. I want a girl who's strong."

"Why strong?" she asked.

"I want a wife who's strong enough to help build a home, put up husbandry sheds and barns and to build rock walls," he told her, and he could tell that she was glad he wouldn't be marrying her beloved Hanna. He continued. "I woke early this morning. There was very little light, just enough to see my way across the room. I had just awakened from a dream that I could not recall but the feeling was still with me. It was a lovely sense of being... peaceful, tranquil," he said looking at Kuerze. He knew by the softness in her eyes that she understood and by that look he knew she deeply loved her husband, David de Brebon.

Leeuw continued, "I felt the presence of a woman with skin as soft as the feathers of waterfowl. I felt loyalty and compassion, I felt..."

Kuerze put her hand on his arm. "You have felt the aura of love. You are fortunate to be a sensitive young man who recognizes that there is a very thin line between our waking world and the world in which we dream."

"Yes." The feelings he had for Kuerze were quickly resurfacing, making for an awkward moment that she too felt. They were both silent for a long while. Without telling him to follow, she walked from the office into the main recreation hall where the impromptu social had taken place just hours before. He followed her. The girls were gone now, returned to their dwellings or places of servitude where they would anxiously await their fate.

Kuerze was thoughtful. She turned to Leeuw with a brilliant twinkle in her eye. "You're going to the New World aren't you?"

Leeuw smiled proudly, "Yes. I am."

SIXTEEN

1636   Continued

Leeuw returned home... alone. He thought of the girl he chose for a wife, wondering how he would explain it to his mother. How could anyone understand his feelings, or his need to have a woman who needed him? He thought of the girl's name, Hester, and understood why that name would be a good choice for the illegitimate child born of a slave. But he longed to rename her. That would surely upset his mother. But Leeuw knew how kind hearted both his mother and father were. They would take the girl into their hearts and dote over her like one of their own children. What would break their hearts was his plan to leave Holland for the New World. He chilled at the thought of walking aboard a ship and sailing across the Atlantic with his new wife. He thought of the political situation in New Amsterdam along the Hudson River and recoiled at the thought of how he would need to position himself as a member of the Dutch Reformed Church. As a Jew he was not welcome in New Amsterdam. But as a representative of the Dutch East India Company and a member of the Dutch Reformed Church, he would be highly respected.

It would be months before he would be leaving. That would give him time to get his affairs in order and prepare his new bride. Leeuw fell down onto his bed. He had so much to think about and so many plans, the most pressing being his bride. He felt he could not have a lavish wedding nor one with many people. He knew that many in attendance would scoff behind his back at his choice for a wife. If the Sephardim had boycotted the butcher just because he was Ashkenazi and not Sephardim, wouldn't they boycott his marriage to Hester? He remembered hushed rumors about the Sephardim of Amsterdam frowning on his grandfather Daniel's marriage to his grandmother, Ruth because she was Ashkenazi. Fortunately, she had been a highly respected Akevian. But if Ruth had resided in Amsterdam, her dead body would not have been welcome alongside the Sephardim.

It was late afternoon and he tossed in his bed. He tried to fall asleep, hoping that a dream would come to him. He prayed deeply. After prayers of an hour Leeuw knew what he must do. He rose and cleaned himself up. He put his finest suit of clothes on and though hungry and in need of a meal, he walked into the cool evening air and out into the hustle of Amsterdam. He went straight to the de Brebon residence and pounded on the door. Soetste answered it with alarm.

"Shalom Soetste," Leeuw said angrily. "Please inform Kuerze I am here to see her."

"Yes Sir," Soetste said, then nodded and led Leeuw to the greeting room. Leeuw felt dwarfed by the large paintings. Amsterdam had become obsessed with painters and the de Brebon's were no exception. Large beautifully gilded frames held colorful scenes of the Mediterranean and others the Orient. One painting in particular caught Leeuw's eye. It was one of their largest paintings and it depicted the encounter between Rebekah and Isaac. Leeuw marveled at the artist's ability to capture the delicate feelings between the two.

"That is my favorite as well," Kuerze spoke from half way down the hallway that was quickly growing dark as the evening sun disappeared and Soetste had yet to light the candles. "What brings you out so soon after our meeting?"

He walked toward her. Each time he saw Kuerze de Brebon he grew more and more in love with her. He wondered how he could ever face his father with the thoughts that ran through his mind for the woman twice his age, the woman who had captured the heart of his father. He wanted to hold her and brush her soft graying hair from her dark eyes. He wanted to place his lips upon hers, still so chaste. And from that deep place where young men yearn for the bodies of women, he wanted her. He longed to delight her and give her an experience she'd never had. Each time they met, a silence between them grew as they enjoyed thinking and feeling of one another, a feeling lost in any concept of time, or age and in the knowing that it was fleeting. They silently devoured each episode as if it were their last.

"So," Kuerze broke the silence, "You have come because?"

Leeuw could not look at her when he spoke. "I've come for the girl, Hester."

"Tonight?" she asked aghast.

"Yes, tonight. I want to marry her... tonight," he said firmly, still evading her eyes.

"I'm not sure I can arrange that..."

"Yes you can," he said harshly. "I need to do this... tonight. I don't wish to elaborate on the circumstances that prevail me to make such haste. But if I must..." He put his hand on his heart and lowered his voice to a more respectful tone. "I am a Jew who poses as a Dutch Reformed Christian who wishes to marry an illegitimate half-Negro half-Jewish servant girl. My parents will insist on a Jewish wedding."

"I see your dilemma but haste is never a wise choice," she said, contemplating his wishes.

"Oh but it is for me," Leeuw insisted. "My hastiness has often brought great fortune. There are times when you know something is right and you make that choice and you do it quickly without remorse."

"You are so much like your father," Kuerze said. Emotionally exhausted, she walked to a small bench in the entry hall and sat down. "Although..." she said mischievously. "I would enjoy inflicting a little revenge on your father," she laughed and looked up at him.

But Leeuw knew she was not sincere.

"Though it would be quite fitting. It would make us even, your father and I. Don't you agree?"

"I'm surprised you harbor resentment," he said, waving his hand about the room. "You've done well to marry Monsieur de Brebon."

She smiled. "Yes and I love him very much... Leeuw, I will honor your request. I will send Soetste to retrieve her, after all, he is her brother."

Leeuw's heart sunk. He wasn't sure why but that knowledge brought great anguish.

There was not much silence before Kuerze spoke again... very clearly. "They are very close. When you leave for New Amsterdam you will break both their hearts. And no... you may not take Soetste with you. He's part of our family."

Leeuw nodded and took a deep breath. "I need to find a rabbi and then a Minister."

"You're going to be very busy tonight," she warned. "Leeuw..." she stopped him before he left. "I wish you well. I will have Soetste go immediately. He's fond of you. He'll be pleased with the news."

"Shalom," Leeuw said, placing his hand softly onto hers. "And thank you for your graciousness."

She nodded and watched him walk to the doorway without looking back. It felt as if her young heart walked out that door with him. Just before the door closed he turned and gave her one last look. It had grown dark in the hallway and all that could be seen were the shadows, but from behind her Soetste came with a large array of candles that lit Leeuw's bright blue eyes. And in that light reflected one solitary tear that rolled down his beautiful dusky skin.

Leeuw waited nervously for Rabbi Maronne. Hester was given a beautiful dress, probably from Kuerze, who'd insisted Soetste attend the wedding of his sister. Hester was extremely nervous but wonderful things must have been said about Leeuw, for though she was surprised she appeared happy. She kept her eyes on Leeuw, until he looked back and then she would look away. Which was fine because he was miserably nervous himself. The wedding was in the back room of a Sephardic man who said he would deal with the repercussions later, referring to the uproar sure to arise from gossip in the Jewish Quarter. The man left as soon as the wedding party arrived. Leeuw presumed the man would use the local tavern as an alibi.

So there Leeuw stood, next to Hester who stood next to Soetste and the three stood in front of Rabbi Maronne. Leeuw sensed the rabbi was waiting for something. He fiddled around and created distractions to stall. Eventually, the door behind them swung open and in walked David de Brebon. Leeuw would not have thought that much of it until he saw the tenderness between the Monsieur and Soetste and the *unmistakable love between a father and his daughter.* Monsieur decided this was no time to deny the truth and gave Leeuw a piercing look. Leeuw looked at Hester who smiled bashfully. Leeuw looked at Soetste. He nodded with refinement and pride. Leeuw looked at Rabbi Maronne. Leeuw did not dart for the door. But as he stood solemnly he was reminded of a dream he had as a child. He had gotten caught and tangled in the ropes of one of the large shipping vessels. A pulley raised his young body up to flap in the wind. His mother heard his cries and woke him. He remembered her words. *Do not be afraid Leeuw, you are safe in your mother's arms.*

After their vows were said, Monsieur de Brebon took Leeuw aside to speak with him. "I know this comes as a surprise to you."

"Yes it does!" Leeuw said in a loud whisper.

"Well, you should have investigated first. I'm surprised you didn't. There are many who know," Monsieur de Brebon said in a tone that stated he was quite proud of his ability to have procreated such fine people as Soetste and Hester.

"Does Kuerze know?" Leeuw asked.

"Oh no, nor does Hanna. They must never know. Our life is perfect the way it is, this would ruin it."

"What about Hester's mother?" Leeuw looked back at Hester. She was still very nervous.

"Once I knew she was with child, I sent her away. She lives well, I see to that. I keep her in Paris. When business with Parisian Royals takes me there, I see that she is..." he paused and said with great pride, "taken care of."

"I'm sure you do," Leeuw said snidely. If he'd known in the morning what he knew now, he wouldn't have felt guilty desiring his wife. Now, if his fortunes permitted, one day he would send for

Soetste and bring him to New Amsterdam. He had no interest in sparing the feelings of David de Brebon.

"I'm familiar with the status of your family," Monsieur de Brebon told him. "My daughter has been well placed. I could not do better nor be more pleased."

"You know my family?" Leeuw was confused. His family was angry that David de Brebon had taken the long-held Soeira family position of Brenger.

"I knew your great-grandfather, Jacques," David de Brebon said smiling.

Leeuw gasped. "You knew my great-grandfather?"

"Yes. Quite well," Monsieur de Brebon said, sticking his chin in the air proudly. "Jacques schooled me as a lad. He's the one who taught me the ways of a Brenger."

Leeuw sighed. All these years his family bore a grudge against de Brebon and it had been Jacques who unintentionally handed the coveted position to someone else. Leeuw wondered if the evening drama would continue into the night.

As soon as Rabbi Maronne finished with the marriage ceremony, Leeuw swept Hester away to another home where a Christian friend stood waiting at the door.

"Hurry!" the young man said, quickly ushering them into his home.

Hester was confused but accustomed to keeping quiet. She did exactly as she was told, making it easier for Leeuw who'd not come to terms with his selfish behavior.

"Did you get the papers?" Leeuw asked his Christian friend.

He nodded and took one last look before closing the door. The young man's father was a Dutch Reformed Church minister who would be away for a few days administering to a congregation halfway between Haarlem and Amsterdam. His wife accompanied him.

"Remember, these are complete forgeries. You did *not* receive them from me. I have changed the name of the minister to another here in Amsterdam," he looked gravely at Leeuw. "They won't think to trace it back to me. I've already written you down in the church register. I went there this afternoon. Don't ask how I was able to get in there and do it, it was not an easy task. I hope I spelled both your names correct."

Leeuw looked carefully at the document. There wasn't much to it, just their names and the date, Dutch Reformed Church and the name of the minister. "I'll hang on to it and not show it to anyone. I will only need it once in Amsterdam, when I book passage," Leeuw said looking gratefully into his friend's eyes. "But I will use it often when I take my bride to the New World," he said, finally acknowledging Hester, who had not known of his plans. As desperately as she tried to remain stoic, the revelation that she would be leaving Holland left her stunned. Yet, if she knew the sea of change that awaited her in the distant lands, she may have welcomed the adventure. If Leeuw could have foretold his future, he surely would have never left Holland.

Leeuw's Christian friend warned them, "Please, do *not* reveal where this document came from. I will deny it to my grave. I will say you stole it if I have to."

Leeuw handed his friend a small, heavy bag of coins. He nodded, pleased that he did not have to remind Leeuw that he'd done the deed for a price.

"Thank you for the kindness you've displayed toward myself and..." Leeuw looked at his new bride, not yet able to say *wife*, "Hester."

Leeuw, relieved that the night was over, admired his young bride. *She has the wisdom of someone much older. Who is she?* He had no plans for consummating their marriage, he'd not prepared himself for that, nor her. First, he would allow their love to grow. As they walked along the dark streets of Amsterdam he pondered her past. *Had her chastity been violated?* She glanced up, as if she knowing his thoughts.

When they arrived at the door to his home, he knelt, feeling for the hidden mezuzah. He was proud to be a Jew but in Holland he continued to pose as a Portuguese merchant who attended church. Once inside, he fumbled in the dark for his favorite candleholder. The light shined brightly on his small bed which he gave to Hester before making a bed for himself on the floor. With only a flimsy blanket and a straw mat beneath himself and the cold floor, Leeuw realized that the discomfort of the day was not yet over.

"Tomorrow, we'll gather your possessions. I am a kind man..." he sighed, "and will be a worthy husband."

She smiled faintly and nodded. He blew out the candle and fell into deep slumber. Hester did not fall asleep until the dark brought the light of a new day. Leeuw was pleased to find her sleeping when he woke. He stood over her, gazing at his new wife.

SEVENTEEN

1636   *Continued*

It had been three weeks since Leeuw married Hester. He had still not touched her. Nor had he been able to get her to talk. They were a comfortable pair despite Hester's subservience. His own mother, Anabela had a mind of her own, he found that missing in Hester. But Leeuw was optimistic and thought that maybe his mother could help. Hester's obedience did though, enable him to attend to business without worrying that she would leave. He was half-way through their emigration process to New Amsterdam. He would represent the Dutch East India Company. It was time to take Hester to Akev to meet his family and break the news that they would sail to the New World in the summer. His only comforting thought was that one day they might follow him.

"Tomorrow we will go to the hamlet of my family. Have you heard of Akev?"

She shook her head no, and then hesitated. Leeuw assumed she'd heard of it. If she'd lived her life with the Sephardim, she'd certainly heard of Akev.

Hester quickly learned to take advantage of the freedom that came with being Leeuw Soeira's wife. She went to the market every day for fresh fish and produce. He delighted in her food preparation skills and teased her by calling her *Hester de Cuisine*. She seemed to like that and the more he praised her abilities the more delicious the meals became. They were becoming fond of one another on a friendly level.

"Hester," he said to her one day, patting his knee, his signal for her to come and sit on his lap. "Come, we need to speak."

She'd grown fond of his confidence and was always happy to sit on his lap. One day, she mustered enough courage to touch one of his thick, blonde unruly curls. Today, she sat down and looked directly into his bright blue eyes.

"I'll be taking you to meet my family… our family," he said. Her dark eyes continued staring into his… arousing him. He looked to the floor and continued. "There is a long list of things we must do but there are things that we must change about you… about us." She smiled. The awkwardness of the previous weeks had grown into affection and Leeuw had begun to think about consummating their marriage.

"I'd like to change your name."

"My name?" He could see she was disappointed.

"I'm sorry but I want to give you a name more suited for our new life."

She nodded but he knew she was obliging him because that's what she was trained to do.

"I'd like to name you An," he looked into her eyes, loving the warmth that flowed from them. "She was the Sumerian god of the heavens."

"Heavens?"

"When you look to the sky or the heavens you'll remember this moment, it your rebirth," he said, having a hard time concentrating. He longed to forgo the talk and make love to her. "We will give you the Dutch version… Antje. Your new name will be Antje. From this moment forward I will call you Antje. When anyone asks, you are to tell them your name is Antje Soeira." He shifted her weight upon his lap, "my wife."

She looked at him dubiously and for the first time he felt her questioning his domination. He felt childish but stood his ground. "You will also tell anyone who asks that you are Portuguese and French."

She gracefully accepted the new rules and as her mind drifted to thoughts of her new identity, Leeuw reached over and kissed her softly. She responded well to his first kiss and the weight of her well-rounded body upon his was arousing. He gazed at her breasts, so near his head. She would respond to any advances he made, he was sure of that. She desired him as he desired her. He'd chosen well and for that he was proud. But they must cultivate new ways of thinking before they meet his parents or appear together in the streets of Amsterdam. She must memorize her new identity and he wanted no errors.

"I know that you've lived and worked in the homes of the Sephardim. The Dutch think of us as Portuguese Merchants. Is this correct?"

She nodded.

"And I'm sure you know that we are Jews who came north, usually from Spain or Portugal."

She nodded again.

"And I'm..." he started... but she interrupted.

"Also known as Marranos," she told him. And when he nodded she added, "And Jews from France. My father is from France."

"Yes, he is," Leeuw agreed. "But he is still Sephardim. I don't know his family history but I'd be surprised if his ancestors were not from Spain."

She'd not thought of that.

"You've had religious instruction?"

"Yes. The family that I lived with insisted that I study with their daughters. I was required to attend to the sisters' needs, but when it came to studies the family was firm about my studying too."

Leeuw was pleased that she was opening up. He was interested in knowing all she was willing to divulge about her past. But he had a more important topic to discuss.

"Do *not* tell anyone that you are the daughter of a Jew, a Sephardim or a Marrano. *Never*," he insisted. "I'm sorry if this frightens you but it's not time for us to reveal our roots. Not yet. We pretend that we belong to the Dutch Reformed Church. Do you understand?"

"Yes."

"Please, wife of Leeuw Soeria," he said teasingly, trying to make it fun. "What's your name?"

She looked at him with a dubious eye, which he'd begun to find attractive. He'd wondered how he could live with a woman who never disagreed with him, but her personality was emerging. He wondered what lay beneath her deep brown eyes and soft brown skin.

"My name is Antje. I'm French Portuguese and I belong to the Dutch Reformed Church."

He smiled, especially when she added, "I am the wife of Leeuw Soeria."

EIGHTEEN

1636 *Continued*

"Time to rise Antje," Leeuw told his wife, who lay comfortably in bed, while he still slept on the floor.

He stood over her. His mop of hair was thick and hung in his face. His demeanor was grouchy. She rolled over, turning her back toward him. "I need to sleep."

"You've been sleeping all night. We're going to Akev today."

She rolled back over facing him, making sure to reveal one of her luscious bronze breasts. She'd grown fond of teasing him. She was no fool to his continued erections. She felt them each time she sat on his lap and kissed. He'd thought her too shy. And surmised that she may have suffered from abuse. But the more he got to know her, the more he realized, she had not been underprivileged.

"I thought you were used to getting up early in the morning. Didn't you care for two girls?" he asked her.

"Yes, but the family was very good to me. They treated me well. The girls were my friends and we all took care of each other," she told him with that pleasant smile of hers.

He'd wondered if men had taken advantage of her, but that was obviously not the case. *Had she led a glorious life?*

"You are just as spoilt as Hanna de Brebon," he told her. "Rise child," he said teasingly.

Antje returned to her obedient persona, finished with her play-acting. He had no way of knowing that she'd been doing her best imitation of the pampered sisters she was assigned to. She'd dreamed of the luxury of staying in bed until she was fully rested. Her job had been to rise early and lay out the clothes for the sisters then go to the kitchen and spend a good portion of her day cooking for the family, along with two other household servants. The only thing Leeuw was growing sure of was that she'd not been physically mishandled. She was inexperienced when it came to matters of the flesh but he detected she was longed for his touch.

Antje looked back at him while she rose. Her linen nightdress fell over one shoulder. He wanted to pull her thickly-matted shoulder length hair into his face and inhale her natural perfumes. Revealing her well-defined shoulder was a calculated move and was too much for him. He rose and came from behind her, kissing her shoulder softly. She turned and he kissed her soft brown cheek. She turned fully around and facing him, they kissed. Antje had never kissed anyone before and Leeuw couldn't help but notice her awkwardness. She tossed her head down and her thick black hair flopped over her face in large mats of curls. He delicately pulled several of the curls from her face and held her chin in his hand. His blonde hair contrasted sharply against her black hair but his dusky skin melded nicely with hers. Their beauty in the streams of morning light that pooled its way into the room, would have enticed Amsterdam's painters. But no one was there to see the lovely sight of two lovers about to consummate their marriage.

He was strong and muscular. She was strong but in a feminine way. He had wanted a strong woman, he had told Kuerze that. But as he stood with Antje now, his quick heavy breathing blowing warmly into her ear, he no longer thought of having a wife who would build rock walls, carry water and milk cows. Leeuw wanted to protect the flower of a woman he'd chosen for a wife. He took her hand and led her back to the single bed. He laid her down on it and she instinctively lay on her back. He brushed her thick curls away from her face again and smiled lightly at her beauty. Her mouth was full and contoured as if the hand of the creator had taken special care that day, to draw the most perfect lips. Her almond shaped eyes turned up in each corner. He kissed her forehead and then kissed her lips again. They were warm. Her breathing was a heavy, soft panting. He kissed lightly about her ears and down her neck. Her body tightened as the shivers ran across her shoulders and down her back. It wasn't easy for him to maneuver her legs apart so he could enter her. She looked puzzled. He tried to be gentle when he placed himself inside her, between her legs, but he too was clumsy. She winced as he broke the flesh of her vulva. He was excited he was inside of her. His heart pounded loudly and he began to sweat as he penetrated lightly at first but soon he became more rhythmic and lost himself in the act. Antje was confused, not knowing what to feel but she soon felt the warm sensations her body was designed to feel. She watched Leeuw's face and could see that he was off in a distant trance and that her body was bringing him great pleasure. She felt a

363

pressure and soon realized that he'd released himself inside of her. Exhausted, he dropped his head and chest upon her breasts. He held back great tears and she felt a sense of wonderment.

"I love you, I love you," he cried and nestled deeper into her warm body.

She took her hand and stroked his hair, telling him, "I have never heard anyone say that they loved me. I have heard it thousands of times but never was it told to me. I'm not even sure I understand what it means."

Startled, Leeuw rose and looked into her serious eyes.

"Can we try that again? Soon?" she asked.

He laughed and lay back down on her chest. "Oh, I do love you Antje. This is the beginning of splendor," he said before they both fell asleep in each other's arms.

After awakening, they gathered a few provisions and walked to the establishment that chartered carriage rides to the outskirts of Amsterdam.

"We'll ride in this one," he said choosing the finest of all the carriages.

She smiled and they cuddled up closely and rode through the afternoon to Akev. The weather was warming and it signaled to Leeuw that it would not be long before they embarked on their journey to the New World, New Amsterdam, where he thrilled at the thought of the unknown adventures that lay ahead.

Leeuw had the carriage driver drop them off at the old spot where all the men of the Soeira line had been dropped off in years past. It was no longer necessary to take the long walk into the hamlet. The road had been extended right up to Akev, but Leeuw wanted to enter the ancient way. He wanted Antje to get the feel of his community, isolated from the rest of the world. And as they had for his grandfather and his father before him, the little children of Akev came to greet them. Full of smiles and questions, the children promised to run ahead and run down to the water where his mother, Anabela and father Seba had moved into the old shack that his grandfather Daniel and his wife Ruth, Leeuw's grandmother had habited until their death. The children who ran ahead would shout of their coming. Anabela would have just enough time to run her fingers through her silver hair and Seba would rise from his chair and lay down the book he was reading. Leeuw thought about his father and had no plans to mention his fondness for Kuerze; there was no need for discord between father and son. The children would probably innocently question Antje about her dark skin but she would be treated with respect by his parents. It was good to see Akev again and Leeuw could tell that Antje was happy and comfortable to be there. Her head turned back and forth looking at the variety of homes and businesses.

"I have never seen such a place," she told him, her pleasure in being there evident in her flashing eyes and bold smile. "Each and every home is different. Where did all these people come from?"

"They came from everywhere and they made their homes from the materials that were affordable and abundant in that era. See the one there?" he pointed to a tiny wooden house surrounded by flowering hedges.

"Yes, is that the oldest one?"

"It's the very first home in Akev. It was built by my ancestors, David and Magdalena Soeira. They later built a larger one," he pointed at another old wooden home. "But this first house, it's very special to all of us. When they first began building the community, it was a refuge for families fleeing the Inquisition in Spain and Portugal. Many of the families who fled were unable to bring their possessions. There were some prosperous families that moved here too. They sold their belongings when they were able and left, knowing that that Spain and Portugal were no longer safe. They left behind large ranches, with livestock and orchards. Sad to leave but happy they could live here in peace. It's still a secret community. You notice there is no synagogue."

"Yes, and I see a church," she said pointing to the little building with the cross.

"There are several homes we use here as synagogues. Unfortunately, we all assume a Christian identity. Someday we'll build a synagogue. That will be a proud day. You see that area down that way, with the green grass and the trees?" he asked her.

"The one covered with tulips?"

He laughed, "Yes, that's the one. There are far too many tulips. It's a favorite spot for all of us. It was selected one-hundred-and-fifty years ago. When it's safe to worship as we please, we'll build our synagogue there."

She held tightly to Leeuw, her trust complete. Their lovemaking had seen to that. He had made consequential decisions and would need to make more. He was satisfied that he'd placed his bride's name on the forged certificate as her new name, Antje and not Hester. The details of his life were convoluted but had been necessary. It had been that way in the Sephardic community long before he became one of the characters in the act that they called life. The lies that they had to speak had been taught to them as children, their truths revealed only in clues found in nuances, such as their names. His new life was also steeped in lies but he held firmly to his beliefs. Though he would forge a new path into a new world, he would never abandon his roots. His family had given him the name of Leeuw, one who descended from the tribe of the Lion. Though for generations the lion would lay forgotten, it would one day be remembered, when it rose from the truth of the golden age of Amsterdam as the most important clue that his descendants would have to know who they were, where the family had come from and why they had to lie. For they were the children of the Lion and yes, they had to lie.

The End

Turn the page for a sample of **Book Two**... **The Guild**

When Soetste's arm brushed against a vase of roses perched on Kuerze's armoire, flower petals fluttered slowly to the floor. She'd asked him days ago to remove the vase, but the statuesque servant had been preoccupied with his plans to escape the mansion, perched high above the River Amstel. Though not a free man, Soetste knew no one would question where he was going, for he was the faithful servant of David de Brebon and his wife Kuerze.

Soetste was the son de Brebon bore with an African slave he kept hidden in Paris. Not a nice thing for a son to walk out on his father, but nor was it kind for the son to be the butler, doorman and head of housekeeping for his father's mansion, propped upon one of Amsterdam's more picturesque canals. And provided he was not apprehended, Soetste would prosper. He knew as much about investments and connections, as any merchant.

The massive door closed sharply. Soetste felt a pain in the pit of his stomach. Inhaling his first breaths of freedom, he hurried down the street, knowing exactly to whom he would make his first proclamation.

Leeuw Soeira pulled nervously at his blonde, thick, unruly curls. His beautiful dusky skin and pink cheeks were flushed. His bright blue eyes strained to look at the commodities listing where he saw the name of the ship he'd invested in, with a line drawn through it. Pushing his way along the crowd of men, he confronted the clerk who'd just drawn the thick black line through the name of his cargo ship.

"What fate has she met?" Leeuw asked anxiously.

"Thieves took the cargo, not much to salvage. See her yourself, she's damaged and not quite all the way to the harbor. Captain's in a pitiful way, his crew's enraged."

Leeuw slapped his papers against his leg, bit his bottom lip, turned and walked out into the streets that reflected warmth from the afternoon sun. He headed toward home in Amsterdam's Jodenbuurt neighborhood where his wife, Antje, would humor him and they would relax upon their balcony and enjoy the evening as they watched paddleboats meander down the canal. It was Shabbat evening and though they did not flaunt their Jewishness, they would enjoy the luxuries for which they'd labored, and in secrecy they would light the candles and speak the prayers.

Antje sat upon the balcony railing and watched the river flow. Leeuw had met her through Kuerze, whose work at the Almshouses supplied dowries for the growing population of daughters of *Portuguese Merchants*. The merchants had found comfort in the arms of African slaves, with no intention of raising the illegitimate children from such unions. Posing as Portuguese Merchants, these men of Sephardic Jewish descent had escaped Spain, Portugal or both. If a young woman could prove she was the daughter of a Sephardic father, the Almshouse monetary fund was overflowing with guilt money. The young women were provided with a dowry and found new lives in Amsterdam's Cryptic Jewish community. Antje was one of those lucky young women. But before Antje was dining with the wealthy elite of Amsterdam, she was a servant girl, washing and preparing wardrobes for others. Knowing her own past, left her uncomfortable hob-nobbing with the wives of affluent merchants.

Leeuw put his hand on Antje's soft cheek. She turned toward his touch until she caught the smiling face of her brother, Soetste, among the crowd below. Leeuw bent down to see to whom his wife was smiling. He smiled too, for he was very fond of Soetste.

"What brings your brother to our neighborhood?"

"What matters is that he's here. I always long to see my brother's smiling face. He's my entire family."

"Except Monsieur de Brebon, of course," Leeuw reminded her of her father, whom they did not take pains to see, as it would identify him as her father, a risk de Brebon could not afford.

Antje, only seventeen, still maintained the enthusiasm of a child. "Come, come, Soetste!" she called out.

Soetste made his way up the three flights of stairs of their narrow brick home. Leeuw could see his brother-in-law was elated about something.

"Don't keep us guessing. What brings you out on Shabbat?

"I'm going to Akev."

"Akev? Who's sending you to Akev?" Leeuw asked, referring to his ancestral hamlet south of Amsterdam, created as a haven for the Sephardim fleeing the Inquisition.

"I'm sending myself."

Immediately, Leeuw knew Soetste's intentions, knew he would be unable to talk him from it, and knew the kind and intelligent man would prevail. *He hoped.* Leeuw also knew that de Brebon's wife would be unhappy to discover that Soetste and Antje were her husband's children. De Brebon would be annoyed that Soetste left, but would keep quiet while Kuerze turned Amsterdam upside down looking for the handsome servant whom she depended upon and ironically had grown to love like a son.

"She'll not stop until she finds you," Leeuw warned.

"Perhaps," Soetste said stoically. "But my wish is to be a free man."

The three sat quietly watching long narrow boats paddle up the canal. Amidst the festive nature of the Shabbat's eve, they found peace.

http://www.amazon.com/Guild-Hesters-Goodwill-Lions-Trace/dp/1484916697